CLANBOOK:

Ventrue ™

By Richard Dakan

CREDITS

Written by: Richard Dakan
Developed by: Justin Achilli
Mind's Eye Theatre Systems by: Deird're Brooks
Editor: Carl Bowen
Art Director: Richard Thomas
Layout & Typesetting: Brian Glass
Interior Art: Steve Ellis, Leif Jones, Vince Locke, Christopher Shy and Andy Trabbold
Front Cover Art: John Van Fleet
Front & Back Cover Design: Brian Glass

735 PARK NORTH BLVD.
SUITE 128
CLARKSTON, GA 30021
USA

CLANBOOK: Ventrue

CONTENTS

TO FAIL AND SUCCEED

Casper Johnson pressed the elevator call button for the fourth time in nine seconds. He knew rationally that it didn't make a damn bit of difference, but he was in a hurry. The elevators at the Hyatt Plaza knew he wanted one of them, and they would send their representative in due time. Just like politicians, elevators worked on their own schedules and made you wait for them. Unlike politicians, elevators didn't yell at you when you kept them waiting. Not that Mr. Van Dorn would yell at him. He'd just stare, which was actually much, much worse. At least it was worse when Van Dorn did it.

Casper wasn't the only person waiting anxiously for the elevator. The Hyatt was a madhouse tonight, just as you'd expect for the biggest party fundraiser of the year. The mayor was due to arrive any minute, while three state senators, six states' representatives and a would-be national senator were all downstairs boozing it up with lobbyists from every big bank, industry and special-interest group in the state. He knew all about that, because, as a lobbyist himself, that was exactly where he'd been too until a few minutes ago when he'd had to cut Representative Friedman off in mid-anecdote by glancing at his watch. 9:02. He was two minutes late. He had 13 minutes to round up Councilman Mackie and get him up to suite 1225.

Now at 9:16 (a minute late!), he pushed the call button a fifth time with Mackie standing beside him.

"Fuck. He's gonna kill me," Casper muttered under his breath.

"What was that?" Mackie asked, obviously a little nervous himself.

"Oh, just cursing these elevators, Councilman," Casper replied. "They've been slow all week, and I know you're a busy man. Sorry about that."

"Well, I don't suppose Mr. Van Dorn will mind waiting a few extra minutes, will he?" the lean young councilman chuckled. A former high-school teacher turned politician, Mackie had won office at the tender age of 36 on a platform of education and above-board politics. A year and a half later, though, he faced re-election and found he needed money. Bake sales just didn't cut it any more. So, like nearly every other councilman before him, Doug Mackie had agreed to meet privately with Matthias Van Dorn, investor, captain of industry and the largest private political contributor in the city. Of course, not many people outside of Casper's lobbying firm knew this last fact. Mackie was about to find out.

The elevator doors opened finally, revealing a car full of portly men and women wearing suits and tags that read "Hello, my name is _____." Mackie looked like he wanted to wait for another car, but Casper dove in, pushing the crowd back and making room for the councilman. He opened his mouth, almost ready to order him into the car, but Mackie came of his own volition. Two-and-a-half minutes later (9:22!), they stood before suite 1225. Before he could even knock, the door swung open to reveal Van Dorn's assistant, a sharp-featured politico named Spencer.

Spencer just nodded and stepped aside to allow the two men entry. Mackie and Casper nodded back. Five more steps brought them into the suite's salon before Mr. Van Dorn, who stood by the window, looking out over the city. He turned to meet them, his impassive eyes fixing them each with a glance. Shivers ran up Casper's spine, but he was used to that. It happened every time he met the billionaire client. A quick look to his left told him that Mackie felt it too, although he obviously wasn't used to it. The councilman almost took a step backward.

Matthias Van Dorn wore a dark gray suit, a subdued purple tie and perhaps the most polished leather cap-toes known to man. His pale, angular features and short-cropped blond hair looked decidedly Nordic and refined, although he spoke with no discernible accent. He locked eyes with Casper for a moment, and the lobbyist's heart filled with dread. He wanted to run away and hide in some dark hole, maybe beneath the porch at mama's house back in Louisiana. He'd been late. This was a bad thing. But the moment passed as quickly as it came. Van Dorn smiled to Mackie and extended his hand in greeting.

"Good evening, Councilman Mackie. It's such a pleasure to finally meet you."

"The pleasure's all mine, Mr. Van Dorn," said Mackie, who suddenly looked very gangly and awkward next to the urbane and refined industrialist. "Mr. Johnson here has told me so much about you and your interest in the city's welfare. I'm happy I could find a few minutes to spare for you."

Ha! Casper thought, *if you only knew who was sparing time for who.* He doubted that Mackie's comment sat well with Van Dorn, but the stern man showed no sign of displeasure.

"Yes, I do thank you for meeting with me," Van Dorn said, all smiles and grace. "I hope it wasn't too much of an inconvenience."

"No, no; not at all."

"Excellent. Please, sit down. Would you like a drink?"

"No thank you, I don't drink," Mackie said a little too quickly as he sat down in a chair opposite Van Dorn. Casper and Spencer remained standing, trying their best to remain unobtrusive. Mr. Van Dorn did not abide interruptions during his meetings. Casper felt for the phone in his pocket to make sure he'd turned it off, just in case.

"Councilman, where do you stand on the upcoming 215? The rezoning issue?" Van Dorn asked, already well aware of the answer.

"Well Mr. Van Dorn, I'm opposed to it. The Laurel Park neighborhood is one of this city's success stories. It needs more schools, affordable homes and restaurants, not factories." Despite Mackie's initial unease around Van Dorn, he slipped back into politician mode easily, speaking on automatic.

"I see," Van Dorn said, his tone still genial. "The neighborhood certainly has improved immeasurably since I first moved to our fair city. Tell me, though, did you realize that unemployment in that area has risen steadily over the last three quarters?"

Mackie frowned. "I have to dispute your facts, sir. Unemployment in this city is at its lowest point ever."

"Oh yes, city-wide that's true, but it's up in the Laurel Park area. Up quite a bit if I recall correctly. It seems to me that the area needs jobs more than schools."

"Yes, well..." Mackie looked confused, disoriented. "That makes sense I guess...."

Van Dorn locked eyes with Mackie. "Would you say the neighborhood needs the proposed industrial park?"

"Yes. The neighborhood could benefit from the industrial park."

Van Dorn's gaze never left the councilman's. Neither man blinked. "How do you plan to vote on Tuesday?"

"Well...."

Van Dorn kept talking. "It seems to me, that if you think the voters of Laurel Park need more jobs, then you should give them to them." He paused to emphasize his final point. "You will vote for the rezoning measure on Tuesday. After all, you've come to realize that it's better for all involved. You'll want to tell anyone who asks that this project will reinvigorate the area's stagnating economy." Van Dorn stared at his untouched bourbon-and-water, motioning to Spencer. "At least that's how it seems to me. Do you agree?"

"Yes...that seems to make sense. I'll have to think about it," Mackie said distantly.

Spencer moved forward, withdrawing a checkbook from his coat pocket. He handed it and a pen to Van Dorn as Van Dorn began speaking again. "Now Mr. Mackie, I think you're doing an excellent job on the city council, and I'd like to contribute to your reelection campaign. I'm sure I have many associates willing to contribute as well. For now, I, Spencer and Mr. Johnson here would each like to contribute the limit to your campaign. It's still $1025, correct?"

"Yes, sir... thank you, sir. I sincerely appreciate your contribution to my campaign." The autonomic political response system was kicking in. "I'm sure that we can all work together to make a better, more prosperous city."

Van Dorn smiled as he rose and shook Mackie's hand. "I'm sure you're right councilman. In the meantime, I imagine you have other pressing business. I'll let you leave now."

Mackie took the checks, shook Van Dorn's hand and vanished out the door with a final vague pleasantry.

Casper was still amazed to see how persuasive Van Dorn had been. He was sure that Mackie would have at least held out for more money if he wasn't going to stand on his principles. His amazement withered, though, when he felt the familiar chill and he realized that Van Dorn had now turned to look at him. Not good.

"I would have liked more time, Mr. Johnson."

Casper felt the sweat begin to seep out of him. He swallowed to avoid stammering. "I'm sorry, sir. Representative—"

"I'll need to see Mister Mackie again soon, to solidify his position. Arrange a meeting sometime next week, after the vote." Van Dorn looked at his watch. "Now I believe you need to round up another appointment for me."

Casper looked at his watch. Fuck! He had to find Senator Gaskins right now. "Yes, sir. I'm on my way." It was all he could do to keep from running from the room. If it weren't for the six-figure pay checks, it just wouldn't be worth putting up with that... *man...*

*   *   *

Casper moved about the main ballroom, looking for Senator Gaskins when his pager started vibrating. 000-911. Damn; his assistant's emergency code. Now what? He pulled out his phone and looked for a quiet place from which to call his office. He ducked into the men's room and hit speed dial.

A second later, his phone flew from his grasp as someone knocked it across the room. It shattered against the wall, and pain flared in Casper's wrist.

He turned his head just in time to see an unremarkable guy with pale skin, slicked back hair and a "Hello My name is _____" sticker grab him by the lapels and shove him into the wall. The force of the blow cracked the tile and at least three ribs.

"What the fu—" was all he could say before the man cut him off.

The attacker locked his gaze and hissed, "*Quiet.*" Although he wanted to scream bloody murder, Casper kept his mouth shut.

"All right, pretty boy. Where is he? Where's Van Dorn?"

As scared as Casper was right then — accosted and possibly in dire physical peril in a hotel restroom — he was more scared of Van Dorn. In fact, he couldn't help but be more scared of his client. He wanted to spill his guts before the assailant did it for him, but he couldn't talk. He tried again, but he just gurgled with the effort.

Still pressing him against the wall, the man asked again, this time staring hard into Casper's eyes. He enunciated every word carefully. "*Tell me where Van Dorn is.*" Casper's head felt like it was splitting. He started to speak, but he couldn't even remember in his panic. Where was Van Dorn anyway? He knew he'd seen him somewhere recently.... He gurgled once more.

"Listen, you fuck," the attacker said. "Tell. Me. Where. Van. Dorn. Is." His hands dug into Casper's arms, bruising them to the bone. That pain was nothing, though, compared to the one in his head.

"Do we have a problem here, gentlemen?" another voice asked. Casper thought he recognized the voice. Who was that?

The attacker turned to face the newcomer. "Get the fuck outta here. This is a private conversation."

Blinded by the pain, Casper couldn't see what was going on. That voice, though — he was sure he knew it. It spoke again.

"Oh yes; I see. Please excuse me." Wait; it was Spencer! Van Dorn's man. Casper tried to shout for help when he realized it, but a rapid series of flat clicks and the wet *spak* of bullets tearing into flesh interrupted him. The pale attacker stumbled sideways with the impact.

Casper opened his eyes to see Spencer drop a silenced pistol and dive forward. The attacker was already coming at him. Spencer knocked him to the ground, driving something long and sharp into the man's chest. The attacker shuddered once and stopped fighting. Spencer rolled off him, stood up and turned to Casper.

"Get the hell out of here," Spencer said. "Don't tell anyone about this. I'll talk to you in a moment." Casper promptly turned away to do what he was told.

*   *   *

Cold. Hard. Casper thought for a moment that he was still on the bathroom floor. No, he could tell it was darker here, even though his eyes were closed. This place's acoustics were different than those in the bathroom as well. The voices' echoes sounded hollow and farther away like they would in a cave. Or in a tomb.

He didn't have it in him to open his eyes just now, even though the cold he felt against his cheek helped soothe the throbbing pain at the base of his skull. After a few deep breaths, the voices ceased to be background noise and suddenly became very important. He had just heard Matthias Van Dorn speak.

"I might as well make sure this night isn't a total waste. It's time to rouse Mr. Almodovar here," Van Dorn was saying.

Casper heard chains rattle close by, followed by a prolonged, wet sucking sound and a sickening pop. The chains

rattled louder, and Casper could hear muffled grunting. What the hell was going on? Where was he? How did he get here?

"Calm down, Mr. Almodovar. Do calm down." Van Dorn's voice carried no hint of irony, and presently, the struggling ceased. Even more surprising, as far as Casper was concerned, was the fact that he found himself calming down as well. His heart stopped racing, his head throbbed a little less intensely. He even managed to open his eyes.

He lay in the corner of some dark, concrete room. A single halogen lamp dangling from the ceiling provided light. A naked man with a gaping red hole in his chest hung on a nearby wall, suspended just a few inches above the floor. If that man flexed his feet, he could probably just scrape the floor with his toes. Casper wasn't surprised to see that it was the same guy who'd attacked him in the bathroom. That made Casper feel even better. Van Dorn stood before the prisoner, his eyes even with the enchained man's. The man on the wall kept his eyes closed and head turned to the side.

"Look at me Mr. Almodovar," Van Dorn said. "You will look at me." The man didn't move. Van Dorn nodded to his left, and Spencer stepped out of the shadows holding a blood-coated wooden stake. He strode forward and took hold of the prisoner. The bastard started to struggle once more, but he didn't have anywhere to go. Spencer drove the stake into the bloody hole in the man's chest.

Casper wanted to vomit, but he didn't want to disturb Van Dorn by being sick in his presence. When Spencer stepped back, Van Dorn took hold of the stake and pulled it achingly slowly from the man's chest, pausing a moment to shove it all the way back in before withdrawing it completely.

"I can do this all night, Mr. Almodovar. In fact, I can do it forever. Now, don't you want to spare yourself all the discomfort?"

The prisoner screamed, his eyes glistening furiously under the halogen light. He howled like a trapped animal. Casper cowered in his corner, not feeling his broken ribs grind together or the deep, purple bruises on his arms. Van Dorn let the chained man thrash about for a bit before halting him with a word.

"Stop."

Almodovar stopped.

"I don't know what it was you thought you were doing, Joachin. I just barely tolerate you as a courtesy in the first place. Now you attack one of my possessions? You interrogate it to get to me? This behavior is unacceptable. You no doubt know enough to think that since I am neither prince nor your sire I

will not destroy you. Think again. You will find that the Traditions extend only to those who observe them. You, sir, have committed a grievous breach of etiquette."

Van Dorn grabbed the prisoner by the hair stared directly into his eyes. Almodovar tried to look defiant, but he lost his composure quickly. Van Dorn had him. "Be still, oaf. It is time for you to answer my questions. Tell me why you needed to see me so urgently...."

The questions went on for a long time, and Almodovar spilled his tale. Casper sat quietly, taking it all in, trying to figure out what was going on. How could the man survive having a *wooden spike* shoved into his heart? *Twice.* And what happened to the bullet holes that should have pock-marked his entire left side? Casper needed answers. Unfortunately, he received none.

When the interrogation ended, Van Dorn turned to Casper. Casper shuddered to behold his employer when he noticed the flecks of blood on Van Dorn's tailored suit. *That won't make him happy,* Casper thought. *Those will never come out.*

"And now for you, whelp," Van Dorn spat through curled-back lips. "I'm not sure whether to punish you for your ineptitude or reward you for drawing out this serpent in our midst."

"If it's all the same to you, sir, I'd gladly split the difference. Don't feel that you have to reward me or punish me," Casper rasped, shrinking from Van Dorn's imperious scorn.

"Actually, I was thinking of giving you a little bit of both. It's an inauspicious welcome to Clan Ventrue, to be sure, but you know my protocols at least, and it will save me from hiring another aide."

"Clan Ventrue? I'm afraid I don't know what you mean." Casper didn't try to get up, but his limbs climbed over each other in a race to escape Van Dorn's closing presence.

"Oh, you'll have plenty of time to learn. Forever, in fact." And then, as Matthias Van Dorn lifted his aide from the floor, Casper Johnson became something else entirely.

Chapter One: The Kings of the Kindred

I have good advice and sound wisdom;
I have insight, I have strength.
By me kings reign, and rulers decree what is just;
By me rulers rule, and nobles, all who govern rightly.
Proverbs 8:14-16

"Our history is our guide," a Ventrue maxim states. Bound by tradition and precedent, the Ventrue rely on their history more than any other clan. They cherish every aspect of it — even (or especially) the parts embellished or fabricated completely. Theirs is a history of conquest, achievement and brilliant tactics. The fact that more than a few of the most esteemed makers of that history still walk the Earth tonight only heightens their reverence for the past. The clan's history justifies their claim to aristocracy. It supports their agendas, it settles their internal disputes, and it causes endless debate. Without it, they would be as a ship without a rudder.

This, then, is the clan's history as consensus. Some dispute individual portions. Members of other clans sometimes dismiss the whole story as pure fiction from beginning to end. The Ventrue stand by its every word, and few can compare with them when it comes to research and the collection of their own history. Not even mythical Caine could know what truly happened, but it is maybe more important to realize that this information is what the Ventrue *believe* took place, a gradual blur from legend to history. In the end, all that

matters to them is that their innate greatness resonates through the ages and reverberates in their wake.

Caine's Chosen

The Ventrue claim to fame begins, quite literally, in the beginning. The most reliable sources state it firmly. Caine ordered his childer to beget the Third Generation; he specifically chose [Ventrue] as the first. In fact, he demanded that Ynosch Embrace [Ventrue], only to sweep the fledgling Kindred from his sire's sway and place it by his side. The young [Ventrue] became Caine's closest advisor and confidant. Therefore, from the moment the Third Generation sprang into being — which is to say, the moment the entire conceit of "clans" came to be — Ventrue could lay claim to have been the eldest them all, a claim to which many still cling in these modern nights.

For a long while, [Ventrue] served at Caine's side, helping him rule over Kindred and kine in the gilded First City. As befit their baser natures, the others of the Third Generation grew jealous of [Ventrue] and his position, particularly the over-ambitious and cunning

[Lasombra]. The dark one (as Caine himself called him then) could not abide even theoretical subservience to one such as [Ventrue]. Others resented [Ventrue's] position as well: the foreign Set, the occult [Tzimisce], the vain [Nosferatu]. For the most part, though, the remaining founders respected [Ventrue] and Caine's decision to elevate him above the rest. After all, no one disputed Caine's wisdom openly in those nights.

Then came the Flood that wiped away the First City and many of the Kindred and kine therein. As the first drops of rain fell from the sky, Caine turned to [Ventrue] and declared that he intended to leave the younger Kindred. Not trusting any of his firstborn, Caine placed the mantle of leadership upon [Ventrue's] shoulders, charging him with watching over the other Kindred, to steward them through the long nights ahead. Ever loyal to his grandsire, [Ventrue] accepted this grave responsibility. As Caine departed, the waters arrived and washed the city away, destroying many weaker Kindred who had been spawned during the city's golden age.

When the baleful waters finally receded, the Kindred sought to rebuild their home. The six Cainites of the Second Generation sought to procure Caine's vanished legacy for themselves, but few among them had ever commanded the Antediluvians' respect or loyalty. In their desperation to be free from the Second Generation, many of the now-Antediluvians turned to [Ventrue] for counsel. Together they slew their sires and set themselves up as rulers, just as Caine had suggested before he left. They then set about building the Second City.

THE WAR OF AGES

At first, the Second City echoed the glory of the first. It became a place where Kindred walked among the kine as gods while the various blood-siblings of the Third Generation set about founding their respective clans. Soon, though, the city became overly crowded, and the Kindred grew restless. Trying to hold the disparate community together, [Ventrue] attempted to listen to and resolve the Cainites' problems — even the depredations of his sister, the witch. Soon the petty bickering turned into violent hatred. Not even [Ventrue] could hold the contentious broods of his fellows together when not a single one of them seemed to want peace. Finally, Caine's chosen successor laid down the law and brought the Kindred into line

through pure force of will. He slew many wayward childer and banished the unruly among the Third Generation, including Set and the vengeful Mekhet. Many resented such high-handed treatment, but none could stand up to [Ventrue's] authority.

For a short while, a tense peace existed within the city. Still, [Ventrue's] heart pined for Caine's assuring guidance. As jealousy and hatred continued to boil just below the surface, [Ventrue] cast his gaze out beyond the city walls. He had sent some of his childer to search for the First Vampire, and some had returned with rumors of his whereabouts. Encouraged by these signs and thinking the city safe under his edict, [Ventrue] left to find Caine and bring him back. He left one of his own childer to watch over the fuming clans while he was gone.

As it turned out, this decision was [Ventrue's] sole mistake. After he departed, the other Kindred of the Third Generation gave in to their own greed and treachery once more. [Lasombra] was the first to break ranks, seizing the opportunity to attack [Ventrue's] childer and claim the city as domain for himself. He did not hold it for long. The other Antediluvians rose up as well, not content to sit by and watch [Lasombra] steal what [Ventrue] had claimed despite their own desires. The battle had begun. [Tzimisce] plotted with [Lasombra], much as their two broods would later unite under the banner of the Sabbat. Lucien drove his brother into torpor and salted the earth where he lay. [Nosferatu] and Set cut Arikel's dead heart from her body and ate it. The fragile peace that had existed under [Ventrue's] guidance gave way to violence and thievery, each night a new treason committed by one Ancient against another. Inevitably, in this climate, the Second City would fall.

Diaspora

Distraught and depressed at the Kindred's failure, many surviving Ventrue moved west, into the Mediterranean. They spread out among the kine, seeking havens from the violence and turmoil that crippled the Second City. Like many Kindred at the time, they set themselves up as gods, heroes and seers among the mortals. Many carried on the clan's legacy by leading kine communities either directly or indirectly.

It was at this time that the Ventrue first learned to respect and even fear what mortals could accomplish if they set their minds to it and could mass enough

Ventrue's Fate

Every clan wonders what became of its legendary Antediluvian founder. Some claim to have killed theirs, others to be in constant contact. The Ventrue admit freely that they haven't heard from their namesake in millennia, at least not so anyone can prove. In fact, most accuse the one known as Brujah — or one of her brood — of lying in wait just outside the walls of the Second City and striking [Ventrue's] head from his neck in jealousy upon the third step of his quest to find Caine.

Ambitious (if heretical) Ventrue have claimed on several occasions that [Ventrue] has risen and promoted their personal play for power. The most famous example of such audacity was the Ventrue Director Vittorio Angelotti, who joined the Directorate's ranks in 1811. With the help of supernatural allies, Vittorio managed to create a very compelling but entirely false appearance of [Ventrue] at a clan conclave. Vittorio joined the secretive Directorate and sat as a member for 80 years, until an aspiring clan member managed to uncover a personal diary that explicated the entire deception from beginning to end. Vittorio disappeared from sight, never to be heard from again.

In spite of such frauds, Ventrue still claim to see signs of their founder's presence from time to time. Most common are Kindred or even mortals obviously operating under intense Dominate by some powerful Kindred. Sometimes, this mysterious puppeteer claims to be [Ventrue]; sometimes he keeps his identity a secret. Theorists have observed a certain commonality to all these appearances that leads many to believe that one powerful Kindred is behind all of them. A stranger appears, usually a mortal or neonate, evidencing powerful Disciplines. He or she always shows up in times of trouble for certain Ventrue, or when rival factions have warred for too long. The stranger helps avert crisis and refocus the Kindred against some common enemy. Whether [Ventrue] or some other clan elder is behind these appearances remains a mystery, but legend and rumor definitely fingers the founder as the interloper, albeit with little verification for such speculation. Some paranoid Kindred think that someone else is using [Ventrue's] "good name" to interfere with the clan. Either way, the Ventrue elders would prefer that whoever it is cease or step out of hiding.

numbers. The lesson came, as did so many in the early nights, with a high price. One of [Ventrue's] own childer, Medon, had set himself up as god-king of a growing community on an isle in the Aegean. He ruled with absolute authority, demanding service from every kine and giving little in return.

Some say that Medon's fate was the result of another Kindred's vendetta, but little evidence supports this position. Most agree that it was merely the mortal mob rearing its indignant head, as it would do time and again down through the ages. What no one can doubt is that the kine burned Medon's palace and staked him out in the sunlight to die an agonizing Final Death. One of the destroyed Kindred's childer escaped to tell the tale, and it spread through the Ventrue community like wildfire. If such could happen to one of the clan's strongest, it could happen to any of them.

Sparta

No one learned to fear the power of mortals better than the Ventrue who took the name Artemis. She, along with a number of other Ventrue, had settled in the prosperous region of Greece called the Peloponnesus. The Dorian Greeks had built on this peninsula the foundations of communities that would become great cities—places such as Corinth and Argos, in particular, and most important of all, Sparta. Artemis — then known by another name — settled in a small rural community of four villages, a few shoddy wooden temples and not much else.

What, then, made Artemis pause in her wanderings at this rustic crossroads that offered so little to attract a Ventrue? It was a man who had a dream for the rough-hewn folk of Sparta — a dream that would transform them into the most feared fighting machine in all Greece. His name was Lycurgus, and he was about to pass into legend. Artemis intended to feed upon the philosopher, but he drew her into conversation, discussing his dream for the Spartans. With Medon's death still fresh in her mind (although several centuries had passed), Artemis saw the potential threat and utility of Lycurgus' dream. She decided to follow a course that so many Ventrue after her would emulate. Rather than try to oppose or dominate the growing power of mortal institutions (and risk being run over in the process), she bought into the Spartan invigoration, following mortal makers of the future.

This Ventrue took upon herself the role of Artemis Orthia, Sparta's patron goddess. She watched Lycurgus

win over the Spartan people and install his fabled constitution. Even she was somewhat surprised when the ambitious Spartans invaded the neighboring region of Messina, enslaving the entire region. Artemis saw in the Spartans many parallels to Kindred existence. A large serf population made progress possible for the Spartans, just as the large kine population made Kindred existence possible. Having so many serfs allowed the Spartans to devote their entire lives to perfecting the art of war. Where most Greek city-states had to spend their time farming or trading to support themselves, the Spartans could focus solely upon the challenges of self-perfection and self-defense. Unswervingly loyal, unflinchingly brave and nearly unbeatable in battle, the Spartans struck Artemis as a flawless model of the mortal potential.

Other Ventrue soon flocked to the Peloponnesus, seeking to work with Artemis to ride the Spartan war machine to power. Each settled in a different city within the region, urging the city leaders toward a conclusion most of them had already reached on their own: better to ally with Sparta than face its wrath. Thus, the Peloponnesian League — a loose alliance of city-states with Sparta at its center — came to be. The second most powerful city within the alliance was Corinth, a rich commercial community. The Ventrue Evarchus claimed this city as his domain and he, too, learned important lessons that the Ventrue would carry with them for millennia to come.

Corinth thrived on trade, particularly in its prized pottery and Peloponnesian foodstuffs. Backed by Sparta's military might, its merchant ships traveled throughout the Aegean and expanded the league's influence and power. Evarchus understood that money had real power over the kine. Kindred had seldom had much use for currency, but in a world where mortal institutions grew more and more expansive, money seemed to be a key to influencing the kine. Evarchus' merchant fleets arguably made him the first truly "wealthy" Ventrue, and others would follow in his footsteps thereafter. All went well, even in the face of two Persian invasions. Sparta, Corinth and the Ventrue Peloponnesian League continued to prosper.

The First Brujah War

Athens and Sparta had fought side by side in the great war against Persia. This war was a mortal concern, one the Kindred had little to do with. In fact, Artemis tried to keep her Spartans from becoming involved at all, but she found that her influence over them indeed had a limit. Proud, brave and scornful of the barbarian Persian king, the Spartans had marched off to war and into history without their goddess' reluctant blessing. Even though they returned victorious, she was not pleased. Nor was Evarchus, Prince of Corinth. In the wake of the war, Athens began to rise in power and rival Corinth's position as the wealthiest trading city in Greece.

Although Athenian ability played no small role in the city-state's meteoric rise, the citizens had a little help from a few enterprising Brujah. Long attracted to innovative thoughts and ideas, several Brujah had settled in Athens to take in its glories. While Pericles built his beautiful city as a monument to Athenian power, these Brujah Kindred sat by his side, helping when they deigned to do so, but mostly enjoying the fruits of Athenian labors. They watched quietly as the Athenians established the Delian League, a powerful military and trade alliance that stood in undoubted opposition to the Spartan-led Peloponnesian League. Meanwhile, Evarchus of Corinth saw his profits decline with each passing year — more so since the Delian League came into being. He did not have to convince the city's rulers that Athens was the problem. They came to despise Athens just as much as the Ventrue did.

Conflict seemed inevitable. The two great alliances finally came to a head, thanks in no small part to the urgings of Evarchus and eventually Artemis. A long, terrible war ensued, lasting decades and engulfing all of Greece in a seasonal struggle. The Kindred held back from battle, preferring not to risk their unlives over mortal assets — yet. The Athenian Brujah could all but ignore the conflict, since Athens' high walls kept the Spartans at bay and the Athenian fleets ensured continued prosperity. Besides, they found the fickle masses of the Athenian Assembly too fractured when they did try to interfere. Their influence over individual members was not enough to sway the greater body of the assembly. Artemis and Evarchus feared attacking Athens on their own without their Spartan troops behind them. Eventually, thanks to the genius of a Spartan general named Lysander, Sparta sank the Athenian navy and lay siege to the city. Athens surrendered after a deadly plague ripped through the population and Sparta had won.

Artemis and Evarchus visited the troops as they marched into the city, fully prepared to take their vengeance on the arrogant Kindred of Athens. It was not to be. The wily Cainites had fled the city, and the first "Brujah War" ended without either side spilling the other's blood. However, it left a bitter taste in the mouths of Sparta's Ventrue patrons. Several Brujah and Toreador called the Ventrue barbaric and power-mad, while the Ventrue came to think of the Brujah as dangerous dreamers with no sense of decorum. The conflict set the pattern for things to come between the two clans.

Like all legendary ages, though, the epoch of Sparta's glory passed shortly thereafter. In but a few short decades, Spartan hegemony fell like a house of cards to the upstart Thebans, whose city seemed remarkably free from Kindred presence. Artemis' temple was burned, and she and her brood fled into the night. Evarchus lingered in Corinth for many more years until he finally slipped into torpor for a few centuries. Awake once more and residing in Greece, Evarchus supposedly exists in the modern nights as but an echo of his greatness during the mythic age.

THE LATIN VENTRUE

When Artemis and Lysander fled west in the fourth century B.C., they found Ventrue among the Romans already established on the Italian Peninsula. The Ventrue had settled among the Etruscans, an ingenious and prosperous people of central Italy, centuries before. The Ventrue had existed there in quiet peace, many claiming a small Etruscan city as her own domain. Then came Collat. Ventrue history credits Collat with leading the revolution that freed Rome from its Etruscan rulers and established the first Latin state. Whether or not Collat actually started the revolution is unknown, but he certainly took advantage of it. He set himself up as the Kindred Prince of Rome and watched his city grow.

Rome's power and sovereignty spread in fits and starts over the next few centuries, expanding to include all the former Etruscan cities and eventually most of Italy. Collat and his Ventrue brood profited from the expansion, following the soldiers into new cities and claiming domains there. It was Collat, though, who set the pattern for future Ventrue in Rome and in the world at large. Unlike many Kindred at that time, he did not rule openly or claim to be a god. The Romans were a religious, superstitious and proud people. They were more likely to stake and burn a vampire than try to coexist with him. Therefore, the Ventrue of Italy maintained a low profile, collecting favors from its citizens and governors and influencing events from behind the scenes by calling on them to repay their debts.

When war with Pyrrhus of Epirus brought Rome into direct conflict with the Greek cities of southern Italy, the Italian Ventrue came into contact with Greek Ventrue who had settled the area, including recent arrivals Artemis and Lysander. Artemis had retired to Athens' ancient enemy Syracuse to lick her wounds and eventually escape from the world into torpor. Lysander

had established himself in the Greek city of Tarrentum. Tarrentum eventually became the focus of Rome's war with Pyrrhus, and, when all of southern Italy fell, Lysander himself fell into the hands of Collat's most promising childe: Camilla.

Camilla and Lysander debated for years. A young Kindred of potent blood, Camilla knew little of the world outside Italy. The war with Italy's Greeks had

exposed the Romans to all manner of new and exciting things, from coined currency to elephants. It also exposed Camilla to Ventrue history and to the way Lysander and Artemis had led their unlives in Greece. Brought up by Collat to believe that Kindred should lurk in the background, he was both horrified and intrigued to learn that Artemis had set herself up as a goddess. Moreover, he was most impressed with the martial might she had helped foster amongst the Spartans. What Camilla learned inspired him….

CAMILLA'S REIGN

With Lysander at his side, Camilla returned to Rome. There he confronted Collat with his vision: a vision of Ventrue not only following the Romans as their empire expanded, but guiding, even directing their legions. What happened next remains a mystery. Camilla and Lysander claimed that Collat saw the wisdom in Collat's plan and decided to step down. Ventrue scholars simply assume that the two young Ventrue destroyed their elder and covered up the evidence. Either way, Collat disappears from the clan's history at this point, and Camilla steps to the forefront.

Camilla took lessons from both Collat and Artemis. He would not set himself up as a god, but he would not hide in the background. Instead he interacted actively with the leading patrician families in Rome and encouraged them to undertake certain policies. The difference between how he interacted with them and how many other Kindred worked with kine was that Camilla worked through proxies rather than as a god or through coarse use of Disciplines. He offered favors in exchange for representation at the Senate (as Camilla was not himself a senator), or he put people in touch with others for similar considerations. When his contacts grew old or fell out of favor, he cultivated others. In this sense, Collat set the precedent for many Ventrue. Rather than bullying their way through mortals, these "enlightened" Ventrue learned to politic in a fashion that not only hid them from the matter, but allowed mortals to think that what the Ventrue wanted was what they wanted.

For example, Camilla was a proponent of building and maintaining the vaunted Roman roads. As many Romans knew, the roads were key to not only travel, but to facilitating trade as well. Without roads, the empire would have collapsed far earlier into tiny, autonomous principalities. Therefore, it was in the interests of the imperial government — particularly those in power — to protect their investment, as the preservation of their power depended upon it. Camilla's task was easy: Simply ensure that enough officials understood the truth of the matter and let it take care of itself. Indeed, Camilla didn't even need to approach every member of the empowered government. Most were quite content to continue growing rich, regardless of Kindred counsel.

Many other Kindred fail to realize that the Blue Bloods don't hoard power, wealth and influence for themselves. Only the most foolish vampire sets himself up as a dictator. The wise Ventrue *shares* power, calling upon favors and offering his services in return. Doing so not only keeps the true master hidden from view, but it also ensures that an enemy can never truly unseat an influential Ventrue from her position of comfort without crippling her vast network of contacts and allies. Rivals may lop as many heads from the hydra as they wish, but the body is what must die to truly ruin a Ventrue.

Camilla's methods made him wealthy and, ultimately, decadent. His ghouls fed and protected him while he tried to rule Rome through mortal proxies. Lysander advised him in turn, although he grew wary of Camilla's decline. He traveled throughout Italy and the Mediterranean, acting as Rome's eyes and sometimes strong hand in Kindred matters. Of course, Lysander had his own goals. His eyes looked constantly eastward to his homeland, which even then was ruled by the upstart Macedonian descendants of Alexander the Great. First, however, the Roman Ventrue faced a greater problem: Carthage.

THE SECOND BRUJAH WAR

Carthage, the new capital of the Phoenician people, had become the predominant city in Northern Africa and one of the most potent trading powers in the Mediterranean. Its colonies extended all the way through the African coast and on into Iberia. It stood as Rome's chief rival in the West, although it had yet to threaten Rome itself. For his part, Camilla cared little about Carthage. His ambitions still remained confined to Italy or possibly to the land that Lysander so coveted. It was Lysander who saw danger in the African city. It was Lysander who saw the Brujah.

The Greek Lysander, who had unknowingly fought the Brujah during the Peloponnesian War, had inherited his sire's hatred of the clan. In his travels on behalf of Rome, Lysander had heard many tales of Brujah walking openly among the kine of Carthage, ruling over them like gods, demanding blood-tithes and sacrifices. Lysander himself journeyed to the city to discover the truth of these rumors, and he was shocked to find them all too true. This behavior had apparently been going on for centuries, and brutal broods of Assamites and Brujah had the Carthaginian population well cowed. By the time of Lysander's reconnaissance, some even planned to expand their infernal practices to Spain and threaten Gaul. Italy would not be far behind.

Lysander returned to Camilla to report what he had found. He no doubt embellished the tales, tainted as his perception was by his own dislike for the Brujah because of their Athenian connection. Camilla, though, was slow to act. He did not feel comfortable engaging the enemy on their own ground, and he was not so sure Carthage was truly an enemy. He had grown complacent in his position, fatted by bloody excess. Lysander urged his prince to take action again and again, but Camilla refused until the weight of Malkavian and Toreador counsel convinced him otherwise in a round about way.

In 265 B.C., Greek colonies occupied most of Sicily, independent from both Roman and Macedonian rule. A scattering of autarkis dwelt on the island, with different clan-broods residing in different cities. The greatest of them all was Syracuse, where Artemis had fled and slipped into torpor and where now a Malkavian prince named Alchias sat enthroned. Alchias did not care about Carthage; he scarcely knew that Brujah resided there. In fact, it was the mortal leaders of the city who started the war. The Carthaginians had intervened in a dispute between Syracuse and the neighboring city of Messina. They not only settled the dispute, they occupied both cities afterward.

Then a Brujah of Dominic the Rogue's lineage came to Alchias, stating in no uncertain terms that both Carthage and the Brujah had plans for Sicily and Syracuse. Prince Alchias flew into a rage at the implied threat, decapitating the startled Brujah envoy. Unsure of what to do next, he fortunately had someone to turn to for advice: the recently awakened Artemis and the bull-dancer Arikel. This coalition summoned Lysander to the city, and together they concocted a plan to engage Rome in a war with Carthage. Lysander returned to Rome to once again plead his case to Camilla while Alchias urged the governors of Syracuse to commit soldiers to the imminent battle.

The result was the First Punic War, a battle that would decide the fate of both Sicily and Corsica as well as set the tone for Brujah-Ventrue relations for centuries to come. The Carthaginian and Roman armies and navies fought for years in an evenly matched stalemate of a war. Carthage made a few forays into Sicily and Italy, but its army was repulsed bloodily on each occasion. Likewise, Roman raids into Africa met with similarly dismal fates. In the end, the mortals finished the war. Rome proved victorious, annexing both disputed islands.

Despite the ostensible victory, Carthage remained a power to be reckoned with, and several cults of Brujah,

Assamites and Baal-revering Cainite heretics still rampaged there. Alchias, Lysander and the now-awake Artemis all put pressure on Camilla to continue the war and follow up on the victory. Rome's prince refused. He had seen what happened when Kindred set foot in Africa: They disappeared forever. Until the Brujah posed a serious threat to Rome itself, he would not act.

CARTHAGO DELENDA EST

The second war with Carthage came 20 years later, and it had nothing to do with Kindred at all. It began in faraway Spain, where only a few Brujah neonates resided with the cruel Lasombra. The mortal Hannibal and his fellow Carthaginians set the city to war on their own by capturing the Roman allied colony of Saguntum. Hannibal then marched east and south across the Alps to invade Italy itself, where he and his army remained for the next 15 years. While Romans and Carthaginians involved themselves in the bloodiest fighting they had ever seen, most Kindred remained silent and stunned. Many Italian Cainites were too scared to leave their cities, and the Sicilian Malkavians and Toreador had their hands full with fresh Carthaginian incursions. The Brujah sat back in Africa and let their human allies do most of the fighting.

Eventually, the Romans turned the tables and forced Hannibal back to Africa. The Roman legions followed along soon after, invading Africa and defeating Hannibal on his home ground.

Camilla and the other Kindred stayed in their havens for this last fight, still recovering from nearly two decades of war in their peninsula. Carthage surrendered and agreed to Roman terms, ceding Spain and making other concessions to the Roman victors. Although upset by the defeat, Carthage itself remained a secure city so the Brujah were content, for the time being.

Romans, Ventrue and the loosely allied Toreador and Malkavians in Sicily alike were not so pleased with the outcome. Lysander urged for a final end to the conflict. The mortal army might have been defeated, but the immortal enemies remained as powerful as ever. Other clans came to Camilla as well, led by the Malkavian Prince Alchias. The wanted Carthage eliminated for good. Meanwhile, the Roman people were being encouraged to fight as well. The famed Roman orator Cato the Elder had an obsession with Carthage. For years he ended every speech he gave in the Senate with the same phrase: *Carthago delenda est* — Carthage must be destroyed. Lysander picked up the refrain and echoed it in Camilla's ear.

Whether it was Cato or Lysander rallying the cause, the result was the same. Camilla agreed to ally with the other clans and eradicate the Assamite-Brujah menace in Carthage for all time. In one of the few instances in which the Ventrue actually provoked a mortal world conflict, Rome once again declared war on Carthage in 150 B.C., five full decades after the end of the last great struggle. The Roman fleets and armies attacked Carthage and lay siege to the city, surrounding it with a wall of troops and ships.

The Third Punic War amounted to not much of a battle for the Romans: a quick siege and capitulation. For the Ventrue, it was the greatest, largest battle they had ever fought. While Roman legions razed the city, Ventrue, Toreador, Malkavian and a few Gangrel officers helped lead the charge and did battle in the streets with the Carthaginian Brujah for five nights. Scores of Kindred died on both sides, along with several thousand mortals. Never before or since has such a titanic battle taken place openly between Kindred. Any lucky enough to have survived those nights can testify that it was a blood-soaked horror beyond all others.

The invaders won the night, albeit at a terrible cost. Artemis herself had led the first foray into the city, and she was torn to shreds by a pack of frenzied Brujah berserks. Prince Alchias was so badly hurt that he slipped into a torpor from which he might never have recovered — his fate remains a mystery. Lysander emerged from the battle scarred but otherwise intact, having taken the final Brujah head himself. Camilla had remained in Rome, but his fledgling progeny Tiberius Carnifex slew an entire cell of Assamites before succumbing to their envenomed vitae. The city surrendered soon thereafter, and the legions began the sack proper. On Lysander's orders, they razed the city to the ground, killing thousands and enslaving the rest. They salted the earth so that nothing would ever grow there again — and so that no torpid Cainite could rise. The war with Carthage was over.

THE SENATE'S FAILURE

Rome's place in the world grew by leaps and bounds after Carthage's destruction. Next came Greece, then Asia Minor, then the Near East, then Gaul, then Egypt. The Roman Empire dominated most of the known world, and Camilla and his fellow Ventrue sat in the center of it all. Of course, so did a great many Kindred from other clans. The Malkavians, the Toreador, the Gangrel and even the Roman Nosferatu had all played roles in defeating Carthage, so they claimed a share of the spoils. Many of these clans already held influence within the newly conquered Roman provinces, and they were not about to give up just because the mortal government had changed.

For the first time since the fall of the Second City, Ventrue had to learn how to exist in peace with the other clans. Doing so proved more difficult than it would have seemed since the Ventrue themselves had fallen to squabbling with one another. As the Prince of Rome and one of the architects of the Empire, Camilla was without a doubt the most influential Ventrue — if not Kindred — in the world. He decided that such power deserved recognition and that the individual Ventrue scattered throughout the Mediterranean should pay him heed.

This desire for dominance ground against everything individual Ventrue had practiced for thousands of years. Each was used to being his own master, beholden to none, with the possible exceptions of sires or patrons chosen at their own discretion. Certainly they recognized a kinship, but clan hierarchy was more a question of social standing than temporal rank even in those nights. Ventrue held what power and position they could, and damned be the rest of the world. They had no friends, only allies of the moment. As a clan, they came together semi-regularly in a deliberative body not unlike the Roman Senate. This Ventrue assembly body proved even more ineffective than its less-than-impressive mortal counterpart. Factions tore the Senate apart and prevented any real

decisions from being made, while many Ventrue seemed more inclined to make deals and alliances with other clans than their own brethren.

As before with the Punic Wars, Camilla ended up making one of his greatest decisions not by his own design, but rather after inspiration from his mortal counterparts. Together, Julius Caesar, Pompey the Great, Marcus Antonius and Octavian busied themselves with eviscerating the Roman constitution and the Senate's power. Strong men, tired of working within the constraints of an elected government, dragged the empire into a bloody civil war. Decades of fighting later Octavian, emerged as victor and renamed himself Augustus, Emperor of Rome.

Camilla liked what he saw. In the chaos of the civil wars, Ventrue authority within Rome had slipped even further. Members of other clans claimed domains in important cities and isolated the Ventrue position, but individual Ventrue were too divided to do anything about it. The Ventrue assembly had not met for three decades, and it showed no signs of ever meeting again. With the help of his blood-bound brood and his trusted ally Lysander, Camilla set about enforcing a clan unity — at which the two anticipated no end of rankling strife.

An Ancient Grudge

More often than not, Ventrue simply do not get along with one another. Clans tradition demands that they come to one another's aid when asked and prohibits them from encroaching on each other's domains, but beyond that, they often work against each other more than for any arbitrary common good. Clan history has seen some truly infamous rivalries develop between members, some of which have gone on for thousands of years. One of the most famous — a tale sires tell their childer to this night — is the feud between Demetrius of Massilia and Gaius Fabricius of Ravenna.

Greek colonists founded the ancient port city of Massilia (now known as Marseilles) long before Rome rose to power. When the entire south of France fell under Roman authority centuries later, Massilia held out as a free city for quite some time. Eventually, though, it fell square into the Roman Empire, which Demetrius never forgave. A distinguished Ventrue, Demetrius sat as the Prince of Massilia for centuries, nearly since the city's founding. He had worked with his clanmates in Rome, helping them when required and assuring autonomy for his beloved city in exchange. When Roman troops stormed the city in the first century B.C., Demetrius went into a rage and blamed one of the elder Ventrue in Rome, Gaius Fabricius. The fact that Fabricius had nothing to do with the event and that Julius Caesar had everything to do with it did not bother Demetrius. He blamed Fabricius for failing to make Caesar a pawn.

Ever since that night, Demetrius has worked against Fabricius at every turn. Although the Roman Ventrue bore the Greek no ill will at first, he quickly took up the feud on his own in retaliation for Demetrius' constant attacks. Now, 2000 years later, they are well beyond the point of reconciliation. Both have tried and failed to sway the ranks of the clan, to some degree because their rival stood in their way, but also because few outside the drama wish to be dragged into it. Any undertaking in which one involves himself, the other opposes out of venomous spite, even if it is against his best interests to do so. Their acrimony even extends to their progeny, their progeny's progeny and so on. Although both are reputed Cainites of the Fifth Generation, they have been known to take out their aggressions on lowly neonates who can claim a rival's lineage. As often as not, the rival doesn't even know that the poor descendent even exists.

Each justifies his position by citing ages-old treachery on the other's part. Regardless of the feud's legacy, most Ventrue realize that not every move in the Jyhad is grave — some are petty, fueled only by bitterness. Forever is a long time to bear a grudge.

The Golden Age and Transformation

Camilla could not quite mirror Augustus' great accomplishment, and he failed to set himself up as sole ruler of the Ventrue. He did, however, manage to bring many of the less powerful Kindred into line. He established a system whereby the most important Ventrue within a given city or region had "authority" over the younger members of the clan. He claimed a local supremacy for himself as preeminent among the Roman Ventrue, although a number of other powerful Ventrue, including Lysander, had practical autonomy. Obviously, the clan could not have absolute authority over its members — nor was such the nature of Camilla's claim. Instead, the clan served as a guide and resource to its members. It began to take on many of the functions that it has tonight, such as providing a forum for settling disputes, a network for alliance against common foes and a social denominator of contacts and potential allies to help individual Ventrue achieve their personal goals. The clan claimed chroniclers, historians, adjudicators known as "notaries" and "vouchsafes" and even enforcers who could bring unruly neonates to bear if they became a liability to more influential Ventrue.

For the next five centuries, the Ventrue prospered as a clan. As Rome spread its influence, Ventrue traveled in its wake. Ambitious Ventrue, always eager for new lands to claim, spread with the Empire, establishing domains throughout Spain, France, modern-night Benelux and Britain. In the East, where populations were larger, Ventrue came to dwell in concert with other clans throughout Asia Minor, Syria and Egypt. The mortal world saw periods of upheavals and prosperity as Rome went through a long series of good and bad emperors.

If the Brujah mourn the fall of Carthage, so do the Ventrue grieve for the fall of Rome, placing too much emphasis on the short reigns of insane men like Caligula and Nero in the first century but ignoring the wise reigns of men like Vespasian, Trajan and Marcus Aurelius in the centuries that followed. The truth is, Rome did not truly fall in A.D. 476 or on any other specific date. It merely evolved into something else, and the Ventrue followed reluctantly. The same can be said for Camilla, who had overseen Rome and its Ventrue for nearly a thousand years before he finally slipped into torpor. Meanwhile, his trusted aide Lysander moved east with the empire's seat of power, observing quietly the politics of what would become the Byzantine Empire and last until the Crusades.

In the West, the empire dissolved gradually into discrete nations and kingdoms. The Ventrue were there all along, merely exchanging their governors and generals for kings and princes. They had also found a new venue for exploitation, a human institution that showed every sign of some day rivaling the empire itself: the Catholic Church. The Ventrue became involved in the Church, and they Embraced some of the most important Kindred the clan has ever known, such as Fabrizio Ulfila, from its influential ranks. In effect, the clan was now split into two halves: the old guard that had migrated east with the changing focus of the Roman Empire, and the newer Ventrue who remained to take advantage of the growing disorder and the Church's increasing influence on society. A noteworthy minority, disillusioned with the collapse of the Roman Empire, withdrew from the political unlife altogether, preferring instead to observe the passage of time from a cloak of shadows. It is even rumored by some that this faction formed the basis of the mysterious Inconnu.

The Dark Ages

For vampires, anything called the "Dark Ages" has to have its benefits. It certainly seemed thus to the Ventrue at the time. Human institutions, with the exception of the Church, were weaker than they had been in a thousand years. Individual Kindred could exist practically out in the open as masters of their own individual domains and occasional rulers of mortal lands. The system Camilla had devised to unify the clan fell by the wayside as single Ventrue came to care about only themselves once more.

The clan itself split into two distinct halves: the Western Kindred who focused their attention on individual nobles and personal domains, and the Eastern Ventrue who retained close ties to what remained of the Roman Empire in the form of Byzantium. While clan unity might have suffered, few Ventrue cared for such esoteric (and largely impossible) matters. After centuries under Camilla's strict rule, they thrilled at the chance to stretch their wings on their own.

During the Crusades, this split became a source of deadly contention within the clan. Western Ventrue, tied to an aristocracy of Christians and their Roman Church came into direct conflict with Eastern Ventrue and their Greek Orthodox and Muslim allies. Although neither side made any organized effort, a number of small rivalries and contests between Ventrue broke out during this time. In a few instances, Ventrue even came into direct contact, fighting one another openly, sometimes even destroying one another. For example, a faction of Slavic Ventrue ousted Ventrue claiming Teutonic and more Western origins in Eastern Europe, and became known as the Eastern Lords. Caught up in the undisciplined freedom of the Long Night, the clan as a whole was sinking to a low point in its history. Then things became much, much worse.

Buried History

Archeology is a relatively new science, one devised and largely practiced by mortals. As far as many Ventrue are concerned, the relics of the past that aren't already in someone's hands are lost for good. Or that used to be the feeling, at least. Recent finds by younger Ventrue in search of their clan's past have changed these attitudes for many. In a clan obsessed with ritual and history and tradition, items from the past carry great cachet. Someone who can claim to hold Camilla's laurel crown or a stone from the Second City haven of [Ventrue] himself earns the immediate respect and (more importantly) envy of his fellow Kindred. Of course this passion applies generally to Ventrue-related artifacts. Kine or even other Kindred objects (except those with universal appeal, like anything relating to the mythical Caine) hold little interest to most Ventrue.

With their tremendous resources, more than a few Ventrue have funded large-scale archeological digs in sites of known Kindred interest. In order to preserve the Masquerade, several Ventrue agents or ghouls usually oversee such projects along with a younger Kindred who monitors the situation from afar, the better to take care of any leaks or errant pawns among the mortal diggers. Several Ventrue behind such operations claim to be protecting the Masquerade by funding the operations, ensuring that unwatched kine do not stumble upon some secret they should not know. There may be some truth to this claim, but the real reason remains a burning desire to accrue *dignitas* and show up one's clanmates.

The Nights of Fire

Almost every clan found itself caught unawares when the Inquisition came. The Ventrue were hit as hard as any, arguably more so than some because of their high profile. Thousands of Kindred of all ranks and stations met the Final Death during the Church-sponsored conflagration that swept through Europe in the 13th century. As the crisis unfolded, the Ventrue began to suffer the consequences of their disorganization. Swept up in the fear of the witch-fires of the faithful, Ventrue elders took to sacrificing their childer to save their own unlives. Brood patrons left their progeny behind when they fled, hoping that the time spent destroying their hapless childer would delay the Inquisition from reaching them. One French Ventrue even Embraced childer as she fled, throwing innocent mortals turned ignorant fledglings in the Church's path.

In response, these embittered childer resisted in what became known as the Anarch Revolt, something totally unprecedented in Kindred history. Seemingly as one, the vampiric youth rose up against their sires. This threat came close to equaling that posed by the Inquisition itself, since the anarchs usually knew just where and how to find an elder Kindred. Already weakened by the internecine fighting of the Crusades, the ranks of Clan Ventrue dwindled at this point. The anarchs posed a threat that the Ventrue alone simply could not answer, and the Inquisition had proven remarkably difficult to sway.

The Camarilla and the Rebirth of Clan Ventrue

The answer to the anarchs' challenge came, as one might expect, from a Ventrue. Hardestadt the Elder was a prominent member of the clan, made more so by the fact that he had managed to survive the Nights of Fire relatively unscathed while many of his elders had fallen. Like many Ventrue, Hardestadt had a fondness for history. Unlike many others at the time, he also had a vision for the future. He looked back on his own clan's successes, how Artemis had united Kindred to fight

LASOMBRA REVISIONISM

Ventrue historians have not always held a negative view of the Lasombra. In fact, until the formation of the Sabbat, the Ventrue had little to say about the clan for good or ill. Only in the past five centuries or so have historians begun to "find" evidence of Lasombra perfidy through the ages. Now, many Ventrue — even those old enough to know better or young enough to be otherwise apathetic — believe that the Lasombra have been a constant thorn in the Ventrue's side ever since the nights of the First City.

In fact, despite being competitors for eons, the Ventrue and Lasombra did not come into outright, clanwide conflict until the formation of the Sabbat. Since then, both sides have developed rather radical views of one another. The Ventrue see their shadowy kinfolk as obsessively jealous, consumed with a desire to replace Caine's chosen clan as leaders of the Kindred. As far as many Ventrue are concerned, the entire Sabbat and all the conflicts that have resulted are a personal attack upon them by the Lasombra.

The reality of the situation is that the Ventrue collective ego cannot stand the fact that the Lasombra do not acknowledge the genius of their creation: the Camarilla. Moreover, the idea that the "distant second" clan would dare to oppose Ventrue domain in politics, money and other areas of mortal influence galls the Blue Bloods. What right do the Lasombra have to claim such authority for themselves? Moreover, how coarse are they in their methods? The brutal, Masquerade-endangering Sabbat is a threat to all Kindred. How could any would-be leaders risk another Inquisition willfully? Many Ventrue feel that jealousy has driven the Lasombra mad, and that the Lasombra are best destroyed like rabid beasts if they cannot be brought to heel!

against the Brujah of Athens and then again how Camilla and Lysander had entreated many clans and Kindred to destroy Carthage. Here again, the young and radical seemed bent on threatening the established Kindred. Unity was the answer Hardestadt gave.

The Camarilla's creation in 1450 and its history are well known. What few realize, however, is that Hardestadt took this opportunity to centralize the Ventrue clan as well. Some say that Lysander himself helped guide Hardestadt for this coup, although no one can confirm reports of sightings of the ancient warrior then or since. Hardestadt must have had him and Camilla in mind, though, since the Ventrue hierarchy

he proposed showed more than a few signs of classical inspiration. Hardestadt recreated the council of peers that Camilla had begun at the turn of the previous millennium. He and about two dozen respected or influential Ventrue agreed to the charter of the Council of *Ephors* to counsel individual Ventrue and to provide a forum for grievances (theoretically) free from regional bias. By agreement, these *ephors*, also called directors, would keep their identities a secret so that no one personality overshadowed the authority of the council as a whole.

RENAISSANCE AND REFORMATION

After establishing the Camarilla, Clan Ventrue experienced a powerful resurgence that began in the 16th century, and a whole new world of possibilities opened up before them. With most of the anarchs subsumed into the Camarilla, the Ventrue-led sect had the muscle to fight the Sabbat at every turn and reassert its firm presence in Western Europe, which was the place to be at the dawn of the Renaissance, as it turned out.

While humanity rediscovered things Kindred had never forgotten, the Ventrue tested their re-established might. Under the self-sacrificing guidance of individual Ventrue and notable Toreador, Malkavians, Tremere and Brujah, the Camarilla prospered, ensuring a peaceful (or at least safe) environment for the Ventrue to exploit their new potential. Wisely fearing humanity in the wake of the Inquisition, most Kindred still clung rigorously to the Masquerade (just as the Ventrue wished) and withdrew from direct interference in mortal affairs. The Ventrue, however, plunged ahead, although in much more subtle ways than they had used during the Long Night.

It was Robert Kross, a German-born childe of the Inquisition years, who first saw the potential return on investments in the back end of new industries and ventures. An aide to Hardestadt and one of the first archons of the Camarilla, Kross had traveled throughout Europe as part of Justicar Democritus' retinue. He settled in Holland eventually, where he became a silent partner in a number of "exploratory" ventures. Within a few decades, Kross and his mortal partners were making vast sums from trade with the Far East. Meanwhile, Kross' childe, Juan-Miguel Ramirez, repeated his sire's successes in Spain, an investment that eventually paid off in literally tons of gold diverted from the Spanish Empire.

All across Europe, the Ventrue clan led the way in investing in and exploiting trade with the New World and Asia. Although mortals did most of the real work and the Ventrue themselves seldom traveled to their foreign holdings, the Kindred's coffers swelled beyond imagining. It was at this time that the clan earned its much-deserved reputation as the wealthiest clan in the world. The proceeds from those original overseas investments still serve as the basis of many European elders' wealth in the modern nights.

To the Ventrue's chagrin, however, this newfound wealth served to reinforce the schism between the clan and their *antitribu* of the Sabbat. While the Ventrue anarchs had been only a minority of the Kindred involved in the revolt, they certainly did not lack in passion. Even before the formation of the Camarilla proper, many Ventrue dissidents resented the direction many clan members had taken. These young Ventrue thought that their elders had grown rich and complacent. Instead of their noble legacy of nights past, modern Ventrue had chosen creature comforts. In the eyes of the Ventrue anarchs, the elders were no longer an aristocracy but a merchant class.

Elders and more conservative Ventrue, of course, argued that money was simply a *means* to maintain their leadership. The nights of feudalism were waning, they opined. Divine Right was fallible, and the true path to power lay in the new economy.

The *antitribu*, though, refused to relax their position. In their opinion, the mainstream Ventrue had simply taken the path of less resistance rather than the one that had built their august reputation throughout history. From the first nights of the Camarilla to the Final Nights, the *antitribu* have turned their backs on their parent clan like no other. Theirs is not a difference based solely on the tenets of the Sabbat, but a true divorce of philosophy. Theirs is also a rivalry of fierceness matched in vehemence by few other Cainites.

Revolutionary Fervor

Even as war after war tore its way across Europe, throwing governments into chaos and immersing the land in bloodshed the likes of which it hadn't seen in centuries, the Ventrue (and Kindred in general) persevered. They had learned not to attach themselves to any particular mortal king, but rather to the very institutions of government and wealth. Powers and potentates came and went, but the Ventrue presence remained immutable. That is, until the government itself fell.

The Ventrue had been slow to follow up their colonial investments personally, especially in the New World. While Ventrue backers grew wealthy through their British "partners," the Sabbat busied themselves by establishing havens in every major colony along the North American eastern seaboard. Young Ventrue and other Camarilla Kindred looking for opportunities did travel to the New World, but not in numbers comparable to the Lasombra, Tzimisce and other Sabbat-aligned Cainites.

Therefore, the Ventrue were poorly prepared when the American Revolution came. The Sabbat used the mortal revolt to their advantage, sinking their claws into the newly established nation from the beginning. Several Ventrue princes — or "princelings" as the elders in Europe called them — fell to the Sabbat. The War of 1812 offered the Sabbat a platform to strike again, which they did, although with less effectiveness than they might have wished. It soon became clear that these new United States would become the battleground for the two sects for many years to come.

Over the next 50 years, the Sabbat continued to make slow but steady forays into the United States, using their British-Canadian influences to help bolster their position. As often as not, however, they crippled themselves with infighting and treachery that cagey Ventrue were able to exploit by moving into a domain and claiming power in the vacuum left by bickering packs. Losing ground in the East, these Blue Bloods concentrated their efforts in the burgeoning states of the central and western regions; places the Sabbat had not yet infested fully. Chicago, Saint Louis, Kansas City, Denver, Los Angeles (for a time) and San Francisco all became important Camarilla and Ventrue domains.

The Ventrue had never really paid much attention to the issue of slavery. In Europe, it was simply unacceptable among mortals and not particularly cost-effective. As far as many Ventrue were concerned, all mortals were slaves of one sort or another. They had no real qualms about humans enslaving each other. Indeed, some Ventrue felt that the institution made a great deal of sense. When war broke out over the issue — that and "states' rights" — the Ventrue took no formal stance on either side. What they did was seize the opportunity to strike at the enemy while humans waged the bloodiest war in history right in the middle of Sabbat territory.

The Ventrue used what little influence they had in this emotionally charged war to take advantage where they could find it. Coteries of Ventrue-led "raiders" nipped at the heels of both sides of the conflict, sweeping into cities that an army burned and driving out any Sabbat who remained. During Sherman's famous march through Georgia, Ventrue and their Camarilla allies trailed close behind and managed to claim new domains in Atlanta, Savannah and several other cities. Richmond, Charleston and other Southern cities soon followed. Although by no means defeated, the Sabbat cause had been set back in the United States, a condition that would characterize their Great Jyhad for decades to come.

MORTAL WARS

Men, much like Kindred, have a passion for conflict. They fight one another constantly, often over seemingly trivial (at least in retrospect) matters such as transubstantiation versus consubstantiation. These wars tend to take place with or without Kindred involvement. Over the years, Kindred have taken credit for a great many things, and the Ventrue in particular have a penchant for laying claim to certain earth-shaking events. In truth, most vampires attach themselves to a conflict only when men fight on a grand scale. Only the craftiest elder or Methuselah can *cause* a war surreptitiously, but any Kindred can wait like a vulture to reap the spoils.

In ancient times, when Sparta and Athens or Rome and Carthage fought, the Ventrue could rightly claim to have had a hand in such matters. Kindred wielded more direct influence in those nights, chiefly because the populations of these great empires paled in comparison to the modern age. Even then, the humans were usually equal partners in any confrontation. One Kindred, no matter how powerful, is unlikely to cause an entire nation to go to war. Instead, the Ventrue have learned to turn war to their advantage. The Romans and Carthaginians vied for power and influence within the Mediterranean, providing the perfect cover for the Ventrue and their allies to strike at the Brujah stronghold.

Warfare has always brought out the most dangerous aspects of humanity. Masses of troops stand side-by-side, ready to bring death or die trying. It is a dangerous time for anyone, even a Kindred, to be trapped in the crossfire. As modern armies number in the millions, the force unleashed in such a conflict is well beyond the means of any single Kindred or clan to control. In a time when explosives level whole cities (and the Kindred havens therein), tank divisions grind the landscape to dust and airplanes drop death from miles up in the sky, wise Kindred duck their heads and seek cover. Those few who dare to drive a people to war consciously must exercise extreme caution. Once the conflict begins, it takes on an uncontrollable life of its own.

EUROPE ASCENDANT

The 19th century was another golden era for the Ventrue, reminiscent of the first three centuries A.D. when Rome reigned supreme. After the all-consuming Napoleonic wars that opened the century, Britain emerged as the largest power in the continent and eventually the world. Even with the loss of influence in America and the problems in France, Clan Ventrue found itself positioned perfectly to cultivate influence in every part of the world. The British Ventrue, under the "prince," Queen Anne of London, made new fortunes many times over and spread their web of contacts and childer to Africa, India and Asia.

To this night, at least one Ventrue still claims domain established during this century in such Kindred-hostile locales as South Africa, several major cities in India, Hong Kong, Macao and the Holy Land. Likewise, they followed the British army into the Middle East, establishing an early presence in the region that would translate into important investments in the oil industry. By the end of the century, Ventrue around the world could claim to be part of the greatest empire Kindred and kine had ever known.

The Ventrue position in Britain also put them in a prime position to take advantage of England's other great 19th-century triumph: the Industrial Revolution. Ventrue money played a significant role in the nation's industrialization. As far as the Ventrue were concerned, the more mortals in cities the better, especially if they could profit from said mortals financially. The Ventrue scarcely needed to do anything but invest wisely and watch the money pour in. They neutralized the few Sabbat and anarch forays into the burgeoning labor movements quickly, usually by paying off the mortal labor leaders, cracking down on the workers and utterly destroying the offending Kindred.

After the models established by Robert Kross, Hardestadt and other prominent Teutonic Ventrue, members of the clan in Germany took advantage of the growing industrial movement and nationalist sentiment to help unify their homeland under one rule. Chancellor Bismarck did most of the work on his own, never knowing that guardian Ventrue had to intercede to save his life more than half-a-dozen times when backward-thinking Kindred and meddlesome Sabbat tried to eliminate him. By the end of the century, Germany was a growing power, with the Ventrue firmly ensconced therein.

FROM TORPOR RETURNED

Whatever aspect of vampire physiology it is that drives Kindred into and out of torpor, it can be decidedly disastrous, especially on the political front. From time to time, a powerful Ventrue slips into the long sleep, leaving behind a monetary and political empire that needs tending or (more often) suffers dissection by his contemporaries and rivals. When the Kindred rises once more, he naturally craves whatever it is he has missed. In most clans, Kindred accept that torpor has its price. In Clan Ventrue, however, a period in torpor does not revoke a Kindred's rights or, more importantly, his rank. Therefore, a highly respected Ventrue can often return after hundreds of years and expect his position to be waiting for him, preserved by acknowledgement of his *dignitas*.

According to rumor, the most recent clan elder to rise again is Philippe de Margaux, a French Ventrue who last succumbed to torpor in the late 18th century. Embraced in A.D. 894, Philippe has accumulated a great deal of *dignitas*, holding the title of prince on two separate occasions and as a Ventrue archon for nearly three decades. Within the clan, he has achieved the title of *strategos* (the second-highest accolade the clan recognizes). Before he disappeared mysteriously in 1791, he was a strong candidate for justicar. Thinking he was dead at the hands of the Sabbat (who claimed credit for his Final Death), the Ventrue forgot about Philippe promptly, right up until the moment he walked into a convocation of the Directorate in Lyons.

As an established *strategos*, Philippe expects certain rights and privileges from his peers and lessers. Unfortunately for him, the world has no place for him right now. His resources long ago plundered by fellow Ventrue and other Kindred, thrown into a time he scarcely understands, Philippe now struggles just to come to grips with how much times have changed. Various factions now vie for Philippe's support, not because of his influence but because of the rank and *dignitas* attached to his name. Each faction hopes to use his reputation to further its own agendas.

Of course, Philippe realizes exactly what is taking place, and he plays the factions against one another, promising endorsement for favors or providing introductions for resources for the time being until he can establish a new foundation for himself. He has begun to attract a following of talented young Ventrue who see a chance to work with a clan great who can use a hand — and repay their loyalty later. He, in turn, hopes to use their knowledge of the present to restore the glories and honors of his past.

As the 20th century turned, the Ventrue looked ahead to a prosperous future. Europe seemed more secure than ever. They had surpassed or achieved equal footing with the Sabbat in America, and their power seemed on the rise. With continued support from the old world, victory there seemed inevitable. Then came the rest of the 20th century, and everything changed.

Two Great Wars

World War One came as an utter surprise for all involved, including the Ventrue. As assassination mushroomed into world war, the Kindred of Europe — particularly the Ventrue — decided to secure their positions, batten down the hatches and ride out the storm.

The new bloodiest war in history exceeded all expectations and changed the face of Europe and the world. Germany was left a wreck, and much of Eastern Europe had been redefined beyond recognition. The Ventrue stayed well away from the trenches, but their industrial concerns suffered greatly during the war. Politically, Europe was in chaos, and many Ventrue had to cultivate new contacts among the post-war governments. When the Depression settled in a dozen years later, things only got worse. A number of prominent Ventrue, including Robert Kross, left the Old World for the United States, hoping to take advantage of the situation to carve out new territories and shore up the Camarilla's position against the Sabbat. Besides, the state of their old homes had become too depressing to contemplate.

The rise of fascism in Germany and Italy gave hope to many of the Ventrue who remained. In Italy — a nation that had seemingly known nothing but chaos and internal political strife for centuries — the Ventrue fell in behind Mussolini and bought into the propaganda that he planned to restore Italy to the glory of ancient Rome. Sweeter words were never heard by Ventrue ears. Important clan members like Juan-Miguel Ramirez in Spain and Cattarina de Volo in Italy stepped right in line behind the fascist parties and seized the opportunity to rebuild the fortunes and influence they had lost during the war.

In Germany, matters were more complicated. Many Ventrue had strong antipathy toward the Nazi party, chiefly because of its professed "socialist" and "populist" roots. Too many aspects of Hitler's program reminded the old Ventrue of the Inquisition. Coupled with Hitler's known interest in the occult, the elders saw a very real danger in a populist movement steeped in mysticism. If the Nazi party could believe Jews were responsible for

all their evils, would it be such a step for them to believe that vampires had a role as well?

The younger Ventrue felt no such fear. They saw in Hitler what the Italian Ventrue saw in Mussolini: a new hope. The Nazis could restore order, rebuild the industries and armies, and keep the population in line. As it turned out, influencing Hitler was nigh impossible, chiefly because he was so well guarded and so paranoid of paranormal manipulation that no Kindred could get to him. Although many Ventrue benefited from and had local influence within the Nazi party, few had any say in its direction.

When war did come, it quickly threw all Europe back into chaos. The Ventrue peerage of *ephors* were caught on opposite sides of the war with competing interests. For five long years, it was pretty much every European Kindred for himself. Avoid the bombs, take what advantage you can and keep your head down was all the help the *ephors* could give their childer. Meanwhile, Ventrue in America cashed in on the suddenly booming military-industrial complex, and they never looked back. As with the mortal world, World War Two marked a continuing decline for Europe and a rise in American influence amongst the Ventrue.

THE NUCLEAR QUESTION

No single event has given both Kindred and kine more nightmares than the first atomic blast over Hiroshima. In fact, some might argue that the Kindred feared the event more than mortals. Mortals already knew that their lives could vanish in an instant. Now Kindred faced the fact that humanity could, with the touch of a button, wipe whole cities off the map, Kindred and all.

The Ventrue, with their high-level government and military interests, have kept a close watch on the nuclear situation. Although a radical faction of the clan proposed various methods to acquire a bomb for themselves in the early '60s, this plan was quickly abandoned as both dangerous an infeasible. No Kindred trusted any other, not even (or especially…) a fellow Ventrue, with such power. In the chill of the Cold War, the Ventrue shifted their policy toward one of containment. Such weapons belonged in the hands of responsible mortal government and out of the spheres of influence of unpredictable groups like the anarchs and — nightmare of nightmares — the Sabbat.

The fear of a nuclear-capable Sabbat towers over some within the clan. The Soviet Union's collapse, the spread of nuclear technology and black-market weapons to rogue nations like Iraq, Iran and North Korea, and the dangerously lax security surrounding certain nuclear materials all combine to form the stuff of the Camarilla's worst nightmares. Few Ventrue would put it past the Sabbat to nuke a powerful Camarilla domain like London or Chicago just to strike at the sect.

Although no one has any evidence of Sabbat possession of (or even interest in) nuclear weapons, the Ventrue Directorate has sprung into action. It has appointed several watchers devoted to monitoring the spread of nuclear weapons and taking whatever means are necessary to control arms proliferation. With methods much more direct and deadly than those employed by the United Nations, Ventrue agents have eliminated several prominent black-market arms dealers who professed access to nuclear weapons. Then, in typical Ventrue fashion, they absorbed the dead agents' business into their own holdings. The watchers, who make up an informal clique with no official title, continue to operate tonight, although it is transforming more and more into a business venture rather than an anti-proliferation group.

THE COLD WAR

The past 50 years have seen Clan Ventrue reassert itself once more after a half-century of troubles and decline. The clan thrived during the four-decade cold war, taking full advantage of the paranoia on both sides to make massive profits and sink its tendrils into the growing government bureaucracies that came to dominate industrialized governments. Having learned a valuable lesson from the debacle of the Crusades, savvy Ventrue have determined to hold their resources together despite the mortal conflict raging around them. Ventrue on both sides of the Iron Curtain worked in concert, watching their respective "governments" act against one another for the greatest advantage.

Differences arose between the two sides, however. Eastern Ventrue invested their resources and time into the authoritarian governments of the Communist Bloc, but they often found themselves opposed by the powerful Russian Brujah. The Ventrue were particularly fond of the various incarnations of secret police that came into existence, finding them an excellent way to keep the kine in line and under supervision. In the West, the Ventrue concentrated on the recovering European industries, all but abandoning the last of their feudal and noble ties for big business and majority shares in multinational corporations.

When the Cold War ended, the few former Communist Bloc Ventrue who did manage to cultivate some degree of influence found themselves stripped of power just as the governments they supported had been. A decade later, these Ventrue are still trying to recover while Western Ventrue-owned companies step into the dismal economies and invest heavily in national infrastructures. As a result, a number of Ventrue in the East

— particularly in Russia, Poland, Bulgaria and the Ukraine — have turned to organized crime as a new field of influence. There, they run straight into Brujah interests, and the two clans have become engaged in their own mob war over the issue.

In America, the Ventrue enjoyed a particularly profitable post-war era. The rampant fear of communism worked in the clan's favor. They could and did oust uncooperative or unwanted mortals from government easily with simple innuendo and a few loaded suggestions about the person's loyalties. The '50s served the clan particularly well, helping the Ventrue establish a firm base from which to withstand the trials that were to come.

Once again, the Ventrue and Camarilla found themselves caught between two simultaneous threats. The anarchs rose in great numbers on the West Coast, effectively negating any claim of Camarilla domain in Southern California. Timely action taken by Ventrue leaders such as Lodin and Robert Kross helped keep the anarch plague from spreading too far. This rise marked the first successful anarch revolt, although it remains to be seen how long the anarchs can hold on to what they've taken. That claim is certainly threatened in the modern nights, considering the swelling presence of the Cathayan menace in the crumbling "Anarch Free State."

On the Canadian border and to the south in Mexico, the Sabbat continue to present a more serious threat. It galls the Ventrue to no end that the Sabbat managed to usurp Camarilla domains in most of the lucrative cities of the American East, particularly in New England and the Mid-Atlantic states. The clan blames decentralization within the Camarilla and the continuing weakness shown in the face of Sabbat aggression for the losses — wouldn't the struggle fare better with a (Ventrue) warlord? Recent Black Hand excursions into the South have only made matters worse. The Ventrue leadership in Europe has been slow to recognize the problem in the United States, but now the Ventrue leviathan shows signs of stirring, much to the concern of less authoritative clans.

A New Era

Clan Ventrue stands at a crossroads. With the Gangrel departure from the Camarilla, Hardestadt's dream has begun to fray at the seams. The Sabbat appears stronger than ever before, or at least as strong as it has been for many centuries. Clan Ventrue has always provided leadership for the Camarilla, but some say that perhaps it is time to start acting unilaterally, like true leaders and princes in the original sense of the word. Let the other clans follow if they will. They are welcome to come along, but the time for waiting has passed.

With each passing month, this sentiment gains stronger support from the American Ventrue — many of whom are young neofeudalists just having their first taste of power. The more established European Ventrue remain unwilling to commit themselves to such a rash course of action, or unwilling to consider that it has ever been anything but. The Camarilla has worked well for over five centuries, and they think it still has life left in it until the night the heretics' Gehenna comes.

Other Ventrue, both elders and neonates, feel that the clan suffers from a lack of strong leadership. The secretive Directorate does little but foment unrest among the ranks to justify itself and look to its own interests. In response to this claim, a number of prominent elder Kindred, including Robert Kross and several others, have set about searching for the most famous surviving leaders the clan has known: Camilla and Lysander. Once found and revived, either one of these powerful Kindred could change the clan's entire direction. Of course, some claim that both of them are quite awake, that they actually sit on the Directorate this very night. Although there is no proof one way or the other, one imagines that they would reveal themselves in a time of crisis, something they haven't done yet.

Then also are the doves, Ventrue who want to make some sort of peace with the Sabbat. They feel that this ongoing war is utterly senseless and that the two sects are not as diametrically opposed as they seem. For all their professed disdain for the Masquerade, Sabbat still do not wander the streets openly, proclaiming their nature. For all their ties to humanity, the Camarilla Kindred are still monsters that feed upon kine. Indeed, even though Clan Ventrue stands as the leader against Sabbat aggression, it is the clan most similar to the Sabbat's own leaders in attitude and demeanor. Ventrue seldom show anything but disdain for humans as people — the masses are far more vital than the individuals, while those same individuals have value as sustenance and tools. These Kindred argue that perhaps the time has come to reach an accord.

For now, the hawks still far outnumber the doves. Although some logic might lie behind the doves' arguments, logic rarely plays a significant role in Kindred relations. The Ventrue and Lasombra — and the Camarilla and Sabbat, by extension — simply hate each other too much for true peace ever to come about. Some say that the only thing that can ever unite the two sects is a common threat, such as the much-anticipated (but never seen) return of the Antediluvians, an event that seems most unlikely to many Ventrue. Why worry about something that might never happen, when the enemy is already before them?

It will be an important century for the Ventrue. They still wield great temporal power and influence, arguably more than any other single Kindred clan. But that power is waning; the base is crumbling. Unless the stagnant leadership finds a way to reinvigorate itself and the Ventrue as a whole, the decline could well become unstoppable as government and economics make the transition to the global scale. History has shown, though, that the Ventrue do bounce back, sometimes coming through when no one else expects it. Why? Because unlike other clans that claim to be, the Ventrue truly are wholly ruthless, cold and calculating. They are willing to do whatever and betray whomever it takes for them to survive. It is their heritage, their tradition, their history.

And the Ventrue do so love their history.

The New New Thing

Long-memoried and tradition-bound, the Ventrue often have a hard time keeping up with the latest technological developments. In the last hundred 150 years, it has become almost impossible. A Ventrue who went into torpor in 2100 B.C. and woke up in A.D. 1200 would find the world different, but not shockingly so. One who went to sleep in A.D. 1600 and woke up only 400 years later can scarcely believe his eyes. Even Ventrue who rose every night during the transition have a hard time dealing with the changes

The clan as a whole has yet to step fully into the information age. As tradition demands, important meetings should take place face to face. Although high-speed travel makes arranging such meetings easier than it once was, scions of the clan and the Directorate must still come together from many disparate lands in order to make a decision that a conference call could have settled in five minutes. E-mail and even overnight express remain mysterious, almost supernatural forces to most elder Ventrue.

Instead of even bothering to try to understand the new technology, Ventrue have come to rely on their progeny to do it for them. Like kings giving orders to their court magicians, the elders simply state what they want done to the technology-minded youth, servants and ghouls, and they hope it happens. This role naturally gives the in-the-know Kindred a sizable advantage and tremendous influence for their age. In some cases, computer-savvy neonates have access to clan information that Kindred centuries older than them do not know. Still, the clan is far from computerized, and many business records, correspondence and orders are still written on paper. Thus far, it has not proved too egregious a disadvantage for the clan, but as the elders lag ever more behind the times, their position becomes more tenuous.

Chapter Two: The King Is Dead, Long Live the King

'My dear sir,' he said. 'I must beg you to excuse me for my discourtesy. The members of my family have always been peculiarly affected by the sight of blood. Call it an idiosyncrasy if you like, but it does at times make us behave like wild animals. I am grieved to have so far forgotten my manners as to behave in such a strange way before a guest. I assure you that I have sought to conquer this failing, and for that reason I keep away from my fellow-men.'

— Frederick Cowles, "The Vampire of Kaldenstein"

Blood alone does not define a Ventrue. While all Ventrue might stem from the same third-generation progenitor, this fact does not make a Kindred truly Ventrue in and of itself. One need only look to the despised *antitribu* to see the truth of this statement. Being truly Ventrue is a mode of thought, a way of seeing the world and even an unlifestyle. In order to be truly one of the clan, one must act the part.

As members of a complicated clan with serious, intricate and prized traditions, the Ventrue have a number of distinct mores and attitudes that define them. These ideals comprise a world-view that many of the clan's members share. Even those who go against the mold acknowledge these ideals by flouting them. While not every Kindred shares all of these beliefs, almost every clan member is aware of them, and each probably holds many of them dear to her own still heart. Even when one disagrees with a particular philosophical position, she often plays along, for these views define the Ventrue and

dictate their place and purpose in Kindred society — the very society they lead perforce.

Noblesse Oblige

As the original leaders among the third and successive generations, many Ventrue feel that they have ample cause, precedent and justification to lead the other clans (if not rule them outright, in some cases). Their reasoning probably stems from the same justification European kings used to establish their claim to power at one time: divine right. In short, the argument goes thus: Through His vessel, Caine, God chose us to lead the Kindred; therefore, we should. If Caine hadn't chosen us, we wouldn't be in charge. The clan's natural abilities to lead, sway and just plain control others only serve to lend credence to their claims. Caine created them to lead his children, therefore, that is what they must — not should, but *must* — do.

With divine right comes divine responsibility. The Ventrue do not exist to rule over the other Kindred as masters rule over slaves. Far from it. Caine bestowed their many gifts upon them in order to ensure that his other childer had strong, able-minded leadership in times of trouble. Ventrue often refer to themselves as "shepherds" or "stewards" of their fellow Kindred. Many borrow another phrase from the days when nobles ruled: *noblesse oblige*.

Simply put, this French phrase means that the Ventrue feel obligated to work on behalf of their fellow Kindred for the betterment of all the race of Caine. Having been given such great power, position and natural ability, it is their duty to pay society back. The Ventrue throw themselves into unlives of service to the greater cause, which means the Camarilla in the modern nights. As the most influential clan within the sect, the entire movement's existence relies on the Ventrue themselves remaining strong. Therefore, accruing more power and influence to themselves is not so much a selfish act as a noble one. Their strength benefits all si— *five* other clans as well.

Of course, Ventrue feel absolutely no obligation toward those who spurn their help. The clans of the Sabbat gave up any rights to call upon the Ventrue for protection long ago. More recently, the Gangrel too have turned their backs on Caine's chosen. As such, few Ventrue feel any sympathy for these bestial pariahs. The Gangrel made their choice, and they must exist with the consequences. This same principle holds true for individual Kindred as well. When someone breaks openly from the Camarilla — as anarchs often claim to have done — most Ventrue disregard any obligation to them as well, unless they can earn something from it. Obligation is a two-way street after all.

Dignitas

For many Ventrue, the clan first realized the role of leadership fully during the early nights of the Roman Republic. It's no wonder, then, that they take many of their ideas and ideals from their venerable Latin forbears. At the Republic's height, great men accomplished great deeds and built an empire that spanned farther than any empire in mortal or Cainite history had. They fought wars, engaged in fierce political battles and sacked cities for more than just the money or the power. They did it because their *dignitas* demanded it.

Dignitas is a hard word to define. It encompasses not only simple dignity, but also many of the Japanese ideals summarized in the word "face" (as in saving face). *Dignitas* is a person's standing in society, a measure of his accomplishments, his social stature and his honor. For Rome's patrician class, *dignitas* was nothing less than the true measure of a man's self, of his worth as a person.

The Ventrue adopted — and, in turn, helped promote — the concept of *dignitas* with a vengeance. In one simple word, it encapsulated everything that they

had held sacred and important for millennia. The Ventrue see themselves as (and, in fact, they are) the patrician class of Kindred society — the nobles of good birth, breeding and behavior who must act with honor and be treated with dignity. For many Ventrue, as with the early Romans, *dignitas* is all.

As a clan member rises in prominence, his *dignitas* grows with him. It is the sum of his accomplishments to date. The battles won, offices held and alliances made all come together to increase a Ventrue's *dignitas*. At the same time, conflicts lost, insults taken and failures recognized all serve to detract from his status. A Ventrue's *dignitas* can fall just as it can rise. For many Ventrue, the fear and anger associated with losing face outstrip the fear of fire or Final Death. In such a history-minded clan, the loss of one's life pales in comparison to the loss of one's legacy.

Increasing one's *dignitas* is the true goal that most Ventrue spend their nights pursuing relentlessly. Talk of "noble obligations" and preserving the Camarilla sound good, and they are important in theory, but many Ventrue seek to aggrandize themselves on a personal level first and foremost. The Ventrue do not denigrate the concept with any sure way of calculating *dignitas*; they observe no "*dignitas* points" or awards system. It is intangible, like reputation or fame. *Dignitas* grows not only with success but with achieving that success in the right and proper way. A Kindred who reaches new heights of political influence through the standard course accrues more *dignitas* than one who does so at the expense of other Ventrue, the reputation of the clan or simple decorum. Image, tradition and values play as much a role in determining *dignitas* as do money, influence and temporal power.

Aside from breaches of the Traditions, the clan knows few crimes greater than impugning another member's *dignitas* groundlessly. Ventrue take assaults on their stature very seriously. Spreading rumors, taking credit for another's work and insulting a Ventrue without just cause (publicly or privately) are just a few of the ways one can diminish *dignitas*. Doing so is a sure way to make an enemy for all of unlife, and it can indeed be cause for severe punishment or discipline. Centuries-long feuds continue tonight between elders who feel that some idle comment at a social gathering in the 16th century threatened their *dignitas*. Although this example is extreme, it is indicative of a greater trend. In some cases, Ventrue have actually petitioned elders or princes for permission to destroy young Kindred who insulted them foolishly in some way.

Assistance

Perhaps no tradition sets the Ventrue more apart from other clans than their Ethic of Succor. While other clans, such as the Tremere, are closely knit and often support

members, no clan has the same "no excuses, no exceptions" practice of coming to each other's assistance in times of need. Many Blue Bloods credit this tradition as the foundation for the clan's continuing strength. While they might fight and compete with one another, the Ventrue invariably rally and fight as one when the time comes and a crisis is upon them, whether they like it or not.

Observing the Ethic of Succor means ultimately extending a fellow Ventrue aid, should she ask it, regardless of personal piques and desires. Actually doing so can, admittedly, be hard. Many Ventrue have learned how to argue successfully that strengthening their own position and eliminating or pushing aside a weaker rival are good for the Blue Blood in question, and that type of argument mirrors the Ventrue clan's own position vis-a-vis the rest of the Camarilla. Semantics aside, no Ventrue can ever willingly and obviously harm another who requests hospitality under the ethic's auspices, nor would most seek to. The penalties for such behavior are grave indeed, ranging from mere blackballing to oaths of vengeance. Moreover, when a Ventrue invokes succor, the member must answer and do good service. In return, he can expect her to do the same for him.

Respecting other Ventrue means not violating their territory, not competing with them in their established holdings and, most importantly, not impugning their *dignitas*. It also means that a Ventrue gives aid to a fellow when in need, no matter how damned inconvenient doing so might prove to be. This tradition dates back to a time when Ventrue hoarded influence in Rome against all other clans. Although the Ventrue have five "cousin" clans to call upon tonight as well, they often choose to trust only themselves. When a Ventrue asks, you act.

The act of asking is where tradition comes in. Succor can take many forms, especially among Ventrue liberal enough to twist this tradition to their advantage: asking for help, asking for favors, asking for information, asking for a light. Any Ventrue can refuse any of these requests with legitimate impunity. In order to invoke the Ethic of Succor, a clan member must say specifically, "I implore your assistance, cousin," or any one of a half dozen other recognized phrases. Honor and custom bind a Ventrue to help another when the request is phrased thus. However, the beggar had better have good cause. Sabbat had best be banging at the door or rivals staging a corporate takeover or else the Kindred seeking aid risks losing much *dignitas* in her peers' eyes. Requesting aid in a true crisis carries no shame. Requesting aid out of fear or misapprehension does.

It happens occasionally that two or more Ventrue call upon their fellows for succor simultaneously. In such an instance, the eldest Kindred typically receives preference. If the aid-giver feels that he can spare the resources to help a younger member as well, he may divert some aid to his needy cousin. This circumstance occurs rarely. When a Ventrue calls for help, he is in serious need, and he has little time to think of others. An even more prominent or influential Ventrue can, however, choose whom he wishes to help. He might help the elder or, seeing that the elder has adequate resources of his own, he might turn to the neonate.

Failure to assist carries with it attendant losses in *dignitas*, status and influence. Moreover, should a Ventrue complain that another member ignored his plea for help, the aggrieved Kindred has the grounds for a formal complaint. As with so much within the clan, the penalties for this crime vary according to the *dignitas* and importance of the complainant. A neonate who ignores the request of a powerful prince may well face a blood bond or even the Tradition of Destruction. A prince who ignores a neonate might have to pay a fine or grant the youth a boon, according to the Directorate's findings. Still, these events are rare. Ventrue take great pride in helping one another. They not only feel that it sets them apart from and above the other clans, it also means that someone owes them a boon. For the Ventrue even more than the haughty Toreador, boons are better than gold.

Politeness

As the products of five millennia of noble upbringing, class and culture, the Ventrue place great importance on gentility. Ventrue etiquette can become quite complex, especially in Europe where deathless standards persist unto the modern nights. Things are often less formal in the New World, but only by comparison. Even the most casual of Old World cities usually seems stodgy and overly polite by modern standards.

For the Ventrue, politeness means more than just carrying on with traditional ways and means. It serves some very important functions, especially when it comes to making sure that individual clan members can overcome their petty personal differences and respect the social structure. By nature, Kindred are excitable creatures, prone to holding grudges and overreacting to insults. Add in the average Ventrue's regard for his *dignitas*, and politeness becomes not only a matter of manners but a matter of survival. Interacting with one another in a sophisticated, polite and admittedly distant manner helps alleviate the threat of flaring tempers. Discourse becomes less visceral as it becomes slightly removed from reality. With layers of polite gossip and deferential tones separating two roiling egos, tensions become secondary to what is said and the manner in which each party communicates it.

Unless they have a close personal relationship, Ventrue almost always address one another in a formal manner, either by title or surname as the occasion requires. One does not ask personal questions of another without being invited to do so. Polite conversation means no insults (veiled or open), no unsolicited criticisms of equals or superiors, and no speaking out of turn. Interrupting another Ventrue's conversation is most inappropriate. Most conversations begin with idle talk intended to put both parties at ease. Usually such talk has to do with temporal business or social affairs — something everyone can speak about, but that usually does not carry too many emotional attachments. Overall Ventrue conversations tend to sound wordy but pleasant. Few dignified Ventrue raise their voices or ignore another's words. Although she might be seething on the inside, a Ventrue of *dignitas* never shows it.

Control

The Beast: It lurks in every vampire's cold heart, although the Ventrue are loath to admit it. Blue Bloods often tame their Beast with a savage passion and keep it in check as often as possible — indeed, even the most jaded elder probably still harbors some degree of *humanitas*, no matter how minuscule. Some haughty Ventrue even cease to acknowledge the inner monsters' existence at all, claiming that it is a curse that afflicts only other, lesser bloodlines. Others admit to the uncontrollable urges but take pride in their ability to control them. Either way, all but the most callous Ventrue holds self-discipline in the highest regard. Self-control unlocks the door to success, setting the Blue Bloods apart from those who let their emotions rule them. Emotional control, along with all other traits discussed here, helps define the Ventrue.

Slipping into a frenzy obviously stands as the most extreme example of loss of control. Strangely enough, it is the one slip that Ventrue forgive most easily. However much they don't want to admit it, all Kindred realize that the Beast lurks within each and every descendant of Caine. A vampire who frenzies has obviously passed the point of discretion. It is hoped that a Ventrue can control herself better than most under such circumstances, but these things do happen. As long as the out-of-control Kindred does no damage to the Masquerade or the well-being of the greater race of Caine, all is usually forgiven.

Less forgivable are the lesser lapses, perhaps due to their more inconsequential nature. A Ventrue should control every other aspect of his emotions, or at least appear to do so. Anger should not turn into rage, affection into lust or curiosity into desire. Bouts of shouting, the raising of fists in anger, uncontrolled laughter or even — heaven forbid — bloody tears are all consider terribly graceless. One of good breeding, manners and lofty *dignitas* does not debase herself in this manner. It just isn't done.

Aside from being unseemly, losing control usually leads to making mistakes, and the calculating Ventrue cannot abide avoidable mistakes. Leaders must, however, act when the challenge arises, sometimes without all the information they need or desire. Certainly, no one makes perfect decisions all the time. Mistakes under such circumstances do happen; a wrong decision made out of fear, hate, lust or even misplaced loyalty usually remains inexcusable, though. It is beneath a Ventrue's *dignitas* to act in such a way. It violates her obligations to the rest of her clan and the Kindred to let such feelings interfere with her ability to lead by example.

CRUELTY

For all their noble ideals about serving Kindred society as a whole and shepherding the Camarilla through the Final Nights, the Ventrue have a surprisingly nasty cruel streak. This fact stems mainly from the general Ventrue attitude that institutions and ideas are important while individuals (especially kine and non-Camarilla Kindred) are not so vital. Even Kindred of a Ventrue's own lineage, especially younger vampires multiple generations removed, scarcely warrant sympathy or attention. While they still speak of their roles as stewards and noble leaders, the fact is that, when it comes down to it, most Ventrue could not possibly care less about the fate of any given individuals aside from themselves. In fact, many feel the same way toward some of their own childer. As long as the Camarilla prospers (in the individual Ventrue's estimation), what does it matter if a few troublesome cousins perish in the process?

Of course, wise Kindred keep these less than respectful attitudes to themselves. Still, this obvious hypocrisy serves to rally many other Kindred against overly headstrong Ventrue.

When dealing with Kindred society, in which destroying a fellow vampire just isn't done without permission, this cruelty manifests itself politically or socially. Ventrue know no bounds when it comes to making and breaking deals. Their polite demeanor, archaic traditions and noble manner all belie the simple fact that they are willing to do anything for their own benefit — which they defend as the benefit of all Kindred — as long as they think that the goal is worthwhile. That is to say, most Ventrue have the sense not to eradicate contacts and friendships or take great risks for small gains. It's better to lose and survive to fight another night with your resources intact. However, when a Ventrue sees potential profit too choice to ignore, he holds nothing back.

Ventrue cannot help but be somewhat circumspect when they deal with other Kindred; by their own ethics every vampire has some basic rights to existence and even domain. Kine, however, have no such protections at all. For most, humans are like worker ants or peasants as in nights long past. Humans are necessary, but they are interchangeable and readily disposable. One can destroy a family's means of support just to stymie a rival's efforts and not think twice about it. The order to kill a troublesome union boss or frame a politician for blackmail

purposes might come as easily as an instruction to one's valet to press the gray suit for tomorrow night. Even the somewhat more personal process of perusing a mortal's mind for information and then manipulating the memories thereafter carries no emotional stigma for the Ventrue. As individuals, these kine matter not a whit.

It's not that the Ventrue hate humans, or even that they view humans as somehow lower on the food chain and therefore worth killing and torturing, as the Sabbat do. To the Ventrue, humans just aren't worth consideration as anything less than a great collective. Humanity brought about the Inquisition, a single human did not, or so goes another Ventrue maxim. Even though they themselves were once just like these humans, the Ventrue forget that more quickly than most. Unless they see some special spark in a person that makes him a potential resource or even possible ghoul or childe, humans mean little. Exploit them, abuse them, or just plain kill them — as long as the Masquerade remains intact and unthreatened, do what thou wilt with them.

Prejudice

According to their own oral history and annals, the Ventrue have Embraced only those "worthy" of the honor. Nobles, religious leaders and great military men have all found their way into Clan Ventrue over the centuries. The Ventrue have high standards for admittance into their ultra-exclusive club of undead. They want those accustomed to wielding influence and authority, those for whom command is second nature. In other words, they want men for the most part.

While gender plays no noticeable role in a Kindred once Embraced (as the race of Caine is egalitarian if not equitable), it has traditionally mattered a great deal before that fateful night. Women did not command the kind of influence that men had in Western society for not just centuries, but millennia. Exceptions arose, of course, but mostly of the sort that prove the rule. Likewise, some very ancient and potent female Kindred have earned clan honors. However, the number of men far outweighs the number of women, especially among the older Kindred — even in the modern nights. Clan Ventrue is very much an aged and malevolent "boy's club."

The ethnic makeup of New World Ventrue is predominantly Caucasian, with ratios of Nubian, Asian or Hispanic stock similar to those in the mortal world. In less cosmopolitan parts of the world, ethnic diversity is even less prevalent.

Outsiders often charge the Ventrue with thinking and acting old-fashioned. They allege that the clan is stuck in its ways and not open to adjustment. While this claim isn't as true as the outsiders would like to believe, it isn't entirely false either. These nights, most Ventrue are as color- and gender-aware as the society in which they dwell. They would not pause to Embrace an African-American or woman with great potential. Still, such is not the case for some Ventrue. Brought up in another time to believe in their inherent superiority, even death has not eradicated fully such petty concerns of flesh tone and genitalia. These old-guard Ventrue still look down on women, continue to deny minorities advancement and generally hold the clan back because of their anachronistic prejudices.

Unfortunately, Kindred who hold positions of great power, especially in established regions of Europe and the Middle East, have been influential for centuries with only minor interruption. Ancient prejudices still thrive in these domains. A very few still have edicts forbidding the Embrace of certain types of kine, but the progressive thinkers among the Ventrue frown on this less enlightened view. As a result, most have dropped the restrictions (at least publicly). Even so, Kindred of "unfortunate heritage" have a hard time dealing with their prejudiced elders. If the minority is not even of Clan Ventrue, bigoted elders often snub them completely. Ventrue warrant a little more respect because *dignitas* demands it, but few mistake the nastiness that lies behind a patronizing smile.

Clan Organization

Of late, many have compared the Ventrue clan's organization to a corporation. While this simile *seems* (and in some ways *is*) appropriate, it is largely inaccurate. The clan's current hierarchical arrangement predates the modern corporation by many centuries, and it is rather a product of the clan's classical roots. In Europe, many clans still use the Greek and Latin names that have demarcated Ventrue for millennia, while it has become more fashionable in some parts of the New World to use the language of modern business. Both are as correct as they are misleading.

The system borrows heavily from the Roman Republic's political institutions. Although the democratic elements of that system were stripped away long ago, the overall structure and some of the names remain. This system runs parallel to the Camarilla's organization. Thus, someone might hold varying rank within both. Ventrue tend to place more esteem on Camarilla titles than on their all-but-outdated Ventrue titles except at the highest levels (such as the Directorate). Although they care about both, few outside the clan could care less about a Ventrue's internal standing. Always hungry for the respect and devotion of other Kindred, Ventrue naturally prefer to achieve offices that outsiders and clanmates will respect equally.

The Ventrue do take pride in the fact that every clan member has a place and knows just where he stands within the clan in relation to everyone else. Of course, the system is not at all like the Tremere's eldritch pyramid of authority or some military organization. One does not necessarily ascend a ladder of advancement from rank to rank. Rather, members can move through the (largely honorific) system as their abilities and fortunes decree. The Ventrue feel that this system allows them more flexibility and lets them spot new talent within the clan and reward it if desirable. The clan elders often point this latter facet of the system out to young Kindred who are anxious and frustrated at the lackluster success of their own unlives.

The clan's youth do have something to complain about, although the wise ones don't do so too loudly for fear of souring their own chances for advancement. Increasing esteem within the clan takes more than just ability. The elders, particularly the local and international Directorates, approve who advances when. No matter what those elders might tell the clan at large, their decision-making process does not (and never has) relied solely upon a Ventrue's ability and accomplishments. Personal feelings, alliances, jealousies, contacts, bribes, favors and a host of other purely political factors come into play — which is perfectly apropos in the social setting of Ventrue status. Ventrue who want to rise must learn to play the game and not make too many enemies (or make sure that they also have the right allies). Some resent this system. Most recognize it as the exact kind of policy that prepares them best for dealing with the rest of the world in true Ventrue fashion.

It should be noted that almost any Ventrue, unless expressly forbidden by one of the bodies described later, can literally buy into the hierarchy. The various Ventrue bodies manage tremendous assets, most of which are made up of contributions allocated by individual clan members. The lowliest, most impoverished Ventrue could theoretically set aside one Mexican peso per year for support of the clan coffers and reap the full benefits of the hierarchy's recognition. In truth, this sort of thing happens rarely. The higher levels of the hierarchy are very much a venue for the wealthy and influential. For less prominent Blue Bloods, the benefit they have is that they are rarely forced to set aside funds for the clan's greater assets. "The Ventrue have no tithes or dues," as the saying goes, and most young Ventrue prefer to deal with the world on their own terms, at least until the opportunity to join the esteemed ranks of the peerage means more than shining the silver at an elder's soiree.

The Titles

Ventrue love titles and offices, although most would never admit to such emotional attachment to anything, much less a sometimes ceremonial appellation. The Ventrue have made distinct two levels of title: local and clanwide. In each case, the highest-ranking Ventrue have

the greatest discretion over promoting and demoting others through the ranks. There are no elections, and no position carries any "job security."

Clan Titles

The Directorate (The *Ephorate*)

Most young Ventrue have heard about the Directorate, the shadowy body of 12 or so elder Ventrue that has tremendous sway over the clan. Older Ventrue still remember the older name, the *Ephorate*, by which the council was known for many centuries. The classical name comes from the ruling council of ancient Sparta. The clan adopted this name in the Renaissance, since the word "senate" had unpleasant associations for them and seemed inappropriate for a body of less than three dozen individuals. Even in the 21st century, the two titles remain interchangeable, although "Board of Directors" or "Directorate" is becoming somewhat more fashionable.

The *ephors* or directors establish precedent in matters of "clan policy." Just what that statement means is open to interpretation: Certainly, individual Ventrue princes have preeminent influence over their domains. The clan justicar definitely has her own powers, responsibilities and free will. The Ventrue representative to the Camarilla Inner Circle has his or her own authority as well. What, then, does the *Ephorate* do exactly?

For starters, the *ephors* manage several clanwide endeavors and clan holdings. Ventrue have vast monetary reserves spread through banks and secret caches around the world. They own vast amounts of real estate, they hold stock in every major (and most minor) corporations, and they hold controlling interests in more than a few of them. These resources allow them to disperse funds to clan members in need and give them tremendous political and economic clout if they choose to use it. Where a coalition of individual Ventrue might backstab each other into futility or be unable to bring enough resources to bear against a certain situation, the *Ephorate* can act as a guidance council or lending institution. For example, a coterie of Ventrue wishing to establish a global communications network could appeal to the *ephors*, not only for venture capital, but also as a board of directors unaffiliated with the network company itself (thereby assuring the petitioning Kindred that their fellow venture partners wouldn't have undue influence over their own share of the operation). Managing this vast, invisible financial empire alone takes a great deal of their time.

The *ephors* also choose the clan's representative to the Camarilla Inner Circle. The Kindred chosen for this great honor invariably comes from their own ranks, although his or her identity remains a secret (as do those of most of the *ephors*, who work almost exclusively through assistant

Kindred and other agents). This influence over the course of Camarilla politics also ensures that all Ventrue take heed of the *Ephorate*'s will. After all, most of them hope to hold high Camarilla honors one night, be it the title of prince, archon or even justicar.

The *ephors* also set policy for the clan as a whole, for what it's worth. Clanwide policy issues usually center around what stance the Ventrue take on various political and security issues within the Camarilla. When the *ephors* make a decision about such an issue, everyone within the clan is expected to follow their lead. While many Ventrue may ignore such directives easily, the princes, primogen and other visible elders are certainly encouraged to heed them. These policies usually focus on topics such as relations with and actions against the Sabbat, how to check the rising power of the Tremere, what to do about Caitiff and so on. They also attend to more mundane matters, including which party to support in national elections, certain stocks that should be traded at certain prices and other economic and political concerns.

Perhaps the *Ephorate*'s most important power is its role in arbitrating intra-clan disputes. When Ventrue disagree (a common enough event) or one of them violates any of the myriad clan traditions and guidelines, the Directorate has established a process for resolving such problems. The local clan structures take responsibility for handling the smaller disputes, but when serious matters come up or two potent Ventrue collide, the *ephors* have the power to pass final judgment on the matter. Typical disputes involve conflict over domains and areas of influence. Most of the time, the clan leaders let individual Ventrue work these issues out among themselves—such is the way of the Jyhad. Sometimes, however, the *ephors* need to step in, especially in very volatile or far-sweeping cases.

Crime is another matter altogether. When a Ventrue breaks with clan tradition, he risks not only his *dignitas*, but his very place within the clan and even his existence. The two most grave crimes are slaying a fellow Ventrue and failing to heed a call for assistance. Both events come to the Directorate's attention so rarely — although they undoubtedly take place with relative frequency — that the body has full authority over all such cases. When charges are brought, the accused comes before the *ephors*, or possibly only some of the *ephors*, to stand trial. The *ephors* preside over the trial from behind a curtain or two-way mirror, or within darkness so that the accused never sees them or hears them speak. An advocate questions the witnesses and cross-examines the accused. The trial seldom lasts more than a few nights, and the *ephors* may even resort to the use of vulgar Disciplines to find the truth of the matter if the matter is in doubt.

Having established the truth, the *Ephorate* can administer one of several punishments. Final Death is a dire option, since no clan can claim such power over its members, at least according to the literal wording of Camarilla Traditions. In reality, the *ephors* have ordered more than a few Final Deaths over their long history, although they have never admitted to it. The *ephors* can strip a Ventrue of his title, his holdings and his boons, or even impose a term of imprisonment (sometimes with a stake through the heart for good measure). In extreme cases, the *Ephorate* can demand that the criminal Kindred agree to a blood bond either to the aggrieved party or an influential and responsible clan member.

All of these temporal powers aside, the Directorate's most important role is not so easily quantified. The directors set the tone and stance for the entire clan. Their philosophies, leadership styles and political stances are discussed and debated through the ranks, influencing the majority of the Ventrue to some degree or another, as an example of how (or how not to) conduct one's affairs. As the most powerful members of the most resourceful clan, they have contacts everywhere, servants almost everywhere and direct influence in global arenas. Between them, they can accomplish grave feats since their combined power — especially vis-a-vis the mortal world—rivals that of a major government. The fact that few Ventrue even know who sits on the council makes their potential power all the more fearsome and mysterious. If ever a group deserved the title of secret masters, it is the *Ephorate*.

Of course, such grand ideals and practices fall far beyond the scope of almost any given Ventrue's sphere of influence. A neonate whose sire denies his attempts to blackmail a police detective is none too likely to attract the Directorate's attention, and few *ephors* care if some 13th-generation Blue Blood has chosen to flout one principle of *dignitas*. As with all matters political and the very nature of the Ventrue's collective empire, individuals matter far, far less than the moment of the greater body.

The Elders (*Stragetgoi*)

Clan Ventrue has many venerable members who do not sit on the Board of Directors. Some are princes, others primogen, but all have garnered great respect within the clan. Likewise, they are much more public figures than the *ephors*, at least within Ventrue's own ranks, due to their lack of secrecy. No doubt some of those whom the world recognizes as *strategoi* are in fact *ephors* as well. The world, of course, has no way of knowing. Directors or no, the *strategoi* are the honorary "generals" of Clan Ventrue, as their name suggests. They carry out the policies that the secretive *ephors* hand down, enforcing the Directorate's will. For the most part, they are the only Ventrue to have direct, possibly even face-to-face, contact with members of the *Ephorate*.

The *strategoi* effectively run the operations of the *Ephorate*'s quotidian concerns. Each is responsible for a different part of the *Ephorate*'s dominion. In heavily populated regions, this responsibility can apply to just a few hundred square miles, while it can cover a number of whole states in the wide-open plains of the American and Canadian West. *Strategoi* usually make their havens within their territory, often serving as a primogen or esteemed elder. *Strategos* princes are more rare, since their duties to the Kindred of their domain occupy too much time and make it hard to fulfill their other obligations as well as they should.

From night to night, the *strategos* oversees Ventrue business and political affairs in his region in addition to tending to his own needs and *dignitas*. In times of crisis, the *strategos* must step in and enforce the Directorate's policy findings, whether regarding Sabbat incursions, anarch riots or Cainite power plays that threaten Ventrue holdings. They have no official power over princes of course, but they do have the *Ephorate*'s weight and influence behind them, which provides them with resources even beyond their own considerable assets. *Strategoi* can also help arbitrate intra-clan disputes and bring the rare rogue Ventrue to the Directorate's attention. All in all, the *strategos*' powers are somewhat analogous to those of a Camarilla justicar, although extending only to clan Ventrue, of course.

Troubleshooters (*Lictors*)

The *strategoi* themselves seldom dirty their hands with detail work. They determine the best manner for effecting the *Ephorate*'s will, then delegate the necessary tasks to their *lictors*. If *strategoi* can be likened to justicars, then the *lictors* are their archons. Many younger members refer to them as troubleshooters, the individuals in a corporation who move from department to department, fixing any problems they come across. The *lictors* do the same thing throughout the entire Ventrue clan.

Individual *lictors* tend to specialize in particular types of problems. Some have expertise in financial matters, others are leaders, and still others have proven diplomatic records. When a Ventrue elder or consortium in a particular city has troubles it cannot handle effectively on its own (something as a group they are always loath to admit, although it takes only one esteemed Ventrue to call in a *lictor*), they call upon their *strategoi* to send help. That help usually comes in the form of a *lictor*. More often than not, she is enough. Her mere presence as a representative of the *strategoi* (and thus the *ephors*) lends a certain cachet that can help rally the other clan members to solve the problem together under the *lictor*'s direction — something they probably could have done on their own if they were able to put aside their petty differences.

The title of *lictor* is much prized, especially among relatively young (under 200 years) Ventrue who seek a way to increase their *dignitas*. More than one *lictor* has stepped into a city full of warring Ventrue and wound up assuming the title prince when all was said and done. Likewise, a troubleshooter is on the slow-but-sure path toward the ranks of the *strategoi* or even the Directorate, by definition. With opportunity comes risk, though, and the troubleshooters have their share of that, both political and material. Doing the *strategoi*'s dirty work can make one some powerful enemies, and rallying the troops in the face of bloodthirsty Sabbat or anarchs is always risky. For those who survive the experience, however, holding the title of *lictor* is a sure step toward greatness.

Agents at Large (Tribunes)

The *Ephorate* maintains a loose network of contacts and "field operatives" around the world. These Kindred are referred to as both tribunes and agents at large, and they serve as the *ephors*' eyes and ears in Camarilla (and sometimes even Sabbat) cities. They have no official powers or duties, and they often do not even acknowledge their title publicly (a hard thing for any Ventrue). The tribunes tend to be young Ventrue who the *lictors* or *strategoi* have decided show promise. They not only have a strong track record and reputable *dignitas*, they also have a history of respect for their elders and the Ventrue traditions, at least some of the time.

Most nights, tribunes do nothing in their titular capacity. Sometimes, though, they receive messages from the *ephors* (passed on by *strategoi*) that they must deliver to prominent local clan members. In turn, they report to their superiors what takes place in their city. Often, the city's tribunes call upon a *strategos* for help rather than the city's elders doing so. Not bound up in their own *dignitas* as city leaders, they usually have no qualms about asking for help when it's needed. A tribune occasionally calls for assistance when it's not necessary, but few make the mistake twice. The local and clanwide repercussions for such a mistake usually force the wolf-crying tribune out of office and possibly even the city.

Perhaps most important of all, a tribune must be on hand to assist any *lictor* or *strategos* who comes to town. Although tribunes often hold other ranks and titles within both the Ventrue clan and the Camarilla, they are expected to put them aside and serve the *Ephorate* (and its entourage) first and foremost. Doing so can sometimes make local clanmates jealous and angry, but the *ephors* typically reward the loyalty their subordinates show them handsomely.

The Peerage

Not every Ventrue who distinguishes herself becomes a member of the elders' collection of pawns and catspaws. While the goals of the *Ephorate* and its supporters are admirable (in its estimation, at least), few Ventrue wish to tie themselves so closely to the whims of their sires and elders.

The peerage — individual members are known as peers — is a loose but recognized body of Ventrue who have accumulated any but the most minor degree of esteem within Camarilla or the Ventrue social hierarchy. It takes more than the acceptance of the prince to join the peerage, but not much. A sanction by a member of the Ventrue hierarchy, whether local or clanwide, is enough to allow a Kindred to join the peerage's ranks, however. Additionally, a Ventrue peerage is present in almost any city where a Blue Blood makes her haven.

As a group, the peerage exists to further the Ventrue traditions and the concept of *dignitas* — nothing more. By conferring status upon "good" members of the clan, the Ventrue reward those among them who toe the line and make names for themselves without causing undue schisms among one another. For example, a young Ventrue who influences the outcome of a local zoning hearing successfully in order to preserve a city's Elysium might be extended an invitation to join the peerage. An ambitious Ventrue who usurps his sire's interests in his corporate holdings would not.

To this end, the peerage is nothing so much as a social register, a club of Ventrue with impeccably clean (if not impeccable) reputations. Still, the Ventrue place great value on such things — it allows them to set themselves apart from the uncouth among their ranks.

City Titles

Lately, it has become fashionable to refer to the clan organization within a given city as if it were a corporation and assign various business-inspired titles to individual Ventrue. In actuality, this appellation convention is merely an update of the more traditional nomenclature that Ventrue have used for centuries, based upon classical Spartan and Roman political titles. The business model actually reflects very well how Ventrue operate, but many venerable Ventrue — especially in the Old World — still use the traditional names.

Additionally, local assemblies of Ventrue are known as consortiums, although this word has no formal meaning. Some elders use it in place of the word "coterie" when speaking of cells of young Ventrue, while other Blue Bloods use it to refer to any group of two or more Ventrue undertaking a given endeavor. The word has only come into vogue recently — within the past decade or so — because it sounds so much more genteel than "faction" or "conspiracy."

The Board (The *Gerousia*)

The *Gerousia* (loosely translated as council of elders) or Board effectively adjudicates Ventrue concerns within the city. It usually consists of the eldest, most experienced Kindred in the given locality. If the city has a Ventrue prince, he or she likely sits as the head of the *Gerousia*. Otherwise, the clan primogen or other highest-ranking Camarilla title-holder rules the council. One joins the council only by invitation and majority approval by the sitting members. Once a Ventrue ascends to the *Gerousia*'s ranks, he cannot be removed except under the most dire of circumstance (as determined by the clan *ephors*).

In a corporate capacity, the *Gerousia* oversees Ventrue business and political interests within the city, much like a holding company. Indeed, some Boards do incorporate under just such missions. This organizational structure leads not only to managing funds and taking positions, but also monitoring the individual Ventrue's investments and their activities. As a general rule, Ventrue do not compete directly with one another for the same contacts and resources. The *Gerousia* acts as arbiter of any local conflicts of interest that might arise. If it so chooses, the council can demand that a clan member cease his or her efforts in a particular area, and it can enforce the demand as it sees fit. For example, should two Kindred make a play for influence within the local steel industry, the *Gerousia* might hold a hearing to determine who had the rights to said influence, assuming that one of the Ventrue brought the matter to the group's attention. For the most part, though, individual Ventrue are loath to turn to the Board, because doing so implies that they are incapable of asserting their own dominance.

The *Gerousia* holds two types of meetings. Monthly clanwide meetings are usually held the first Tuesday of the month. Every Ventrue in the city should attend these conferences, because the clan discusses new and old business, hears complaints and reports, and the *Gerousia* passes down any messages, edicts or announcements from the upper reaches of the clan hierarchy. The *Gerousia* also holds private meetings on an irregular basis as needed, in which the members discuss greater political or financial issues as well as more discreet clan affairs.

Despite the honor and *dignitas* associated with serving on the *Gerousia*, the council has very little formal power. It cannot order other Ventrue within the city to do anything. Rather, it can, but it has no capacity to directly punish those who disobey. Indirect punishments abound, however. Those who go against the Board's wishes find themselves outcast — and greeting the sunrise in the most extreme cases. Without the Board's protection, other Ventrue can and will assault the anathema Kindred's financial and political holdings. Peer pressure is the Board's greatest weapon, and Board members wield it almost dictatorially.

Managers (*Praetors*)

The highest Ventrue rank within a city's hierarchy, the *praetors* or managers almost always have a seat on the *Gerousia* as well. Each city has one *praetor* at most (if it has one at all) who might well be the prince or Ventrue primogen as well. As the alternate title, manager, suggests, these powerful Kindred are responsible for guiding and managing Ventrue affairs within the city. In order to attend this lofty position, a Ventrue must perforce be not only an elder, but an elder with unassailable *dignitas* and wide-ranging support among the peerage. *Praetors* hold their position indefinitely, and only a *strategos* or *ephor* can remove one from his post.

The *praetor* maintains with his own funds the "public" meeting space where any Ventrue can come to attend the monthly Board meetings. Such a place is usually an exclusive club of some sort, but it can be anywhere the *praetor* chooses, such as a hotel's function space, a skyscraper's boardroom or even the den or office of her own haven. The meeting place's atmosphere and appointments reflect directly upon the *praetor*, so most spend lavishly on providing a luxurious and impressive facility. The *praetor* also chairs these Board meetings and acts as a tie-breaker in all *Gerousia* votes.

Other than these few responsibilities, the *praetor* has no other official powers. Most often, however, he is a Ventrue of great influence within the city, which he may well bring to bear in matters concerning the Board. Merely achieving the office provides him with a sizable boost to his *dignitas*. As the person at the center of all Ventrue affairs in the city, he has access to people and information that many other clan members do not. Furthermore, the rest of his clanmates often turn to him for leadership in any crisis, and they tend to follow his instructions without question (or without too many questions, in any event).

Supervisors (*Aediles*)

Below the *praetors* lie the *aediles* or supervisors. These Ventrue aid the *Gerousia* and *praetor* just as supervisors assist managers in a business. They keep tabs on what the lower-ranked clan members are up to, and they take care of the specifics associated with running a corporation, such as managing nightly financial issues, investigating potential new investments or ensuring that all the bribes have been paid on time. The *aediles* act as spokesmen for their superiors, delivering instructions, requests and orders to the rest of the clan. They also serve as lieutenants in a crisis, helping to organize and lead the troops into whatever metaphorical or real battle is at hand.

The *aediles* are usually experienced ancillae, individuals who have a proven track record and have established their own business and influence domains within the city. They have resources enough to help them carry out their duties without needing help from anyone else. The *praetors* alone or *Gerousia* as a whole can nominate new *aediles*, and there is technically no limit to the number a city might

have. In practice, there are seldom more than three even in the largest cities, and usually only one or two. After all, in a city with seven Ventrue, making half of them officers practically defeats the purpose.

Foremen (*Questors*)

Down in the proverbial trenches are the *questors* or foremen. These Kindred are but one rank above the common Ventrue. Youngish, with some experience, a Ventrue receives promotion to this rank in recognition of some significant achievement that brought him and the clan *dignitas* and improved fortunes. The questors assist the higher-ranking Ventrue by performing basic tasks that keep their investments running smoothly. Such tasks can be anything from opening an account with a brokerage to hiding the bodies of newly deceased union bosses. Often *aediles* assign them tasks with little or no explanation. *Questors* who do their job well can look forward to advancement within the clan as well as personal opportunities they might not have perceived otherwise.

The *questors* sometimes take pleasure in flaunting their position over the common Ventrue. Although they have no real authority over their lesser clanmates, they can rightly point out that they have the ear of the elders whereas most neonates have no access at all. *Questors* spend their nights accruing favors and good will with their superiors, who occasionally throw them a bone to gnaw on. Of course, Ventrue bones tend to be things like hundred-thousand-dollar stock options or important government contacts, so a foreman can do quite well by playing the game.

Associates (*Eiren*)

At the bottom of the pile stand the *eiren*, otherwise known as associates. No matter who their sire might be, young Ventrue have a long way to go before they gain real respect within the clan. The word *eiren* comes from the Spartan word for inexperienced youths, not yet matured by battle and experience into true men, which is exactly how many Ventrue see their younger clan members. They have excellent breeding and valuable skills brought from their mortal lives, no doubt, but they are ultimately nothing more than fledglings who need experience to temper and shape them into true Ventrue.

Eiren have little respect, but, then again, they have few responsibilities. Although sometimes referred to as associates, these young Kindred do not have any official jobs or tasks that they must perform. If a *questor* or higher-ranked Ventrue asks them to do something, they may choose to refuse, of course. The Ventrue can think of no better way to ensure that one never leaves *eiren* status, but no one has the power to *force* the neonate do anything. Most, however, do what they're told, all the while trying to find some way to extend their own influence and increase their *dignitas*. One must work within the system to ascend its ranks. As a rule, the Ventrue do not reward mavericks.

Investors, Partners and Nonmembers

Naturally, not every Ventrue is a lackey or a scion of a given city's Board. Those Ventrue who invest with the Board might not hold a title within the organization, but that does not make them janitors. For those who do not attach themselves to the Board, unlife continues as it would for any other Kindred. Indeed, many Ventrue who place themselves outside of the local and clanwide hierarchy rise to great station in the Camarilla. Likewise, nothing prevents them from accumulating accolades on their own (see the "Going Solo" sidebar). Ventrue do not force their hierarchy upon their members; they simply encourage their members to avail themselves of its vast resources and make their own contributions.

The Embrace

The Ventrue reserve their blood for those whom they consider truly worthy, those who stand head and shoulders above the herd. Only men and women who have something that strikes the potential sire as admirable deserve consideration. Even then, most do not make the cut. While every Kindred has her own feelings when it comes to choosing childer, the clan as a whole does have its own standards to which all new Kindred are held. Neonates who fail to meet the clan's benchmark find themselves shunned by their blood-siblings, left out of important opportunities and otherwise disadvantaged. Many would-be sires discuss their potential childer with their elders, often their own sires, before the Embrace, thus gauging the new Ventrue's acceptance into proper society.

Tonight, especially in the West, the noble's time has passed. Formerly potent human bloodlines now give birth to anemic, spoiled dilettantes who have never governed anything but a paid servant and a trust-fund allowance. Since the concept of the noble class began its decline two centuries ago, the Ventrue have shifted their attention to less well-bred but more promising classes. In the modern nights, rare is the Ventrue neonate who can claim titled blood except by coincidence. Although they consider themselves the nobility of Kindred society, the Ventrue care little for mortal titles any longer. It was always the power that came with the title that drew them.

Government

Although stereotype portrays the Ventrue as the consummate undead businessmen, the clan actually feels quite comfortable within the halls of government. Politics and business have long worked hand-in-hand, and money

Going Solo

Players and Storytellers, don't feel like a Ventrue character must have a litany of titles to be an influential or interesting persona. Most Ventrue have little more than a peerage behind them, and most neonates have yet to accomplish even that.

True, the Ventrue organize more than most other clans. Yet, even with the Ventrue, clan is not a rigidly enforced concept. No Blue Blood sergeant is going to kick down the door of a character's haven and stake her for not adhering to Ventrue Bylaw 517-a.

The Ventrue hierarchy exists for two purposes. First, it allows Ventrue Kindred to pool their resources and reap greater benefits than any individual Cainite would likely be able to accomplish. It is an investment club, political lobby, high-society association, union and social contract all rolled into one. Second, it allows the scheming elders to… well, you're better off not knowing that.

Many Ventrue make their fortunes without undue reliance on the hierarchy. They choose to do so for any number of reasons. Some Blue Bloods would rather not indebt themselves to others of their kind. Other Ventrue prefer to have sole control over their own assets, rather than relying on a hidden cabal of hoary elders to do what they think is best.

The Ventrue accord no shame to their blood-siblings who work outside the system. Of course, it's harder for them to be recognized by others… but not every Ventrue needs the validation of his associates.

has always played an important role in determining policy. Still, government's raw power — the authority to accomplish goals by decree, the ability to sit in judgment over others, the expectation of having one's commands obeyed — appeals to many Ventrue sensibilities. It is no wonder, then, that successful politicians often make great Ventrue.

Of course, Ventrue very seldom Embrace successful public officials. The sudden inability of a sitting or former Senator to walk about during the day would not go unnoticed. The modern world's elected officials stay in the public eye too much. Only rarely would a sensible Ventrue Embrace someone so exposed to the public, since the person's death must invariably be faked (or some other cover story must be created) to explain the person's disappearance. Even then, most Ventrue feel that the risk of someone recognizing the new Kindred far outweighs the benefits of having him within the clan's ranks.

Instead, the Ventrue set their sights on political advisors and accomplished bureaucrats who know the ins and outs of government but who aren't well known outside their own intimate circles. Besides, the advisors tend to have as much or more actual power in modern politics than the elected figureheads they represent. They run the show behind the scenes, make the deals and even determine policy. Of course, this is exactly how the Ventrue themselves try to influence the kine political landscape.

The Ventrue Embrace these career politicians for their expertise, mindset and experience, not for any personal power they currently wield. Politics is too ephemeral to Embrace a person just because of the position he occupies at the moment. The Ventrue use their vast contacts, sycophants, allies and loyal ghouls to address such issues. Childer with government experience become Ventrue because they know how to lead. They can make decisions, tell others what to do, analyze a crisis and exercise diplomacy. Such neonates are usually marked from their Embrace for greatness. Their sires train them to take on the mantle of responsibility, both as Ventrue and among Kindred society as a whole. Ultimately, they are the clan's future and their sires' prestigious progeny, if they can learn to wait a few centuries.

BUSINESS

Managing and making money has become second nature to the Ventrue in the past few centuries. The clan elders recognized long ago that power in Western society was shifting from hereditary divine right to the new, moneyed aristocracy. Acting with what some might consider uncharacteristic acumen, they concentrated their efforts on understanding and mastering the new world of free trade and unbridled capitalism.

And the Ventrue have mastered it. Business is as much art as skill, and it is timeless in most ways. A good businessman will always be just that. However, markets, goods and technologies change, even though the fundamentals remain the same. Therefore, the Ventrue have long monitored the ranks of big business for new childer, always looking for competent protégés to help expand their ever-increasing financial holdings. Banking, real estate and long-term investments are well-traveled ground, but the Internet, biotechnology, managed health care, foreign market cultivation and day trading are new fields that need new expertise.

Unfortunately for the newly Embraced, financially savvy Ventrue are chosen almost solely for their ability to make the clan money, unlike government experts who are Embraced for their leadership qualities. Granted, money is very important to the Ventrue, but ultimately it is just a tool. Having substantial funds lets the Blue Bloods achieve their goals in every other field. However, a distinct prejudice toward such Ventrue remains, especially among the noble-born elders. They view these "bankers" as little more than artisans. They are clan members, but of a lesser quality, probably not cut out for the clan's legacy of noble guidance of the race of Caine. As a result, neonates often have a hard time making a name for themselves. Any successes in business are simply what the clan expects of them, and they usually have trouble succeeding in other venues, where more experienced Ventrue build their own *dignitas*.

ORGANIZED CRIME

Society has always had its criminal element, and less ethical Ventrue have long acknowledged these humans as potential clan members. Ancient prejudices and an inclination toward nobility meant that, for millennia, few self-respecting Ventrue would even consider Embracing such ill-bred kine. In the past century, organized crime has come into its own in the West, transcending individual criminals and becoming that which Ventrue respect most in the mortal world: an institution.

From a certain standpoint, organized crime figures make ideal recruits. Most have experience wielding autocratic power, making tough, ruthless decisions and working behind the scenes to influence the mortal world. They certainly value money, and moreover, they have experience using it to circumvent other kine and their institutions. Furthermore, unlike public officials, they use their power out of visibility, away from the public eye. Therefore, their disappearance from the ranks of the living does not attract much attention.

Despite having all these fine qualities to recommend them, organized crime leaders have several important strikes against them as far as most Ventrue are concerned. First of all, they tend to be uncouth, uneducated and disrespectful of tradition, particularly those sired within the past five decades. Even those who do not fit into this stereotype find themselves the victims of prejudice. As soon as a noble-born or MBA-trained Ventrue discovers the Kindred's criminal past, she tends to view him with scorn immediately. As a result, most crime-boss Ventrue have a hard time rising high within the clan's ranks unless they show exceptional ability combined with proper decorum.

Few mobsters retain their ties to their old gangs for more than a few years. It is possible to continue running a gang as a member of the undead since few underlings can question their leader's decision to meet only at night. Eventually, though, the ties must become less obvious. Often, the Ventrue nominates a successor, usually a groomed underling or even a ghoul, to run the organization in his absence. Using this technique, a few Ventrue have managed to reap the benefits of their gangs for decades. Most however, must use their skills to make their own fortunes. They must make the most of their underworld influence and contacts to open other avenues for achieving *dignitas* if they hope to rise within their clan.

MILITARY

In nights long past, nobles and military leaders were interchangeable. Tonight, most nations in which the Ventrue hold sway make a firm point of separating political leadership from the military. Kine with armed forces experience make good Kindred candidates, especially if they have distinguished themselves by achieving rank or numerous awards (the titles and ranks especially appeal to Ventrue sensibilities). They know how to give orders and comport themselves with dignity. They can also take orders, and they have an ingrained respect for institutions and authority. All in all, they have every quality a Ventrue could want.

Well, almost every quality. The problem is that most successful military men and women do not have the right temperament for being Kindred. They often value honor, forthrightness and honesty, qualities that don't lend themselves well to an unlife of murder, treachery and crumbling morality. Put more simply, most don't want to suck blood and stab backs for all eternity. Those who do — the sociopathic mercenaries who join the military not to defend their nation but to kill for money — usually don't have any of the other qualities that Ventrue do admire. Therefore, although many elders scrutinize the military for possible recruits (among other reasons), fewer and fewer Ventrue hail from the armed forces.

LABOR UNIONS

Since they're political institutions by nature, unions represent another fertile field for harvesting new Ventrue. While Ventrue interests usually lined up against the union movements in Europe and the United States for many years, the clan was quick to step in and avail itself of the unions' burgeoning power once these labor groups achieved real power. Although their influence seems to be on the decline in some countries, the labor unions still produce their share of valued Ventrue. Like politicians, union leaders have all the skills a Ventrue looks for: They lead their fellow kine, they know how to deal, and they can play rough if they have to. What's more, it's easier to find a way to make one disappear from mortal life unless he has a very high profile. (And no, Jimmy Hoffa is not a Ventrue.)

Kindred from union backgrounds tend to keep their interests focused on the same issues for which they fought in life. Their intimate knowledge of the labor movement allows them to influence and shift large groups of organized workers to better suit their needs. The only problem is that, as with religious devotees, many labor organizers believe deeply in their cause. Not every gifted union boss works willingly for the other side just because he's now a vampire. Therefore, Ventrue focus their attention on those leaders already compromised in some way, either through personal avarice or via blackmail.

Their mortal-world training and experience make union leaders well suited for existence as a Ventrue, but their all-too-common working-class origins do not. The aristocratic Kindred in the clan (of which there are many) naturally look down on these blue-collar rabble-rousers. Even if the new Kindred manages to act the refined and noble part, he still faces discrimination based on his background alone. This plebian taint can hamper one's ability to accrue *dignitas* and position within the clan, if not outside it. The problem fades gradually with age, and some groundbreaking union organizers from the 19th century have succumbed, shedding their utilitarian values and rising in status.

CLERGY

Religion and Kindred have a long, uncomfortable history. The fact that devout, suspicious kine tend to congregate in churches makes them less than hospitable to vampiric influences. And yet, religious leaders have held great temporal power for many, many centuries. As an institution, the Church (of whatever faith or denomination) appeals to Ventrue sensibilities — especially the rituals, the traditions, the moral authority and the popular influence. As for individual clergy, the Ventrue can pretty much take them or leave them.

Compared to the situation just a few centuries ago, religion has lost some of its power in the Western world. At one time, bishops were favored vehicles or targets for Ventrue schemes, along with nobles. Times change, though, and now clergy members pale in desirability compared to the other kinds of kine. Still, they have something that most do not: moral authority. Many Ventrue see themselves as a Platonic ideal when it comes to Kindred behavior. They feel that they define how a Kindred should view, exist in and interact with the rest of the world. Religious leaders have that same certainty that their ethical code can build a better world. The Ventrue like this righteous self-assurance.

Old habits die hard, and the Ventrue still hold Kindred from the clergy in high regard within their ranks as a rule. Those from more traditional, established faiths and spheres of influence usually have the proper attitudes and manners to negotiate the rarefied circles of Ventrue society. Likewise, those with a grounding in ritual and hierarchy acclimate quickly to the Byzantine politics of the Damned. Kindred with religious roots tend to go far in the clan, finding few doors closed to them out of prejudice. The only exceptions are the few childer from the more radical or reactionary fanatical sects. Many Ventrue find these individuals crass, base and uncouth, and few are ever even considered for the Embrace. The handful who have joined the clan have had a hard time of it from their blue-blooded brethren.

ACADEMIA

As any college professor can attest, the halls of academia do not hold much temporal power. Except for the heads of large universities who might have local or statewide political gravity, most academics are confined to mere thoughts and words without the deeds. Why, then, would the Ventrue take interest in such individuals? For the most part, they don't. Occasionally, however, a Ventrue decides that an insightful thinker or innovative engineer could prove useful, and he Embraces an academic or two, plucking them from their libraries and throwing them headfirst into the occult world of the Kindred.

Academics (at least the ones who would interest a Ventrue) know how to think. They have problem-solving skills and a wealth of experience dealing with others in a structured setting, and they often have a way with words and ideas. They also know how to research a problem and determine its base causes. Moreover, the Ventrue clan's traditional and historically oriented social structure makes having a trained researcher on your side a definite political asset. Finally, quality academic candidates know how to both explain things to others and convince them of their point of view. In other words, as the Ventrue see it, academics know how to make other people think the way they want them to think.

A one-time professor who joins the clan does so on a less than even footing. Unless they have other qualities (such as noble birth or aristocratic upbringing), most Ventrue tend to regard them as curiosities or hopelessly specialized. Nobles find them pedestrian, businessmen see them as little more than tools, and politicos see them as irrelevant daydreamers. Thus an academic without real dynamism finds himself confined to supporting and advisory roles. Most academics find such roles comfortable and familiar. Their blood-borne ambition is tempered by a lifetime of contemplation. Eternal unlife, supernatural powers and what money and influence they might earn as Ventrue are usually more than enough to satisfy such progeny. With whole new vistas of Kindred-oriented research open to them, they have plenty to occupy their time and talents.

OTHERS

The above categories *by no means* define the limits of which kine the Ventrue Embrace. They are just tendencies. The clan always keeps an eye open for talent and ability, traits that can be found in the most unlikely places. The media has provided its share of recruits, as has the entertainment industry. Talented writers with the power to sway audiences, clever assassins and even well-connected athletes and teachers have made their place among the Blue Bloods. Even "common people" can have that certain spark that attracts a Ventrue's eye or ignites his long-dormant passions. The Ventrue observe no restrictions, only customs and prejudices. Most Ventrue do not believe that all men are created equal, and only among the staid elders do neonates sometimes find it hard to shed the taint or distinction of their former lives.

FEEDING RESTRICTIONS

"Why has Caine cursed you thus?" asks a fisherman of [Ventrue] in one of the apocryphal *Night-Tales of the First City*. "Why not drink from whomever you please?"

In fact, the Ventrue do just that — they drink as they please. Rather, they drink *only* what they please. Their aristocratic tastes have grown so rarified over the centuries that they feed only from a specific kind of kine, even under the most dire of circumstances. As for Caine cursing them, well, the Ventrue would never admit to such a fault. In fact, they do not consider themselves disadvantaged at all (at least not that they'll acknowledge in mixed company). Their feeding preference is simply a matter of choice for them, as well as a sign of good breeding.

Of course, there is more to it than that. If it were just a matter of choice, some Ventrue, somewhere, would be crass (or practical…) enough to choose to drink from anyone at all. No Ventrue exist who fit this bill. Even a Ventrue Embraced under unusual circumstances, who never again has contact with her sire or clan, still has feeding restrictions. Moreover, the restrictions transcend consciousness. A Ventrue in torpor cannot imbibe non-Kindred blood that does not match her tastes. Even at the brink of Final Death, she vomits the vitae up rather than ingests it.

Where does this irksome restriction come from? Little evidence has surfaced to show that Caine actually cursed the Ventrue. Rather, it appears to be a taint in the Ventrue blood, something acquired from the destabilized nobles the clan has Embraced for so many centuries. At the same time, a mental component exists as well. The Ventrue does have a chance to make a conscious decision about her feeding preferences. Having made the choice, changing it becomes almost impossible (with a few notable exceptions discussed later).

Immediately after her Embrace, the Kindred is open to all possibilities. Indeed, for a few nights Ventrue can in fact feed on any vessel they please. It is not until the Ventrue takes her first taste of vitae that she considers truly exquisite that a choice is made. This choice does not usually happen when the Kindred is ravenous with fledgling hunger, but rather the first time she has an opportunity to choose prey in a timely manner, to really enjoy the feeding. That first taste is so thrilling, so entrancing, that the Ventrue's palate will never again settle for anything that doesn't compare.

Theoretically then, a Ventrue who stayed on the edge of frenzy every time he fed could avoid ever acquiring restrictively selective tastes. That person would have to have an indomitable will and enjoy hunting on the edge, and he would ultimately frenzy at the wrong moment and bring about terrible consequences. Very few newly Embraced Ventrue even realize it's an option, and only a handful in recorded history have tried it. Needless to say, all met predictably gory ends.

As a result of their finicky ways, the Ventrue have a remarkably refined sense of taste. From a mere sniff, they can determine readily whether or not blood is palatable to them. Like a master sommelier, they can even discern basic aspects of the person's age, health and diet. Where Kindred vitae is concerned, very experienced Ventrue can determine even such esoteric values as clan and age, with possibly even a guess at generation with an accuracy that would make any Tremere blush with jealousy. This ability is not a matter of supernatural power, but rather a result of years of experience paying careful attention to not only blood's supernatural benefits, but its less tangible qualities as well.

The one instance in which a Ventrue might have some hope of changing her tastes comes when her particular blood type is no longer available. That is to say, not available *at all*, in any way, shape, form or place. Such circumstances are rare, since most Ventrue prefer blood from specific types of humans. For those whose tastes run more precise — such as those who prefer the blood of a particular nationality — the situation becomes complicated. Indeed, more than one Ventrue has fallen into the cold arms of torpor once vessels of his chosen caste or nationality have vanished from the world altogether. In some nigh-apocryphal cases, individual Ventrue have become attuned to the taste of one specific mortal's blood — woe to them if they cannot adapt their tastes once her favored vessel meets his inevitable end.

Perhaps the most famous example is the notoriously cruel and crafty Roman Ventrue known in modern accounts as Democritus. Originally Embraced to help fight the ongoing war with Carthage, Democritus developed a taste for Carthaginian blood. A century later, when victory finally came and the Romans had destroyed the city utterly, the victors burned Democritus' blood supply as well as the city proper. He found that the residents of the newly built Roman Carthage did not suit his needs. Democritus soon slipped into torpor. When he awoke, he found that his need for Carthaginian blood had vanished. He soon acquired a new predilection, this time for residents of Byzantium, and has fed well on the city's residents ever since. Now, even though the name has changed, the blood of its citizens still satisfies.

THE AGOGE

No matter how many mortal years might have passed before their Embrace, newly created Ventrue are no more than babes in the woods, compared to the history of the clan. The responsibility for preparing a neonate for his release falls squarely upon the sire's shoulders, but the local body of the clan often plays a role. Siring a competent, confident and proper Ventrue means learning from everyone, not just parroting the sire's instructions—or prejudices.

The Ventrue term this training period the *agoge*, after the ancient Spartan education system. Renowned in nights long gone as the most comprehensive and demanding means for schooling youth in the world, the *agoge* is a fine metaphor; Ventrue relish drawing the comparison between it and their own strict teaching style. Although young Ventrue do not sleep on straw mats or train constantly for warfare like the Spartan youths did, they do face mental and emotional challenges that are every bit as trying. They must learn the ins and outs of Ventrue etiquette and traditions quickly, all while learning to master their undead potential and discover their place within Camarilla and Kindred society.

Note that the *agoge* does not always take place. In the tumultuous modern nights, many would-be sires simply lack the time to introduce a new childe to the intricacies of her legacy. These "latchkey" progeny often have difficult times adjusting to their grim fates.

THE NEWLY RE-BORN

Unless a given childer was a ghoul or had some other association with Kindred, becoming an undying parasite can be quite a shock. Most Ventrue give their offspring a few nights to adjust to their new state, feeding them either their own blood or some from their private herds. During this time, the Ventrue explains the situation as he or she sees best. This indoctrination is a matter of personal preference, and the *agoge* traditions do not proscribe a particular approach. However, sires are encouraged to emphasize to the childe that he has become part of a very exclusive, very noble, very *responsible* family. Great opportunities are available to them, but they come with important obligations.

THE CHOICE

After a few nights, once the childe has grown accustomed (however minimally) to her new existence and has a body full of precious vitae, the time has come for her to choose her preferred blood type. Traditionally, the sire escorts the childe among the kine for an evening, although this tradition has become less prevalent in the modern nights. The childe looks over the massed humanity and listens to her heart and palate. She eventually finds a kine who calls to her, whose aroma she cannot resist. Sometimes with the sire's help, the childe feeds. In so doing, she chooses the blood that will sustain her for all time.

THE TRAINING BEGINS

The honeymoon period is now over. The new vampire embarks upon her journey into the bloody world of the Kindred and Ventrue. For at least a week, sometimes much longer, sire and childe closet themselves away from the world. The sire lectures, presents books to be read and trains the childe in all the basics, including how to use blood to heal or increase physical attributes, how to feed without leaving a mark, what the Traditions are, the history of the Camarilla, clan history and hierarchy and so on. The *agoge* demands that the sire test her childe constantly, quizzing her on facts and challenging her understanding. Many sires prefer Socratic tests, as well, teaching their childer more as they assimilate previous knowledge. Failure or missteps result in withering insults and even physical pain. All told, this experience is not pleasant; a single omission in reciting one's ancestry may result in a week's denial of vitae.

PRESENTATION

The first training phase ends when the sire feels that the childe has learned enough not to be an embarrassment to him in public. In accordance with Camarilla tradition, the sire presents the childe to the city's prince, formally inaugurating her into Kindred society. Every available Ventrue in the city attends the presentation ceremony and watches the neonate closely. Afterward, the Ventrue gather alone and praise or criticize the childe's performance. The neonate meets the rest of her clanmates here, probably for the first time.

THE TRAINING CONTINUES

At this point, most sires would cut their childer loose, since they are no longer accountable for the neonate's actions, according to Camarilla traditions. Not so for the

BIRTH INTO DEATH

A curious custom, observed by many Ventrue and even a few Kindred outside the clan, is the recognition of one's deathnight (as opposed to birthday). While some Ventrue find the observance of such things needlessly vain, most enjoy the ritual, both for its pomp and for the opportunity to host or patronize a party. The practice has come very much into vogue in the Final Nights, as it allow the Kindred to forget for a time the impending prophecies of Gehenna that many spend so much effort on ignoring. Sires may throw lavish fetes for their childer, elders host grand soirees at their estates and even a few princes have been known to step down for a brief period, allowing a toastmaster to spoof them and become prince for a night.

Ventrue. For them, the process has just begun. The peerage holds its sires responsible for its childer for quite a while, until the neonate has completed the *agoge*, in fact. During this extended training session, the neonate often dwells with the sire or in a haven the sire provides. A few promising individuals do strike out on their own, but even they find themselves under what feels like constant supervision.

Even as the sire continues to test and train her childe, the other clan members may well step in to "help." The new Ventrue often spends at least some time with many local members of the clan. Even fellow Ventrue who feel personal enmity toward the neonate's sire join in schooling the fledgling occasionally. Each lectures and then tests the neonate, who must receive the Blue Bloods' approval before moving on. This process usually takes several months, and sometimes years (depending upon how many Ventrue participate and how thorough they are), but it gives the neonate a broad perspective of the clan and a basic understanding of the "corporation's" holdings and influence within the city. At this point, the Ventrue is still excluded from Board meetings and other clan gatherings, but their sires often apprise them of clan business.

The Test

Finally, the sire poses a challenge to the neonate. The young Kindred must go forth on her own and establish a domain of influence within the city without the assistance of any other Ventrue. Doing so can mean setting up a moneymaking arrangement with some industry or corporation; it can entail establishing contacts and influences within some political or governmental institution or for the truly daring; it can also mean earning a boon from another Kindred in the city.

The neonate has total freedom as long as she operates within the Traditions and, equally importantly, does not impinge upon any other Ventrue's sphere of influence (unless said Ventrue chooses not to participate in the *agoge*, in which case the neonate doesn't really need his approval). This last restriction can make the final test quite difficult, especially in cities where other clan members have already claimed many of the choice opportunities. When the neonate is finished, she declares her victory to her sire. The sire judges for herself whether the neonate has succeeded. Only if she agrees does she recommend the neonate to the *praetor* and *Gerousia*. She is then scheduled to appear before the entire clan at the next full Board meeting.

Coming Out

Finally, the neonate stands before her assembled clanmates and tutors. She then gives a full accounting of herself, clan traditions, history and how she met the final challenge. Ritual then has the assembled clan vote on

whether the neonate should be accepted into the clan. In reality, only the dullest sire places a childe before the Board without first making sure that the *Gerousia* finds her acceptable. The assembled clan then assents to the Kindred's acceptance unanimously (those still strongly opposed may remain silent if they wish). The *praetor* then asks the neonate a series of ritual questions devised by any Ventrue who cared to proffer one. In answering them, the neonate also recites her lineage and promises to uphold the traditions of both the clan and the Camarilla.

Once the formalities are finished, the celebration can begin. The acceptance of a new Kindred into the clan is a cause for great rejoicing among the Ventrue. Since the *agoge* practically guarantees that the new member has abilities and talents that can benefit the clan's accounts, it means that the Ventrue as a whole have just grown that much stronger. They have one more committed (albeit young) ally to turn to when times grow dangerous. The celebration, complete with rare blood of the neonate's preference as well as other entertainments, usually lasts through the rest of the night. These parties are, as one might expect, usually Ventrue-only affairs, held in the most exclusive venues and attended under high security. (One headstrong prince is rumored to have brought his Malkavian lover to one, but the rumor is terribly vague on *where*.) Surrounded by such opulence, wealth and power, the newly accepted clan member cannot help but feel that she is now part of something very special indeed. Surrounded by so much blood and so many walking corpses, most cannot help but feel they are also part of something very malignant.

On Their Own

Once the party concludes, the neonate returns to her temporary haven for one last day. From the next night forward, her fate is her own. The other Ventrue no longer hold her sire responsible for her actions and mistakes. Although many develop strong ties to their sires, neonates may now deal and compete with anyone, inside or out of the clan. Having passed the final test, she has a domain to call her own, a base upon which to build both her *dignitas* and holdings. It is a heady, wonderful feeling for a short while.

Then reality sets in. She soon begins to realize that the pleasantries and camaraderie of the coming-out party have disappeared and that the cruel, hard facts of Ventrue internal politics now predominate. Nightly, the unquenchable thirst for vitae rises in her gorge. As a neonate, she has no power and no rank. She needs allies, connections and arrangements to help get ahead. The struggle that was unlife in the *agoge* suddenly pales compared to the fierce freedom that surrounds her. But she is up to the challenge; she no doubt relishes it. After all, it is in her blood. She is Ventrue.

Protocol and Manners

Anger is impolitic. Impoliteness is a sin.

The Ventrue take etiquette very seriously, especially when interacting with one another. Dealing with coarser Kindred sometimes requires less dignified speech patterns, but discourse with one's own esteemed colleagues should always be as respectful and elegant as possible. After all, you would expect nothing less from *them*.

Respect drives the myriad Ventrue protocols. A Kindred's *dignitas* demands that others accord it to him and that he, in turn, accord it to everyone else whose *dignitas* demands it (which is to say almost anyone else of Ventrue blood, or at least members of the peerage). A dignified, proper Ventrue would never dream of insulting openly or even snubbing a clan member in good standing. Those sentiments are best left deep in the discourse's subtext. Only when a Ventrue has shamed himself do his erstwhile peers unload their scathing comments and biting remarks in response, an act in which they take malicious glee, if only because of its rarity.

The Laws of Decorum

As a clan devoted to proud detail and tradition, the Ventrue have managed to accumulate a code of conduct large enough to fill several weighty tomes (not that they have ever collected them thus). "Suggestions" can be found that govern everything from what color clothing to wear at Board meetings (dark blue, gray or, if you must, black) to what kinds of presents to give at deathnight celebrations (expensive but not gaudy jewelry is fine, antiques from the Kindred's Embrace date are gauche — except when they aren't…). All together, these rules work remarkably well at a) making the clan seem very stodgy indeed, and b) making sure that the clan members don't let their egos embroil them into bloody, frenzied brawls with their clanmates. All agree that avoiding "b" makes "a" a small price to pay. Presented here are some of the more important and commonly applicable rules by which Ventrue behave. The most important rule of all, though, is to make sure that one is never caught breaking one of these gentle suggestions openly.

Greetings and Casual Conversation

Always address another Kindred by his title, if he has one. If he has multiple titles, address him by Camarilla title rather than clan title in mixed company. A Ventrue with no title is addressed by his surname (e.g. Mr. Rubin, Ms. DeKoonieg).

Shake a man's hand, kiss a woman's. Women should simply let their hands be kissed by men and kiss fellow women on the right cheek.

Defer to your elders in all things. Wait for them to acknowledge you before speaking.

Never interrupt another clanmate while he speaks, even if you are his elder.

Never take offense when an elder interrupts you, even if it is rude.

Always look into an elder's eyes when speaking or listening to him. Doing so shows not only interest, but trust that he will not use the gifts of Caine upon you.

Personal affairs and business interests are best left as just that — personal — unless a Kindred opens the discussion himself.

Other Kindred are not nearly so interested in your personal achievements as you think they should be. Crowing shows crassness.

Do not raise your voice, use expletives or otherwise debase the discourse.

That said, avoid conversation on the modern "Inter Net."

A Ventrue's blood preferences are a private matter. One never asks.

CLAN AND BOARD MEETINGS

The highest-ranking Ventrue in the meeting presides over it. If two attendees have the same title, the eldest Kindred takes precedence. If the eldest defers, do not challenge him on his deference.

A younger assistant (usually an *aedile*) actually conducts the meeting, listing off the points on the agenda, recognizing speakers and otherwise taking care of the minutiae. This arrangement allows the presiding Ventrue to ignore the organizational details and concentrate on the greater issues at hand (or simply sleep through the meeting if he so chooses).

The agenda is always set beforehand and made available to all attendees. The presiding Ventrue must approve any variations from that agenda.

As each matter is brought before the body, the lowest-ranking Kindred always speak first on a matter. Elders or those of equal standing may interrupt the speaker politely to ask questions or make comments. Those of lower rank must wait until the speaker finishes and then address any questions not to the speaker but to the Ventrue conducting (not presiding over) the meeting.

If a vote is called for, the body votes as it spoke, from lowest to highest rank. Secret ballots may be cast, at the presiding Ventrue's discretion.

When the agenda is complete, attendees can suggest topics for the next meeting for the chair's consideration.

Do not interrupt; do not joke at another's expense. No shouting and no base language is ever appropriate. Tempers will remain in complete control. Meetings are most solemn, and not a venue for levity.

PUBLIC APPEARANCES

Ventrue should always dress and comport themselves with the utmost dignity in public, no matter the time of night or situation.

One should never disagree with one's elder in public, especially when lesser Kindred are about.

Following that, one should never disagree with one's equals or juniors in public either. Always show the world a united front.

Never speak of clan business to outsiders under any circumstances.

Treat other Camarilla Kindred, no matter their clan, with as much respect as you would expect them to show you. Do not sink to their level, nor allow yourself to be baited into exchanging taunts with a rapscallion or anything else so unseemly.

DISCIPLINES

Do not enforce your will or charms upon another member of Clan Ventrue unless absolutely necessary.

If the fellow Ventrue in question is in good standing with his peers, it is hard to conceive of a time when it would be absolutely necessary.

Eavesdropping upon another's thoughts, defiling their memories or toying with their emotions are all quite rude, but sometimes necessary if one's subject is not a Ventrue.

Should an elder demand access to your mind and he is within his rights to do so, do not resist.

Only a prince, justicar, *praetor* or *strategos* (or *ephor* should one such as you meet one) is ever within his rights to demand access to your mind.

ASSISTANCE

Come to a Ventrue's aid when he asks. This Ethic of Succor is inviolable.

Never begrudge or besmirch a clanmate who asks for aid. It is his right and your duty.

Never call for aid unless you actually need it. Esteemed Kindred have little tolerance for wasting time.

One does not remind another of his previous requests for succor in casual conversation.

Remember that you, too, might be in need of your clan's assistance one night, and act accordingly.

Difficulties and Disputes

The Ventrue show a united front to the rest of the world — or at least they pretend to. They claim unity of spirit and purpose as a single great clan organized toward lofty goals, such as upholding the Camarilla. Their strict internal etiquette helps promote this image. Always considerate, always politic, the Ventrue seem ice-cold in their self-control and clan discipline. The truth, as one might imagine, is quite different. The Ventrue have internal difficulties and rivalries as divisive and passionate as any clan or sect in the Kindred world. The childer of Caine are emotional, jealous, ambitious and monstrous individuals by nature. Add into this volatile mix the Ventrue obsession over personal *dignitas*, and it's a wonder the whole clan doesn't tear itself apart.

To date, however, the Ventrue haven't torn themselves apart, chiefly because most have the sense to realize that they're better off together than fractured. Thus the stifling etiquette, inflexible hierarchy and internal mechanisms for dispute resolution. All of these factors help the Ventrue work together and not only survive as a clan but thrive. However, problems simmer constantly just beneath the surface, waiting to embroil the Blue Bloods in numerous deadly Jyhads.

The Courts

The Ventrue decided long ago that they needed an impartial forum in which to settle disputes between clanmates without violence. Likewise, they needed a system that would preserve the *dignitas* of both sides, reducing (if not eliminating) the bitter acrimony that ensues whenever two Kindred come into conflict. These concerns resulted in the current Ventrue court system, an ad hoc dispute-resolution forum that combines one part debate, one part arbitration and one part showmanship.

The clan maintains no permanent courts or judges. Instead, anyone within the chain of command — which is to say, anyone recognized as a peer or greater — can petition his superiors to convene a court as the need arises. Before a court comes into being, all the parties must agree to it. One Ventrue cannot normally force another to come to court. Only the *ephors* can compel compliance thus. However, an elder in the clan may suggest that the two disputants resolve the issue among their peers, a suggestion that wise Ventrue heed without complaint.

The two disputants then agree upon someone to preside over the hearing. If feasible, this arbiter should be someone who outranks both of them, but someone of equal rank can serve in a pinch. Few Ventrue of *dignitas* would agree to have a lower-ranking Kindred preside over them. The arbiter convenes the court, which traditionally lasts just one evening. Any Ventrue in the area can attend, and when two powerful Kindred contend, the gallery is usually full, sometimes hosting guests from hundreds of miles away. What follows is a structured debate in which each Ventrue can make his case, call witnesses and display his rhetorical skills.

Ventrue cite historical precedent to bolster their case, relying upon research-minded compatriots to cite the tradition on which they depend if they can't find it themselves. A Ventrue must always speak for himself, and he can neither use an advocate, nor consult with others while the court is in session. The arbiter may not ask her own questions, although the disputants may question one another in turn. In order to avoid impolite, possibly insulting queries, all questions are addressed to the arbiter who then rephrases them for their intended subject.

When all is said and done, the Ventrue lay their dispute at the arbiter's feet. She then withdraws to consider the case before her. It is forbidden for anyone, even an *ephor*, to communicate with an arbiter while she deliberates. The court convenes again on the following night, and the arbiter delivers her judgment. Her decision is not binding unless the two disputants agree. Disagreeing, however, is considered a grave challenge to the arbiter's *dignitas* as well as duplicitous on the disputant's part. After all, he already agreed to abide by the arbiter's decision. Only the most foolish of Ventrue would ever ignore a court's decision unless he had absolute proof that someone had tainted or corrupted the process. Even then, he would probably be better served by petitioning a new arbiter for a secondary court.

The Young and the Old

How does one succeed to higher rank in the hierarchy if none of her superiors ever retires? The short answer is that she doesn't. She achieves that rank on her own or hopes that someone is unlucky enough to meet Final Death. That's the price one pays for an eternal unlife.

This glass ceiling is the most common complaint voiced by members of the clan by far. The young Ventrue have no place to go and no room to advance. All the choice domains are taken. Whatever shall they do? The elders hear these same complaints time and again. Other clans, especially loosely knit ones like the Brujah or Malkavians tease the Ventrue neonates for it constantly. The neonates themselves feel stifled and repressed. Oh, what a burden to be a neonate in the Camarilla's most prominent clan, an immortal who can bend minds to his will and cow mortals with but a thought. Can anyone imagine anything worse?

The fact of the matter is, it has always been thus within the clan, and it will no doubt always be thus. This problem is one that Kindred of every clan face, but the effects exacerbate under the strict Ventrue hierarchy, in which the ambition to achieve ever-greater heights burns so much stronger. Still, the clan has survived this trial for millennia; certainly it can continue to do so tonight. So say the elders.

The elders might not be correct any longer, though. The world has changed in recent years, and new challenges face the Blue Bloods. The most important difference is in the kind of kine who become Kindred. The 21st century is not a patient time. Ambitious, powerful people expect results not this decade but this *year*. The Ventrue "youths" want more and more — and they want it sooner.

Furthermore, more Ventrue stalk the night now than ever before. Part of this growth is natural, since populations of Kindred and kine have grown increasingly over the centuries. Part is not. With increasing incursions by the Sabbat, the Camarilla's loss of the stalwart Clan Gangrel and the generally hysterical mood among the Kindred, Ventrue have been Embracing new Kindred in record numbers. This indiscretion creates more foot soldiers to do their elders' business and enforce its agenda, but those foot soldiers are ambitious, and they won't stay satisfied servants forever.

Search for Solution

The youth versus age problem perseveres not only because of elder apathy but also because of a centuries-long quest to find an answer. Quite simply, the problem seems intractable. The established Ventrue have no need or desire to relinquish what they have, and the up-and-coming "progressives" have no need or desire to curb their ambitions. Many credit the stern Ventrue hierarchy, the clan's impeccable manners and blind adherence to tradition with staving off bloodshed and internal conflict for so long.

The only immediately feasible solution, one that has worked in the past, is for these young Ventrue to find new forums for achievement. Young Ventrue tend to rush (although not without planning and forethought) into newly open markets or areas of influence. In doing so, they have a distinct advantage over other clans seeking the same prizes; the Ventrue have the might of their whole clan in support. The elders encourage their youth actively to expand the clan's holdings wherever and whenever they can. The clan's power not only grows, but the youth no longer complain about the lack of opportunities. The Internet, global commerce, new technologies and even the evolution of previously valueless markets all provide a fertile bounty of resources for innovative and quick-thinking Blue Bloods.

Other, more extreme options have been employed from time to time. When a young Ventrue becomes too ambitious or too vociferous in his complaints, a world-weary elder might decide that enough is enough. No, Final Death is not the (usual) answer, but a blood bond can be. The most volatile Ventrue meet this fate, often before they even realize what has happened. (It is remarkably easy for a Kindred to discern a particular Ventrue's feeding preferences.) Blood bonding a fellow Ventrue forcibly is a serious offense, though, and neither party is liable to retain his *dignitas* should he resort to such manipulation of the Curse of Caine. Furthermore, only the *ephors* can authorize such treatment. Ultimately, most Ventrue consider this measure a last-resort, useful only in the most extreme cases.

The Outsiders

Some people just don't react well to others. Occasionally some Kindred refuse to play along, despite the choosy sire, the rigorous *agoge* and their gracious (at least to their faces) Ventrue peerage. They want no part in Camarilla politics or clan hierarchies. They don't give a rat's ass about *dignitas*. Thrilled (or sometimes crushed) to be undying — and unwilling to work within the system — they strike out on their own. The Ventrue quickly disavow these malcontents, often referring to them as caitiff or, in some cases, *antitribu* (although this last is not always technically true).

A Ventrue who disdains his clan cannot expect any of the traditions, rights or benefits accorded to members in good standing if he makes a public display of his bitterness. Not only may clanmates refuse assistance to an outsider, they often go out of their way to make unlife more difficult for him. Although the Camarilla's Traditions still apply to him — protecting him from breaches of the Masquerade, and such — enterprising Ventrue usually find some way to take care of such troublemakers. Almost half disappear within a year of their renunciation of the clan and its precepts, either because they fled of their own accord or because their former brethren resolved the issue for them.

Redemption always remains an option if the Ventrue shows true contrition and throws himself entirely at a merciful Ventrue's feet. Often a blood bond or a step toward one is part of the bargain. Even then, it takes a long while to earn the Ventrue trust once it is thrown away. Still, more than a few outsiders return to the fold in time, realizing that the Ventrue do indeed have much to offer, camaraderie and protection being more scarce amid a world of predators than they first imagined.

CLIQUES

Aside from their established hierarchy, Ventrue also organize themselves along their own social lines. Clanmates with similar interests find one another, not only within a city but around the world. Although Ventrue seldom actually like or trust one another, they do see the value in social gatherings, both to keep current with news and trends and to make important contacts. It is easier to gather when one has some common interest with her peers, for the Kindred has something to distract her from the disgust, hate, anger, envy or general mistrust she probably feels toward the other Kindred in the room.

VINTAGE CLUBS

As Kindred of rarefied tastes, Ventrue appreciate the subtle differences in vitae, even within the strict confines of their restrictions. All kine are not equal, and different bodies provide blood as varied as the wines from different vineyards. Just as a first-growth Bordeaux is incomparably better than a supermarket jug wine, so, too, a human who has lived and eaten well or particularly exemplifies a certain type produces vitae far more succulent than a less desirable vessel.

Ventrue tend to keep their blood proclivities a private matter, but individuals with similar preferences become aware of one another inevitably. In densely populated regions like Western Europe or the East Coast of the United States, Ventrue with the same restrictions sometimes come together to share particularly choice vessels. Called vintage clubs, these groups of Ventrue meet irregularly, usually for purely social reasons (although politics and business invariably creep into the affairs) or even for the sole purpose of savoring a delectable selection.

Individual vintage clubs usually meet in secrecy, even from other Ventrue, and they seldom consist of more than half a dozen members. The group's patrons often compete with one another to see who can bring the most succulent vitae to the "dinner." Some of the older groups that have been meeting for centuries even go so far as to actually breed and cultivate vessels for flavor. For instance, an Italian group that feeds only on the descendants of Sicily's Moorish conquerors has within its ranks a wealthy Kindred who has contrived for himself a public image as a philanthropist with an interest in history. He chooses young children based on breeding, heritage and lifestyle and adopts them or sets up trust funds for them until they mature to a ripe age and are fit to drink.

One may join a vintage club group by invitation only, of course. Only those who have a proven record for discretion as well as a sensitive palate for fine blood can ever hope to meet their exclusive ranks. The great secrecy attached to membership means that few Ventrue outside

a group even know that the cliques exist. Since members inevitably form bonds of kinship or at least camaraderie, they often make hidden allegiances and deals of which other Ventrue and Kindred cannot easily be aware.

Chess Societies

Many Ventrue love chess, not only as a game, but as a metaphor for life and unlife. Elder Kindred often refer to mortals as pawns, to political gambits as moves, to victory over a rival as checkmate, and so on. Even the wicked Lasombra acknowledge the Ventrue's love for "the game of kings." The game itself has a cultural and intellectual mystique that feeds the Ventrue ego and sensibility. It is a game of absolute strategy in which randomness plays no role. If only existence from night to night could operate thus.

Metaphors and wishful thinking aside, many Ventrue enjoy just playing the game. In many cities, Kindred often come together for an evening to play and socialize. Periodic chess nights, often held in Elysium, offer a chance for Kindred to come together, scheme, chat and test their mastery in a controlled environment with their favorite allegorical board game at hand. When Ventrue play (as with all things), it is considered bad form, a loss of face, to become too emotionally involved in a game or to trumpet one's victory. Although the Kindred might seethe inside, showing outward emotion — be it joy or sorrow — is a sure sign of a pedestrian nature.

Becoming active in the Ventrue chess community takes commitment. One must spend a great deal of time becoming very good at the game just to stay on the same level as the other players. Playing poor chess is as gauche as wearing a black belt with brown shoes or not holding a wine glass by the stem. If you come to play, you had best play well. For those who do play, matches can become terribly important. Chess master Ventrue often settle disputes over a game rather than by duel or clan trial. It's far better to test a matter on the completely fair board than in the vagaries of battle or a political undertaking.

Although victories in the games parlor do not compare ultimately to true triumphs in the world at large, Ventrue do attach serious *dignitas* to high-caliber games and respect those who play well. For the most part, the Ventrue look down upon other games, even equally challenging and distinguished ones like Go. Chess has the combination of style, Western tradition and grace that Ventrue value. It is, as they see it, their game.

Olympians

For most Ventrue, the kine are, individually, something not worth considering. They are cogs in the great and terrible machine of humanity. As such, many members of the clan (particularly the elders) take no small delight in manipulating humans for their own amusement. They pit humans against one another like emperors with their gladiators, or as many prefer to think of it, as the gods pitted Greeks against Trojans. Thus, Ventrue argot has come to term such Kindred Olympians, not for their god-like stature but rather for their penchant for sometimes petty but usually interesting diversions.

Not being actual gods of ancient cultures (for the most part), Ventrue seldom grow so capable or influential as to pit entire nations against one another. For amusement, they usually settle for individuals. Olympian groups meet as they will, sometimes coming together every decade or two for a game, sometimes engaging in contests that go on for years. Their sport comes in two types: man versus man or man versus the world. In the former, each Kindred chooses a single human as his or her champion. They then try and influence events so that their pawn wins over their rivals' pawns. This trial is seldom something so obvious or unrefined as an actual gladiatorial contest or a fight to the death. Rather, the contests usually revolve around matters like achieving success in some business venture, procuring victory in a legal matter, or even influencing the outcome of political contests.

In a man-versus-the-world contest, one Ventrue takes the side of the player. The unfortunate kine caught up in the game finds himself beset by all the trials of Job and more as the other Olympians strive to bring him down, be it financially, legally, mentally, socially, or all of these combined. The sole Ventrue defending the kine does what she can to help him survive for a preordained time. Olympians often wager heavily on such contests — not only money, but influence, boons, status and even more rare commodities.

More than a few Ventrue find the Olympians' activities distasteful and even dangerous. However, since a number of elder and respected clan members enjoy these contests from time to time, they continue unabated. As long as no Traditions are broken — particularly the Masquerade — and no Ventrue interests are harmed, the clan as a whole considers the Olympians pastime innocuous if unpleasantly jaded. After all, the lives of a few kine matter little to the world as a whole.

Philosophes

As a rule, Ventrue do not spend much time pondering the imponderable. They have important affairs in the temporal world that require attention. Some, however, find or make the time to sit down with their fellow Ventrue and discuss the more esoteric aspects of existence. Meeting as it suits them, these armchair philosophers usually spend their time hashing over the same old concepts that Kindred have argued about for millennia. What are we? Who was Caine? Are we Damned? What of our one-time humanity? And so on and so forth.

Where Ventrue philosophy groups different from many Kindred thinkers is that the Ventrue usually try to find practical applications for their discussions and conclusions. They spend a great deal of time arguing back and forth about concepts like obligation, duty, divine right and *dignitas*; all of which play an important role in Ventrue society. *Philosophes* can provide the moral and intellectual authority for a prince or other power to act in some cases, or they might provide the moral basis that affects the outcome of a peer trial. Much like mortal churches sanctioned crusades and wars, a persuasive philosophy can give an elder the justification to strike out at his enemies or consolidate his power.

Seldom do enough philosophically minded Ventrue make their havens in a single city to form such groups. Rather, the members travel on occasion to meet and discuss issues, while exchanging thoughts by letter (or possibly e-mail) when not in each other's company. These circles of thinkers can come to have significant but subtle influence within a region if their members provide potent enough philosophical proofs. One of the most famous groups, the British Lantern Club, is now widely credited with conceiving of most of the clan's policies in England throughout the 17th and 18th centuries. Their power fell only when others came to realize that they had it. The princes resented them as meddlers, and, in a fit of reactionary thought, they took to rejecting out of hand any idea the Lantern Club proposed. This pattern seems to hold true. Ventrue *philosophes* can wield influence up until the moment others realize they have it. Then it vanishes or is accounted for in other ways….

Gossips

It might span the globe and cross cultures, but Kindred society is actually quite small in comparison to the mortal world. As a sub-set of the vampiric whole, Ventrue society is that much smaller and closer. Additionally, Clan Ventrue is one of the most integrated clan cultures aside from the Tremere, and it seems like a group of individuals who either know everyone else or at least know someone who does. Three degrees of separation might be more than one needs to connect this noble clan's members to one another.

As anyone who's attended a school or worked in an office knows, familiarity breeds not only contempt, but gossip. Despite their noble airs and impeccable manners, Ventrue can and do tell tales as often as any other group of social beings. Indeed, gossip within this clan achieves levels outstripped by only the acid-tongued Toreador. Of course, as with most matters Ventrue, clan gossip usually has some

practical application and revolves around topics of politics, business and *dignitas* rather than who's sharing blood with whom and who Embraced her rival's protégé out of spite.

Groups of gossips (sometimes referred to derisively as "gaggles") exist throughout the clan's every level. Consisting of loose alliances between acquaintances, brood siblings and business contacts, the Ventrue grapevine spreads rumor and fact with nearly as much abandon as the Internet, and it has done so for millennia. The members of such groups might not even trust or like one another, but many subscribe to the common belief that sharing information benefits all. Most Ventrue try to join at least one such circle, and some of the best-connected Kindred participate in dozens.

The exchange of information usually takes place at casual social gatherings, but it is also carried on by more impersonal means such as messenger, letter, phone call or e-mail. Society dictates no rules or obligations or set standards for such groups. Rather, by mutual understanding, the members agree to share what they learn. The unspoken truth is that no one expects a member to reveal something if doing so is against his own interest. Of course, the mere fact that it might inconvenience a fellow member seldom prevents others in the group from revealing such secrets. Such is the harsh unlife of the rumor-monger.

Diplomats

As a clan, the Ventrue have a problem when it comes to fulfilling their self-proclaimed role as leaders in Kindred society. For the most part, they don't much like other Kindred. Pleased with themselves, their own ethos and their clan's good manners and form, many Ventrue have little patience for Caine's lesser get. They observe protocols as well as they can, or at least as well as they have to. However, more open-minded Ventrue seek out the other clans and do their best to build bridges between the leaders and the followers. The clan refers to them collectively as the diplomats.

The diplomats do not organize into groups but rather consist of like-minded Ventrue throughout all echelons of the clan. They seldom have formal or even informal gatherings, although they do tend to keep each other apprised of their efforts and successes. Their status is entirely unofficial, and the appellation "diplomat" is never used outside clan-only conversations. Even then, its most common use includes a liberal dose of irony or derision. As far as the rest of Kindred society is concerned, they are simply gracious, maybe overly talkative Ventrue.

What do diplomats do then? They make contacts, pure and simple. They show the rest of the Camarilla that the Ventrue are not all stiff-shirted snobs who care about nothing but their own power, position and prestige. These outgoing Ventrue ask other clans what they think, listen to their complaints and concerns and offer to pass them on to the preeminent Blue Bloods. Although they have no official power and their loyalties likely remain consistent with other Ventrue, offering a word of kindness to the less-favored clans helps the Ventrue smooth over some of the feathers they tend to ruffle in the course of a night's work.

One does not train to become a diplomat, or even set out to do so. Diplomats simply develop naturally, when a particular Kindred finds himself relating to those of other clans better than one might expect. Elders notice this kind of behavior. One might ask the Ventrue to keep up his contacts, or in fact to broaden them and thus become a kind of de facto representative-cum-public-relations figure for the clan. In effect, the Ventrue becomes a low-key, high-class evangelist for his clan. He becomes the accessible one to whom the other clans can talk.

Diplomats tend to share a unique world view, and they succeed with one another much better than they do other Ventrue. They tend to obsess about public image and argue against courses of action that might make the clan less popular with its fellow Camarilla members. They often work together and exchange notes and references in order to accomplish the greater goal of stabilizing the Ventrue position among the clans. For example, a Ventrue with particularly good relations with Clan Brujah might well help a fellow who needs some help avoiding the ire of a Brujah harpy, while he receives a valuable reference to the Nosferatu in return. While frequent association with outsiders sometimes casts a shadow on the individual's reputation, the good he does the peerage when it needs it only helps increase his own *dignitas* eventually.

Innovators

It's the constant complaint within the clan: The elders have a lock on power and influence; they've claimed the only worthwhile domains. The young have nowhere to go up the ladder unless someone meets Final Death, a fate no dignified Ventrue would wish upon another. In order to find a place for themselves and accrue whatever *dignitas* they can to their young stature, many younger Ventrue form their own private cliques that are part alliance for mutual advantage and part group for safety in numbers.

Elder and ancilla alike often refer to these groups as innovators — the former with some amusement, the latter with all sincerity. Innovators see themselves as the clan's future (which is not necessarily true) and the cutting edge that can take the Ventrue where they need to go (which may well be true). In many cases, these groups have all the energy and intellectual fervor of a revolutionary cell or an entrepreneur. Giddy with their newfound power, eager to make their mark, they scheme and dream together in hopes of realizing their goals.

In many cases, these groups' meetings become little more than bitch-sessions, a forum for young Ventrue to express their frustration without fear of offending their elders. More than most Ventrue social groups, innovators often observe secrecy within their ranks. They hold the meetings to be as sacred as the confessional — or at least a non-disclosed board meeting. Without such a devotion to discretion, the groups would not serve their important cathartic role. Elders react to this need for privacy in various ways. Some use technology or spies to try to discover what goes on at meetings. Others, more assured of their power and position, let the neonates do as they please in this matter. They will grow out of it in time.

Indeed, almost all of them eventually do just that. Most Kindred start to distance themselves from innovator groups after a few years. By that time, they might have their own holdings, responsibilities and even childer to look after. Besides, no Ventrue of true standing associates herself with such youthful cliques, so if one wishes to appear strong, she must distance herself from the Young Turks.

Occasionally, however, a group of innovators does distinguish itself in some way, such as the West Coast group that managed to get an early footing in the computer industry over a decade ago, or the group that set out for the New World five centuries earlier. Once they have gained the prestige and *dignitas* they sought for so long, these successful few usually become exactly what they contested for so long: established Ventrue with holdings to manage and power to wield in the face of aspiring young innovators who would take it all for themselves.

VENTRUE AND THE MORTAL WORLD

Ventrue, and all Kindred really, exist in two different worlds. First and foremost, they prowl the world of the Kindred and the clans, a world where sects and cities clash after dark; a world with which many Kindred, especially the Ventrue, spend much of their time and energy dealing. They also stalk the mortal world, variously referred to as the real world, the sleeping world, the world of the Canaille or just plain humanity. It surrounds the Kindred, influences everything they do and, in fact, sets the stage for all their various struggles and triumphs. The mortals are the land Kindred walk upon, the money in their accounts and, of course, the blood that sustains the undead. Without mortals, no vampiric world could exist at all, much as Kindred might wish to deny it.

The Ventrue are the first to admit to humanity's power and importance in both realms. The whole Camarilla exists as a means to protect the Kindred from an awakened

and vengeful beast known as humanity. The Inquisition taught this lesson well. At the same time, many Ventrue see Kindred as a whole as immeasurably superior to kine, and themselves in turn as superior to other Kindred (if not immeasurably so). How, then, do they reconcile the two opposed views that the humans must be feared and yet are worthy of little more than casual consideration? Simple. They respect the institutions while they ignore the man.

Such attitudes shock many Kindred. They claim that such belief is little better than that of the gore-spattered Sabbat, or they claim that the Kindred are not gods to toy with mortal lives. Such "soft-heartedness" usually meets with hand-waving and sneers. The Ventrue do not revile the mortal world — they accept it as a tool or defer to it as a necessary ritual to observe, much like mortals view eating food and eliminating wastes.

INSTITUTIONAL POTENCY

Humanity's strength lies in its numbers. One-on-one, a human is little match for even the youngest Kindred. In groups, humans still might not match an elder's fearsome powers. In armies, wild mobs and great social movements, though, nothing can stand in their way. The kine have a remarkable ability to work together, something of which few Kindred can boast. They submit themselves willingly to a greater goal, to a higher purpose or (at the very least) to a more powerful master. The Ventrue admire this one quality the kine possess: their ability to suspend their egos and ignore their own needs and desires.

In effect, the Ventrue try to do the very same thing with both their own clan and the Camarilla. Thus far, they have succeeded to a certain degree, but it is a constant battle against chaos and individual avarice. The Camarilla lost the Gangrel just recently, a significant blow to the Ventrue's most famous creation. Likewise, internecine struggles and interpersonal jealousies within the clan itself keep the clan from working as a whole in the way it could. Even the Tremere with their fabled hierarchy cannot come close to approximating the discipline, devotion and cooperative edge found in any given national armed force in the industrialized world.

Therefore, the Ventrue have great respect (and even fear) for human institutions. Although they might influence key individuals within a group, the group moves on with purpose and power. Subvert a local election, and Democracy continues. Pay off a member of law enforcement, and the justice system rolls on. Blackmail a priest, and the Church still thrives. Kill a soldier and another rises to take his place, gun blazing. The idea and institution comprises more than the sum of its parts, and the Ventrue must acknowledge that power. Dealing with and blunting the force of such concentrated human force takes great effort, tremendous cunning and dauntless will. Ventrue have done it before, they have manipulated whole systems for their own purposes, but it is never easy. It is like playing with fire. If one is not supremely careful and aware, the fire will burn its master.

INDIVIDUAL IMPOTENCY

On the other hand, a single human is nothing. Unlike many Sabbat, who see humans as mere food, the Ventrue have no respect for individuals because of their minds. The Ventrue excel at Disciplines that shape, alter and arrest the thoughts and feelings of others. No other clan compares to them when it comes to expertise in such matters. Even the youngest Ventrue learn quickly to influence and twist the human mind. Mature ancillae and elder Ventrue can quite literally control a kine's every action or determine their every thought, should the need arise. How can one have any respect for someone whose very mind is yours to do with as you please?

This kind of arrogance comes naturally to the Ventrue, and they encourage it. A certain amount of self-confidence, assurance in one's own power and superiority is a valuable tool, especially when it comes to mind- and emotion-control techniques. The Ventrue must feel that he can conquer the kine intellect with ease if, indeed, he actually hopes to use his Disciplines effectively. This attitude serves only to heighten the Ventrue's prejudices.

Clan culture reinforces the disdain toward individual kine. Ventrue seldom refer to humans by name unless absolutely necessary. Usually they speak about mortal affairs in terms of the institutions. "Chase Bank has some interesting new business possibilities," or, "The mayor's office reports that our proposal will pass." When they do speak of individuals, it is usually by the person's title, or his function if he has no title. "The police officer will not be a problem," or, "My informant tells me there is a new supplier in the neighborhood." Without names, the personalities become interchangeable. It does not matter what kine fills what role, as long as the Ventrue can pigeonhole where the kine fits within the greater human scheme.

Such is not to say that Ventrue ignore human beings as people entirely. Certainly, they are aware of names and even spend a great deal learning about the personalities, histories and foibles of influential mortals. However, they view all of these things through their lens of disdain. This particular human, weak like all humans, has these extra weaknesses and these extra strengths. Ultimately, though, "He is just a kine, and therefore his blood or property is mine should I choose to take it."

OF INFLUENCE, POWER AND CONTROL

One of the most common misconceptions about the Ventrue, even within the younger ranks of the clan itself, is that they somehow control humanity. The idea that a few Kindred, no matter how powerful, could determine the course and fate of gigantic human institutions is bitterly laughable to the clan's elders. They know just how far their powers can go and where they end. Perhaps a Ventrue prince really could determine everything that went on in his city once upon a time. However, the nights of fifth-generation Kindred ruling over Greek city-states of 30,000 citizens are long gone. Tonight, kine cities claim populations in the millions, nations in the hundreds of millions. Control over such masses can only be dreamed of, not realized.

Even on a local level — say, the police department or the city government — utter control cannot exist. One does not rise from his daily sleep and press the "arrest rival minions" button on some remote control. First of all, the Masquerade prevents any such overt seizure of power, but even if no such restriction existed, the task would defeat most. The kine know when something is not right on a grand scale. A few cops on the take or a politician who lets himself be photographed with a nose full of powder while bound in leather restraints are easy to come by and expected to a certain degree. Placing a whole system in the service of one Kindred or clan would send shock waves through that system, awakening that dangerous human impulse. Complete control, at least for more than a few brief nights, is not only nearly impossible to achieve, it's a foolish desire to begin with.

Influence. The Ventrue truly understand and use influence. The fact of the matter is that control is more trouble than it's worth most of the time. Even the Ventrue, who have so many business and other ties to the mortal world, do not really care about most of what humanity does with its days. Why try to control something, spend all that energy and time, on something that affects you maybe once a year — once a decade even? It's better to have a few key levers in place, people you can put pressure on to make something bigger happen when you need it.

What, then, is influence? It's knowing a clerk in the file room who is eager to pass on information in exchange for a few bucks or the keys to the boss' Benz on the weekend. It's having a janitor in your debt who has the keys to every door. It's being able to make a payment into a numbered account and have a congressman vote no on a bill. It's knowing the right prostitute who makes a cop think twice about reporting what he just saw. It might even be a corporate executive who happens to be a ghoul, blood bound to you. Influence is subtle and relatively low-maintenance. You don't need to spend your nights handling affairs in the mayor's office, arms spread wide, talons clicking fiendishly. You just need to know you have an open nerve, a pressure you can apply when the time comes.

POWER AND POWERS

As for power, it is another word that has ceased to have meaning, or that has at least lost the meaning it once had. Power means quite literally the ability to do something, to make something happen. Any elder can tell you that the only power he truly has emanates from his person. The only thing you can ever be sure of is yourself. Your soldiers might flee, your contacts might disappear, and your agents might betray you. Aside from yourself, you don't really control anyone. You can push them in a certain direction — maybe even push them *really hard* — but it is ultimately them, not you, who is doing "the thing" whatever it might be.

In the same way, the clan does pay a price when it uses its mental and emotional powers. Repeated use of Disciplines on a single subject set can have only two outcomes over time. The subjects either grow resentful, suspicious and dangerous, or they become complete emotional and mental thralls. The first is obviously undesirable, and the second is little better. Mortal tools who lose their initiative and free will are less versatile than their mentally capable counterparts, and they tend to rouse unwanted suspicion among friends and co-workers. Furthermore, using Disciplines takes time, energy and effort that the Ventrue could be using other places. Using vampiric powers also leaves telltale signs — signs that perceptive Kindred can read all too well. Why let the Tremere or the Sabbat know with whom and where your influence lies by using such heavy-handed tactics? Finally, it means that the clan has fallen to its last resort; that there was no more subtle way to handle the issue. Graceful Ventrue *hate* to eliminate options with such a vulgar "trump card."

Instead, the wise Ventrue holds his power in reserve until it is needed most, waiting and watching for the precise moment when the smallest nudge of force can have the greatest effect. Until that moment comes, he uses other means. Having wealth aplenty, it is often easier to just outright buy the solution he wants. On the flip side, threatening someone's ability to make money can prove an even greater motivational force. An exchange of simple favors, *quid pro quo*, can succeed where money cannot. Should these more reasonable methods fail, the threat of force (as opposed to its actual use) still has power to persuade. Only when other, less exposed and demanding options fail does a crafty Blue Blood turn to his arsenal to obtain his goals.

THE PATH TO POWER: A VENTRUE PRIMER

How, then, does a young Ventrue strike this balance between carrot and stick that the elders seem to have achieved long ago? He learns the basics during the *agoge*, absorbing different takes on the issue depending on who's doing the teaching. However, almost every member of the clan agrees upon some basics. With so many traditions, it is no wonder that the Ventrue have an "acceptable" path to power along with everything else. While not every Ventrue fledgling follows the course laid out here, many do. Moreover, most are measured according to just how well they do.

ESTABLISHING A BASE

This process begins in the final stages of the *agoge*. The Ventrue sets out on his own to found a base for his future power and position. The first, most important thing a Ventrue must find for himself is a secure, comfortable and respectable haven. The peerage attaches great significance to the appointments that surround an individual Ventrue. One's haven should be suitable for entertaining visits by elders, sires and clients alike (although the first may never actually visit, their servants might). Mansions, penthouses, even private clubs are all acceptable. In addition to this very public (within the Kindred community at least) haven, a prudent Ventrue maintains a number of secret, secure havens. Indeed, some never sleep at their acknowledged "haven," but maintain it just for appearances' sake.

As far as possible, everything about a haven should be legal, paid for and have no strings attached. The less reason mortals have to look into the ownership and use of a building, the better. Many young Kindred take out traditional mortgages on their havens, both to avoid arousing suspicion and because they usually don't have enough cash to outright buy a proper haven.

When it comes to negotiating price, having loans approved and other financial issues, a little discretion goes a long way. Totally mesmerizing a realtor into selling a Kindred the home for a quarter of its value will raise suspicions, but a few polite words and entrancing smiles can let him know the absolute lowest price and perhaps bump that down a little more. It can also ensure that the seller favors the Kindred, no matter who else might be interested in the property.

These abilities come in useful later as well, particularly when a Kindred has made certain security and light-proofing alterations to the building that he would prefer the local building inspector ignore or forget. The same is true of contractors who help build secret chambers or install security systems. Wholesale memory wipes raise questions and suspicions. Bribing the contractors, renovating a "rumpus room" in the basement instead of a "sealed vampire sepulchre," take more tact but pay off in the end. Likewise, contractors tend to do the work faster and cheaper for someone whose mien doesn't involve voice-mail tirades or threats of unholy supernatural power.

SECURING SUSTENANCE

Having established a place to sleep, the Ventrue must next look to the matter of blood. For Ventrue, more than any clan, doing so is a real challenge. The feeding restriction can make one's unlife very difficult. Moreover, when one's enemies discover the true nature of these restrictions, matters can grow quite dire. Every young Ventrue should establish a steady herd from which he can feed and an emergency supply on which to fall back.

Establishing a herd takes time and effort. The larger the pool of possible candidates the better, so the pragmatic Ventrue finds as many excuses as possible to fraternize with the appropriate mortals. Doing so often involves devoting time and resources to causes, clubs and social groups in which the Kindred might not otherwise be interested. Crafty Ventrue always find a way to turn this expense to some advantage. Indeed they must, for if others see the Ventrue lounging about with a particular set of mortals for no obvious benefit, they can deduce the true cause easily.

In order to hide their blood proclivities from inquisitive Kindred, many Ventrue try to find some larger social group or cause that their required blood type associates with as well. Since the Ventrue have so many contacts with mortal society, many interact with so many different groups that it is hard to pinpoint any one as their food source. It is also common sense for Ventrue to pretend or allude to feeding on individuals from whom they could never actually imbibe, thus further occluding their need's true nature.

As a last resort, every Ventrue should have the right blood type on hand in a secure place or person. Having a trusted personal assistant can help satisfy this need. Most also keep the right kind of blood stored in reserve at their havens. For those who can afford it, the best option is to keep the right type of person under lock and key in one's haven, always available. A few cruel Ventrue have even had their vessels put into induced comas and stored away in hospital-like pantries. One had best hide such emergency resources well, though, not only to secure the blood but also to avoid unwanted, prying mortals from wondering just what those bodies are doing there, anyway.

THE IMPORTANCE OF MONEY

Often, but not always, Ventrue come into unlife with some resources of their own. However, while a two-story house and four-car garage may impress the guys at work,

they mean little to a clan of millionaires. It's time to leave the office and the 401(k) and start acquiring some serious investment capital.

Money is very important to the Ventrue. It serves some of the same place keepers for the clan that it does in mortal society: It's a measure of status, power and accomplishment. A Ventrue is not successful unless he has great wealth, or so it seems. At the same time, it's not important at all. Most Ventrue, especially the higher-ranking Kindred, take it for granted. They have had so much of it for so long that they no longer even consider consciously where it comes from, or even bother spending it. Chances are, if they need to buy something or someone, they have the funds. Such should be the goal of every new Ventrue: to acquire so much wealth that wealth ceases to matter.

That goal is easier stated than accomplished, of course. Investments take time to mature, companies rarely make stockholders millionaires overnight, even in the nights of unpredictable Internet stocks. All the traditional, mortal means of becoming rich work just as well for the Ventrue, too; better, even, since Kindred have much more time to weather market cycles. However, investing doesn't do you any good if you don't have any money to invest. Fortunately, Ventrue have other assets at their disposal and a few tried-and-true methods exist to bankroll an ambitious Kindred's future career.

At the most base level imaginable, a Ventrue can always just steal money. Considered crass, low-class and shameful, theft is nevertheless easy and sometimes necessary. Walk into a department store, a grocery store, a liquor store or even a bar. Look into the man behind the counter's eyes and ask him for all his money; it's his ass on the line unless Kindred start making a habit of it. Watch out for security cameras and don't try the same trick twice, but it will do in a pinch. The down side is that, aside from the shame factor, it's nearly impossible to get one's hands on real, Ventrue-sized amounts of cash this way. Ventrue want and deal in millions, not 10s and 20s.

Fortunately, rich people can be and are fooled into giving their money away all the time. The Ventrue can take money for all kinds of reasons that the rich won't even begin to suspect. Ventrue in the modern age prefer especially charities and political contributions. In both cases, a clever pitch or magnetic personality can open up checkbooks, especially when combined with the vintage wines and gourmet foods of a fundraiser. The more traditional but equally useful venue for fund raising is the Church, where the faithful gladly (and tax-deductably) tithe large chunks of income. The advantage for all of these methods is that the people who give do not expect any material return. They think they're buying political influence or salvation or good press or just giving money to feel good about themselves. Few ever check to see what becomes of the money.

It is not surprising, then, that most Ventrue sit on at least one charity or other fund-raising board. But the best and most lucrative cash cow is and always will be straight-forward business. Once a Ventrue puts together a strong business plan and some start-up capital, he can achieve almost anything. Need new investors for a start-up company? In tough negotiations with a potential partner? Having labor problems? A cool Ventrue can solve any of these and a hundred other common business problems with a sit-down conversation. Tact and demeanor haven't harmed the Ventrue in their millennia at the front of the Kindred pecking order.

A fledgling with an influential or connected sire may even entreat his mentor to "borrow" from the Ventrue coffers or the sire's own accounts. While many other Blue Bloods would look down upon this bit of silver-spoon "cheating," those same Ventrue would no doubt have availed themselves of similar opportunities had such been open to them. Some sires, though, would also refuse such requests, wanting their issue to prove themselves. Others would gladly provide the "tools" for their progeny's success, looking forward to basking in the glow of their *dignitas* and their own peers' envy.

All this takes time of course, but not too much. Within two years of being Embraced, the vast majority of Ventrue are wealthy (if they weren't already). Within a decade, all but the dimmest (or least concerned) command assets worth millions of dollars. It's expected. If you don't have so much money you never have to worry about it again by your 20th Embrace anniversary, something is very, very wrong.

THE SERVANTS

Unlike many other clans, the Ventrue sometimes employ vast numbers of mortals directly. Within a hazy chain of command, the clan has easily 10 times as many kine as Kindred, a figure that does not include the thousands more over whom various Ventrue have some degree of influence. There are two reasons for this practice. First, Ventrue do not fear humans as much as most Kindred… or, perhaps, as much as they should. Although no vampire would admit it, most feel uncomfortable around kine. They worry that they'll make some mistake and give themselves away, bringing down the angry, torch-bearing mob. The Ventrue have less fear because they work among the kine, alongside them, and they often have a hauteur over the Children of Seth that borders on the dangerous or perverse. As they say, familiarity breeds contempt; many arrogant Ventrue certainly have more than their share of disregard for mortals.

Almost every Ventrue has a need for any number of mortal retainers from a basic stable at some point in her unlife. She may have need for the lawyers, accountants and managers necessary to manage her finances. For the most part, these employees can be normal mortals who have no idea that they're working for a Kindred, or even an unusual businesswoman. The wealthiest Ventrue employ dozens of these pencil-pushers, each managing a discreet fraction of their interests without even knowing that the others exist. Hiring and firing them is no different than any other business move in the mortal world.

More dangerous are those with whom the Ventrue works more closely. The men and women who carry out her direct desires, manage her holding companies and deliver her ultimatums. Although they usually have little or no knowledge of the Kindred's true nature, they do know that they work for a very rich, powerful and secretive employer. These employees are almost universally very talented, subtle and well paid. The wise Ventrue virtually always has some hold over these individuals, either through the gifts of Caine or some more temporal method like blackmail — or even something wholly fabricated. This bit of leverage should not be used as an impetus for them to do their work well (they should want to do that on their own) but rather as an emergency reserve in case someone steps out of line.

Finally come the close, trusted servants who know the Ventrue's true nature. Revealing one's vampiric identity to a mortal not only violates the letter of the Masquerade, it places the Kindred in some danger as well. The Ventrue must be very secure with any servants and equally prepared for the "calculated risk loss" should doubts rise about their trustworthiness. It is much easier to find a new servant than it is to undo an act of betrayal. These servants sometimes even work for the Kindred with the hopes — stated or hidden — that their master will Embrace them one night. It even works out that way sometimes, although not as often as each would hope.

As mentioned previously, the most important thing that most Ventrue realize about mortal (and even ghoul) servants is that they are all replaceable. Indeed, should a Ventrue ever come to think of one of her servants as invaluable rather than just useful — as the Blue Bloods comment among themselves — it is time to remove that servant. The Ventrue herself is and always should be the one who matters most. A Kindred who so loses control of her domain that she cannot hold it without a mortal's help is better off dead. And that maxim has been put to the test many times over the course of history.

THE ACQUISITION OF *DIGNITAS*

Haven established, sustenance secured and financing acquired, the Ventrue can now set about acquiring what the rest of his nights will no doubt focus upon: *dignitas*. That single word, borrowed from the Romans, sums up every reason that the Ventrue exist. It means accruing power and influence, winning victories against one's enemies and rising within the hierarchy of peers to attain fame and distinction within the Camarilla, all with the dignity and noble air with which all Ventrue comport themselves.

THE TOOLS

How then does one acquire *dignitas*? Every moment offers new opportunities. A following section details the various arenas in which the clan recognizes and encourages excellence. First, though, come the basic techniques that Ventrue can use to succeed in their quest for recognition and status, the four Ventrue keystones found in every clan member's toolbox: money, information, respect and power.

MONEY

Mortals have risen to power and prominence for eons without the aid of supernatural powers or immortal life spans. Ventrue can and do use the same methods, the most potent of which is money. The uses for money are many and obvious: It buys weapons, security, soldiers and information. It can sometimes buy politicians, juries, law-enforcement, results and even affection. The ability to manipulate it can be a weapon, whether that means freezing a foe's finances or taking over his company in a hostile stock buy-out. Money is the most versatile tool for power in existence, and it is no wonder that the Ventrue spend so much time making sure that they never run out of it.

They key to using money is that everyone (or nearly everyone) has a price. The trick is to find out what that price is, even if they themselves don't know it. Once you meet that price, they'll play if you pay. It is important to note that sometimes that price is a negative. For the very wealthy, the price could well be keeping what they have in the face of possibly losing it all. Moreover, one should always look around for when the price is too high. The person standing next to the subject (a wife, a partner, an adviser) might be more affordable — and perhaps a better investment.

As many a moralist can testify, money and greed can lead to more trouble than good. A clever Ventrue knows how to make money create trouble all on its own. Sometimes, especially when it comes to blackmailing or "manufacturing blame," unexplained money can be worse than no money at all. Anonymous, unknown deposits can lead to troubles with the IRS, make it look like a government official is taking bribes or even arouse spousal suspicions. The money itself can be tainted, the profits from a crime in which the serial numbers are known.

Merely possessing or spending the money can result in grave consequences for the Ventrue's enemy.

INFORMATION

The Ventrue have known the value of information just as long as the Nosferatu have, they just don't see the point in lurking in shadows and sewers to obtain it. In many ways, the Ventrue pursue information with more fervor than they do money, since it is both harder to come by and more valuable. In fact, one of the best things about money is that you can use it to buy information. Knowledge is the key to power. The more one knows about enemies, rivals, possible partners, allies and even their own domain, the more effective their leadership becomes. From stock tips to the security codes for a troublesome rival's haven, the right piece of data at the right moment can change the very whims of Fate.

Since Ventrue cannot often lurk unseen in plain sight like some Kindred, they must rely on more traditional means. Successful Ventrue recognize a few things every Blue Blood should invest in from the beginning, one of which is a talented pool of gossips and informants. Private detectives are readily available, and most Ventrue can find one willing to bend or break the rules for the right price (here, again, the importance of money). Wise employers test them first on a mundane matter like industrial espionage or following and reporting on the affairs of a fellow mortal. Gradually, they draw the mortal into their world, paying far better than any other client. Eventually, they groom a devoted "regular," or at least a dependable resource.

Having invested in an investigator, the Ventrue should retain the latest and greatest surveillance equipment her resources will allow. Technology has caught up with and even surpassed the Nosferatu when it comes to listening in secretly on others' conversations. Even a marginally wealthy Ventrue who makes a few law enforcement contacts can tap key phones, bug vital offices and havens, hire computer hackers or even track an individual's movements easily. Many Ventrue, as is their way, resisted these machines for a long time, but competition brought about by young, ambitious Ventrue have made the use of these devices common among even the most staid members of the clan.

After acquiring the basic tools of information-gathering, a prudent Ventrue also spends much of his existence widening his circle of contacts, informants and amicable associates. Here again, Ventrue politeness serves its clan members well. Not only do the clan's supernatural abilities make it easier for them to win over confidences if all else fails, their manners make them actually pay attention to what others have to say. A Ventrue always listens, at least if he wants to get ahead in unlife. Genteel, even gregarious and free with their money when they need to be, the

Ventrue know how to make contacts and keep them, especially if said contacts have valuable information.

Finally, when other methods fail, the Ventrue always has himself to rely on. If turning on the charm doesn't work and the information is too vital to let go, get it straight from the person's mind. The vulgar uses of one's supernatural resources allow the Ventrue to force a mortal to tell him the truth, with no deception possible. Doing so necessitates careful handling in order to protect the Masquerade, and it has its complications. But when one has to know for sure, this recourse is almost entirely reliable.

RESPECT

Charm and cash aside, every Ventrue needs one other tool in his arsenal in order to succeed: respect. Respect is a two-edged sword, and the most successful Ventrue shave with one edge and cut down their enemies with the other. Turned against himself, respect keeps the Ventrue alert, ambitious and graceful. The Ventrue respects not only the breach of Masquerade and the fangs of his peers through fear, he respects the words of his elders and the competition from those below him. He observes the customs of *dignitas*, or else he respects the consequences his fellows would bring to bear on him should he play the maverick. He rides this understanding, lets it press him forward without succumbing to it.

The Ventrue find external respect — that is, other people's respect of them — much more interesting and comfortable to deal with. After all, humility is rarely a Ventrue's strong suit. Along with an honorable bearing and a mannered demeanor, ambitious Ventrue should cultivate a stalwart reputation. All smile and no bite can cause others to disregard a Kindred, something no Ventrue worth his *dignitas* can abide. Fear can breed respect, as can justness, frugality and even a self-fulfilling aura of success. Respect also keeps others on their best behavior. Finally, having the world (or a part of it anyway) respect him just makes a Ventrue feel good and gives him the confidence to do what he needs to do.

How, then, does one develop such a worthy mien? First and foremost, the Ventrue must never be afraid to take measures to their required ends, especially when dealing with mortals and non-Camarilla Kindred. One does not purchase the essentials for unlife on promises or borrowed money. Of course, a Ventrue should not go around killing or sacking his elders' coffers just to prove that he can. Indeed, doing so not only makes one look brutal or foolish, it is a waste of time and energy. No, a Ventrue should take an extreme measure only when the situation demands it, and then he should not hesitate for a moment.

Death is not the only extreme measure, of course. Indeed, it might not even be the most severe. For example,

a recalcitrant mortal servant might step into line if his family is threatened. A young anarch punk who refuses to acknowledge the pecking order can be brought to heel socially. With the ability to control minds, Ventrue seldom need to resort to torture, but some do anyway, just for the fear factor or for the ease of "clean-up" afterward. Other, less physical, actions can instill fear as well. Blackmail and extortion are favorite tools. Threaten to reveal a man's secrets or erase his bank accounts, and he will most likely cave in moments. The following is only one example of the most important Ventrue truism regarding respect: Everyone fears something, and it is your job to find out what that something is.

POWER AND POWERS

Here again we have that troublesome word: power. The word is so overused that it has nearly lost all meaning of its own in the world of the undead. In the terms of this discussion, power refers to the ability to actually get things done. A Ventrue can have all the money, information and esteemed reputation in the world, but if he can't do anything with it, then what's it all for? The ability to enforce one's desires on the rest of the world is truly a measure of power. The more of the world a Kindred can enforce his desires upon, the more power he has. This topic deserves a more thorough treatment than any in this section. The following are details on how and why Ventrue accumulate real power in a variety of different arenas.

Business

Status in the business world comes not from making money, but from the ancillary influences that attend particular industries. No one cares about how much money a Kindred's three radio stations make him. They do care if he can use them to push a particular political agenda or quash a story about some breach in the Masquerade. Who cares if VentrueSoft had a record-breaking IPO? Can the Blue Blood use the company's technology to help hack into the Nosferatu computer network? Arms sales in a slump? It doesn't matter as long as both sides of a given conflict purchase the same ammunition. Therefore, many business ventures that don't necessarily turn a profit still carry high prestige for the Ventrue who can influence them. In other words, if a Kindred can use it for clan or personal advantage, it brings prestige.

This priority on results and influence rather than profits means that Ventrue do not necessarily have to have legal or fiscal control of a company in order to earn *dignitas* from having it in their domain. It is nigh impossible for a young Ventrue to exert any substantive influence over a large corporation. However, she doesn't need to if she knows several low- to mid-level employees who will give her access to the company's internal information and help acquire inventory or services. Why own the limousine company when a single call to one of the drivers brings the resources to your door?

Starting at the bottom is also a good way for ambitious Ventrue to accrue *dignitas* in the face of an elder population that claims dominion over all the city's most prominent industries. The old-guard Ventrue might have the board of directors and the CEO in his pocket, but he probably has no idea what's going on at the loading docks. If she's careful, a new Ventrue can come in and make a play for influence at the ground floor. She accumulates real power over inventory and the use of freight trucks, both of which have many practical uses.

Even in the extreme cases, when and if the elder finds out, the case goes to Ventrue court and an arbiter makes the final decision. As often as not, the young Ventrue can make a case for herself that the elder was not exploiting his dominion effectively, and she gets to keep what she earned. On the down side, she has an elder angry with her, and she loses great *dignitas* if the case goes against her. No one ever said that Ventrue politics was for the faint of heart.

Local Government

The Ventrue try to sink their talons into every aspect of a city's government, hoping to populate it with spies, informants and agents. Actually, it sounds more insidious than it really is. Most of these "catspaws" do not even realize to whom they're reporting or where the money's coming from. Nevertheless, one can often assume that a Ventrue-connected mortal works somewhere in any branch of local government, from law enforcement to the property appraiser's office. Obviously, not every government employee is the secret minion of the vast conspiracy of an undead shadow government, but neither do they need to be. One does not always need direct access to the zoning board when a more anonymous assistant will do. Here again, as with business, it's not whom you influence but what you can accomplish. The Ventrue care about results.

At the top of the heap sits the city's mayor and or city council (depending on local laws). As elected officials, the Ventrue try to steer clear of using too much direct power against such public targets. Moreover, these high-ranking officials have so many interests pulling at them already that it can prove difficult for a single Kindred to establish reliable influence. Besides, most of a mayor's job consists of dealing with issues the Ventrue could not care less about. A conditioned servant needs constant direction, something no one has the time to give. Still, at least one Ventrue in the city—usually the prince or *praetor*—often keeps an "open line" to the mayor. They have established contacts that can yield them direct contact with the city's leaders on short notice. Most already have established relationships, but those who don't may fall back on their mental and emotional powers in an emergency.

The problem with working through the mayor or city council or whatever other authority exists out there is that it takes a great deal of energy, and it actually usually proves quite inefficient. The leaders themselves do very little. They order others to do those things, people who order underlings to carry out the leaders' demands, in turn. It's far more efficient, and less obvious, to go to the person who ends up performing the task in the first place. Not only are lower-level government officials more accessible, they're almost always easier to influence. Why have a mayor put pressure on the D.A. to drop a legal case when having the property clerk lose the evidence sees the case thrown out of court? Why put pressure on the police chief to assign extra patrols of a certain neighborhood on a given night when you can pay off-duty cops to do it for you? The examples are endless.

Moreover, it is important to have the individual parts of the political machine under one's sway because, as often as not, the city leadership has very little authority to make anyone actually do anything. Elected officials come and go, but the entrenched bureaucracy remains the same. Someone is certainly going to want to have members of offices like the tax collector, the property appraiser, the code-enforcement division and the department of motor vehicles in his favor. All of these positions provide valuable services, from fake identity documents to the necessary permits to build new havens (or evict troublesome rivals from their current abodes). Even public services like the fire department deserve the resourceful Kindred's attention. After all, a few wrong turns or missteps by a friendly firefighter can result in an enemy's haven burning to the ground while the Ventrue's receives prompt attention.

In order to establish these vital influences, the Ventrue must do a little research and find out who actually has the power to do things. Who signs the work orders, and who carries them out? Who has the passwords to the computer system? Find out all the basics first before making a move. Often the easiest way to uncover this information is to find and question (or interrogate) someone who has worked there for a long time. Then, Ventrue should develop personal relationships with those mortals in the governmental area over which they intend to establish domain who have the true power. Charm, cajole, bribe, seduce — or Dominate — as necessary.

On a final note, no single Ventrue's influence extends into every part of government. Rather, each Kindred establishes contacts in a particular area. A key element of Ventrue internal politics involves the exchange of favors. If one Kindred has tremendous influence within the police, others will come to her seeking help with police matters.

Clan tradition obligates her to do what she can without jeopardizing her own position. She can of course expect similar favors in return. As a rule of thumb, when a higher-ranking Ventrue asks such a favor, it is given freely and without expectation of recompense. Rank has its privileges.

National Politics

A nation's government is an entirely different affair that most Ventrue have no part in. Unless the Ventrue makes his haven within the country's capitol, it tends to be difficult to affect national policy directly. Even those who dwell around the corner from the president or prime minister's residence don't have an easy time of it, however. National leaders have so much attention, are so public and have so much security that tampering with them is certainly improbable (if not impossible) for all but the most subtle and potent elder. Furthermore, so many influences already pull at a national leader that unless the Kindred devotes his entire being to shadowing the president and whispering commands in his ear, influencing him effectively on a regular basis is not feasible.

The same can be said of national legislative body and other elected officials, although to a lesser extent. The Ventrue often have an influencing effect on those elected locally. This influence is by no means complete, and it usually amounts to something comparable to what a powerful, mortal lobbyist might have. However, the Ventrue should be able to arrange a face-to-face meeting with the legislator if the need arises. Afterward, he should have no problem assuring that her next vote is an informed one. Of course, blatant manipulations and coarse uses of Disciplines are dangerous, and they attract much unwanted attention, both from the mesmerized target and her aides and peers.

The best way to influence mortal politics is by using the same tools mortals do: money and lobbyists. One has no reason to waste valuable energy when money can achieve most of the things a vampire would ever need from a politician. After all, the national government seldom has much to do with the issues that concern Kindred. Most Kindred do not fight open wars or command tank divisions and bombers, nor does any but the rarest of Methuselahs carry our vendettas or grudges with national policy. They do occasionally want federal funding for local highways as a favor to one of their mortal contacts or legal shelter for some business-related undertaking. These needs are not supernatural, and they do not require supernatural solutions.

Having a paid lobbyist on one's staff, for local, regional or national politics, is something many prominent Ventrue do. Usually the Kindred's attorneys handle such dealings. Different Ventrue approach this problem from different perspectives. Most, concerned primarily with local politics, never want any contact or connection with the lobbyist. As long as the job is done, they'd prefer to have their name far removed from the proceedings.

Others, particularly those with a vested interest in national politics, like to work much closer. They often find lobbyists that they can groom and cajole to the point at which they can work with full knowledge of the Kindred's true nature. This way, they can stay on top of the situation and use their own powers to intervene as necessary. Acquiring such a servant is really no different than finding loyal help at home: Conditioning, blood bond, blackmail and bribery all serve as possible motivators.

Crime

Almost any Ventrue could use some criminal contacts of one sort or another at some point during his unlife. Mortal laws do not bind Kindred, and few Ventrue feel obligated to limit their activities to the above-board and legal. With only what remains of his *humanitas* to bind him, a Ventrue may even be prepared to break the law nightly, whether that means ordering wiretaps on someone's phone or kidnapping someone off the street to interrogate him. It all has to happen on demand and in a professional manner. Equally importantly, it cannot connect back to the Ventrue himself under any circumstances.

One should always isolate oneself from actual criminal acts to the fullest extent possible. The justice system is one of those fearsome mortal institutions that can cause great harm to Ventrue, both operationally and personally. Even with adequate precautions, most Ventrue isolate themselves from street-level criminal activities, making requests through trusted ghouls and other intermediaries and extending anonymous favors in return for consideration.

Acquiring criminal associates is easy, although finding skilled ones invariably proves more difficult. Typically, a Ventrue divides his criminal resources into two categories: disposable thugs and experienced operatives. The disposable thugs are street toughs and gangbangers who do violence gladly in return for money. Some Ventrue never have need of such services, but they come in handy for terrorizing mortals, making examples of anarch havens and other brute-force, low-intellect operations. As their name suggests, one uses disposable thugs a few times (or maybe only once) before writing them off permanently.

Professional criminals are harder to come by. They are usually career mobsters or law-enforcement types who have gone over to the profitable side and are a rare breed. They may work in a Ventrue's employ for many years, making good money but not quite enough to retire. They run criminal operations and perform investigative duties. Ventrue who do not wish to trust such sensitive matters to just anyone actually train their own operatives, taking a mortal under their wing from a young age and grooming them for the job. Sometimes — if the mortal lives long enough — he may become a ghoul or even receive the Embrace as a backhanded "reward" for keeping the Ventrue's good faith.

Influence within existing organized crime syndicates is an entirely different matter. Certainly, many Ventrue become involved with such groups, but they run into a great deal of competition from other clans in this arena. Furthermore, most organized groups have already earned law enforcement's detrimental attention. While profit and prestige is attached to having mob influence, one should deal with sensitive and important criminal matters oneself. Better to have no traceable, prosecutable connection with organized crime.

All together, the amount of criminal muscle and expertise available to a Ventrue reflects strongly on his *dignitas*. More than any other arena, the world of crime is chiefly about working around restrictions, be they legal or moral. The ability to accomplish ends, no matter the means, carries great weight within the clan. Of course, it must be done with style, tradition and a certain degree of decorum. Bloodbaths in the streets and Mafia thugs breaking the knees of everyone in a neighborhood do not impress the clan elders. Silencing a truculent reporter without undue attention or arranging the theft of a property deed from a Toreador haven just might.

Society

Once one looks beyond the powerful business, government and criminal institutions, a whole world of mortals practically begs some enterprising Ventrue to come along and grace them with his presence. Ventrue especially prize the ability to sway and set in motion large kine groups. Is a loathsome Toreador planning a tour de force gallery opening for his new protégé? Rouse the religious right for a no-holds-barred protest and boycott. Sabbat setting up one of their infernal churches in the city? Encourage the neighborhood watch to organize a petition and march to oust the unpleasant new residents and demand the old church demolished by the city. As any Ventrue can tell you, the people have power, and sometimes they need to be motivated to use it.

In the nights of history, the Church proved the best means of reaching the population at large. Tonight the same is still true, although not as universally so as it once was. The new gods of popular music, mass-market fiction, television and movies have taken over. The Toreador have made great inroads into many aspects of all these potent media, but the Ventrue continue to make forays into the field, from the business side at the very least. As entertainment and media grow more commonly owned by, operated by and answerable to big business, the Ventrue position has strengthened accordingly.

On the local level, Ventrue can do much with the leaders of individual churches, political organizations and community social clubs. The clan has long involved itself with exclusive societies like the Freemasons and even groups like Elk Lodges and the Shriners. Country clubs and gentlemen's clubs have long served as Ventrue havens and meeting places, as well as a source of contact networks and connected mortals who represent almost infinite opportunities. The Ventrue can make inroads and valuable contacts anywhere people gather to share ideas and establish their group identity.

Using power from such groups is tricky. Social forces are only truly effective when large numbers of people become involved, making the Kindred's visibility an issue. Fortunately for the Ventrue, people tend to stop thinking for themselves when they gather in large groups. A talented speaker with a strong personality can work the right crowd into a fervor and push them into action. Elder Ventrue who survived the Inquisition have seen this phenomenon firsthand. Now, they help teach their childer to harness that power against their enemies — with extreme caution.

THE BEST AND BRIGHTEST

The Ventrue see themselves as the strongest, most important Kindred clan of them all; the preeminent Cainite bloodline. They arguably have the most influence within the mortal world, and they hold the most prominent positions within the Camarilla. Their natural abilities make them the perfect leaders while their traditions, breeding and mores separate them from the rest of the undead rabble that roams the night. No doubt, these claims seem lofty and arrogant, and certainly few others would agree so exultantly, but the fact of the matter is that the Ventrue do have a point. It might not be destiny, noble heritage or "the hand of Caine" working in their favor, but Clan Ventrue very likely wields the most temporal power in the world.

What support exists for this inflammatory claim? First of all, although sheer numbers may work against them, the clan has more influence than almost any other clan. Since the Ventrue have more members in prominent positions, including princes, they can all but govern the creation of Kindred. Most Ventrue are much better than other proliferate clans like the Brujah or the turgid *antitribu* at spending their early years thinking for the future. The Ventrue lead calmer unlives and expand their assets rather than indulging in frivolity or violence.

Additionally, the clan's close ties to mortal institutions give them tremendous power to get things done, achieve their goals and protect their interests and themselves. With perhaps more mortal contact than any other clan, they can place a wall of flesh between them and anyone who would do them harm. The clan's tremendous wealth and contacts add to their potency immeasurably. They can buy whatever and whomever they need, whenever they need it. Even other wealthy clans like the Giovanni and Toreador don't come close to wielding the vast, institutional reserves of the Ventrue.

Also and again, Ventrue hold more leadership positions within the Camarilla than any other clan. Having Ventrue princes generates tremendous clan prestige and opportunities within those cities. Ventrue primogen, seneschals, sheriffs and harpies add even more to the clan's overall strength. Although they might bicker among themselves over minor matters, this vast network of powerful Ventrue can come together and move mountains when the time comes. It is hard to oust Ventrue from power because they already hold so many of these positions. Meanwhile, more up-and-coming Blue Bloods actively pursue those seats not occupied currently by Ventrue. Each decade brings about more Ventrue leaders, not less.

The Ventrue hierarchy and traditions make for one of the most unified clans in Kindred society, behind only the occult Tremere and unwholesome filial nature of the Giovanni. As for the individual Ventrue's motivations, most realize that unity (even enforced by abstractions such as *dignitas*) provides the key to maintaining and expanding their own prominence or comfort. The mere fact that Ventrue can expect succor (or at least a nonhostile approximation) in a crisis puts them head and shoulders above most clans, particularly those without the grace or demeanor of kings.

As the modern nights prove, times change. The physically powerful clans, like the Brujah, still have important roles to play in the Camarilla. The truth of the matter, however, is that modern weaponry has closed the gap between those who posses powerful physical attributes and those who do not. The Ventrue do not necessarily want the martial prowess of the other clans on their side, but rather they have started to even the field physically.

Together, all of these facts lend credence to the Ventrue claim to the title "scions of the Kindred." That's all well and good, as far as it goes. Strongest or no, the Ventrue still need the other five clans to keep the Camarilla functional and viable. They realize as much, and they are even the first to admit it. One fact remains, however. The Camarilla survived the loss of the Gangrel. It could probably even survive the loss of another clan. It could not survive the loss of the Ventrue.

THE CAMARILLA

A Ventrue created the Camarilla, with cursory help from its fellow members. The clan has taken the lead in promoting the sect and upholding its traditions. Much of the clan's *dignitas* is tied to this 500-year-old dream, and the Ventrue elders do not plan to let anything happen to it. As far as the Directorate is concerned, the Ventrue and the Camarilla are linked tightly for the foreseeable future.

The Ventrue see themselves as the sect's stewards. They must lead the other clans; help them meet the Camarilla's standards and traditions. The concept of *noblesse oblige* evidences itself here more than anywhere else. The Camarilla exists for the benefit of the race of Kindred, to help protect them from both each other and the ire of humanity. Ventrue take pride in their duty to Kindred society, and they are generally very serious about the sect and its goals. Some Ventrue believe firmly that they, as a clan, would be just fine without the Camarilla. They have the power and the ability to protect themselves. The other clans are not so blessed. They cannot cope with the kine as the Ventrue do, and they would bring down upon Kindred a new, even more deadly, Inquisition.

THE GANGREL

The loss of Clan Gangrel hit the Ventrue hard — much harder than they have let on to the rest of the world. It is obviously a grave blow to the sect and the clan that leads it. Opinions vary about what to do about the exodus. Some say that the Camarilla should disavow the whole bloodline, curse the Gangrel as they do the Giovanni or any other rogue bloodline. Others want reconciliation. They want to draw at least some of the Gangrel back to the sect and recognize a Camarilla Gangrel body that might not include every (or even most of) the animalistic Kindred, but that at least gives them reputation and restores their name to the sect's roster.

PRETENDERS TO THE THRONE

The Ventrue recognize among themselves two rivals for leadership within the Camarilla: the Toreador and the Tremere. The clan works hard night after night to make sure that neither of these two powerful rivals can usurp its position and authority. First and foremost, it tries as best it can to have close relations with both clans, under the old adage "keep your friends close and your enemies closer."

This tactic might not apply to the Lasombra, but it certainly applies to the artists and the magicians.

The Toreador present the larger threat, chiefly because their areas of influence and contacts with the mortal world come closest to threatening the Ventrue's own. Furthermore, the clan ostensibly has a better relationship with most of the other clans than the Tremere, putting them in a stronger position to rally support (although many Kindred view this situation as one of relative lesser evils). Fortunately, the same is true for the Ventrue as well, who also have a solid working relationship with the Toreador. The two clans see eye-to-eye on many issues of Camarilla policy, and they work together well enough. For now, the two clans observe an uneasy state of nonaggression, and the Ventrue have no systematic agenda for weakening the Toreador. Instead, they play these de facto allies against their mutual rival, the Tremere.

The Ventrue have never had much personal regard for the Tremere, but they do respect the power the clan wields. The Warlocks have so many unknown abilities that many Ventrue — very practical-minded Kindred — become nervous when they have to deal with them. The Tremere make plays for more influence within the Camarilla periodically, but the Ventrue usually beat them back with the most reliable weapon they have: respect. The other clans all fear the unknown, and the Tremere represent a big unknown. They have a reputation as the least trustworthy clan, a fact the Ventrue make sure that everyone else remembers. The Ventrue think they can hold the blood-witches at bay until the Tremere overcome the stigma of their secretive and bizarre reputation.

CLAN RELATIONS

The following Ventrue stereotypes are just that: stereotypes. No Ventrue feels this way about every single Kindred in a given clan. Likewise, not every Ventrue shares the general clan impression. Still, they do shed some light on general Ventrue attitudes toward their fellow Kindred and the rest of the world.

BRUJAH

They are a conundrum: infuriatingly brash when young, infuriatingly clever when old. It's hard to say which is worse. Their strength and commitment are valuable, but their ages-old resentments and furious nature make them unpredictable allies at best. Treat them with respect, but hold them at arms' length, as you would any dangerous animal.

MALKAVIANS

Insane without a doubt, our mentally unstable cousins still provide valuable support to the Camarilla. We have worked with them well in the past, but not when precision is necessary. One must always keep a sense of irony about them as well as one's patience. Ultimately, though, they are second-tier at best, not a real threat or a true asset. Ignoring them completely is often (but not always) the best course.

NOSFERATU

They know what we do, that information is king. Their ability to gather it is amazing, although their obsession with it is somewhat pitiable. Still, they work well for the sect, and they do not necessarily seek our demise. They make fine allies when you can find them, but they're seldom there when you need them (at least not there to be seen). Every prince should have one in his pocket, but one should never be beholden to them.

TOREADOR

Our closest allies and rivals. Fortunately for us, they have their heads in the clouds rather than on the business at hand. Their wasteful obsession with beauty distracts them from more important matters. They are not fools, though, and they can bear down on the problem with appropriate ferocity when a crisis comes. The key to handling them is directing them toward the right goals, which is to say, our goals.

TREMERE

Dangerous, secretive and without dignity. The Tremere's magic sets them apart from the rest of us, but their total devotion to "mystic arts" makes them pariahs and outcasts within the Camarilla. Just as well. If there were any clan in the sect we could do without, it is them, but it is far better to have them on our side than allied with the Sabbat or working on their own. Not as powerful as they think they are, they still merit a close watching at all times.

THE SABBAT

Fools, monsters and traitors to our kind. We have no pity for the Sabbat. The world has no place for them, and they must ultimately be destroyed to the last vampire. Their injudicious, brutal and grotesque ways are a mockery of Caine's legacy and a threat to us all. Were it not for the bitter jealousy of the Lasombra, they would have long ago torn themselves to pieces. We shall do it for them eventually.

LASOMBRA

They have been second to us since the First City, dogging our heels and hoping to pick up our scraps. The play at power, but they understand nothing of its true workings. They hide in shadows and watch humanity from afar, unwilling and afraid to take the bull by the horns. Their influence shrinks with each passing night as their own elders fall to uneducated brutes who know nothing of even the small honor and ability the clan once held. They are a disgrace to behold and worthy of nothing but scorn, derision and most importantly, fire.

TZIMISCE

Incomprehensible monsters one and all, but dangerous nonetheless. That is, dangerous when one meets them alone in a dark alley surrounded by their abominable comrades. Otherwise, they are harmless for the most part. They lose any sense of vision, of purpose, in their uncouth and juvenile fascination with the flesh.

THE INDEPENDENTS

One good thing we can say about the Independents is that at least they have the good sense not to join the Sabbat. Would we welcome any of them into the Camarilla's ranks? With a cautious smile. They are degenerate, base and ill-founded clans, but they deserve a seat at our table. Still, we extend them certain considerations and protections as long as they abide by our rules. While in our cities, they can carry out their pointless existences if they refrain from bothering the rest of us who have more important matters at hand.

ASSAMITES

A curious breed, the Assamites. Gifted with a fervent bent and potent abilities, they waste their unlives with bloody diablerie. We defanged them long ago with Tremere help, but now they seem determined to repay the debt; they slipped that noose and broke our agreement. As such, we can no longer abide them. Until we find a way to chain them once again, trust them only in the direst of circumstances.

FOLLOWERS OF SET

Snake charmers, prone to spreading debasement and dependency. We have no patience for them and their bizarre ways. They taint what they touch, or so they would have us believe. In truth, they seem little more than egomaniacs trying to relive the serpent's halcyon nights from the Book of Genesis. Were they to find a less deluded purpose, they might pose a more present threat. If their presence offends thee (as it should), pluck them out with all the force you can spare.

GIOVANNI

They claim to be rivals to our power and position. Indeed, perhaps they could be if they would leave their crypts and concentrate on the here and now rather than the dead past. This fixation on ghosts and ancestor-spirits is really quite unbecoming. It would be funny if it weren't so grotesque. Still, like any guest, one must watch them when they show their faces in your home. Never let them get a foothold in your territory, and never give them quarter.

RAVNOS

They claim to have honor, but so do all thieves. Their mongrel heritage, their penchant for tricks and their vagabond attitude all make them less than desirable company. Indeed, one need not tolerate their presence at all. Drive them on to the next city — it's better than the filthy bastards deserve. Temper your mistrust of them with pity, however, for they have lost their last chance.

DISCIPLINES

The Kindred's supernatural abilities set them far beyond the mortal herds. It is these powers — coupled with their deathlessness — that give Kindred, and particularly the Ventrue, the right to do as they please and seize what they will in this world. In conversation, the Ventrue seldom refer to their Disciplines by name or even acknowledge their existence openly. Most Ventrue consider Disciplines vulgar and inelegant crutches used by flawed Kindred to enact their will when their own capabilities fail. Even when using very specific powers, they use euphemisms that downplay their reliance on the supernatural gifts of Caine's curse, such as, "I made him see things my way," or, "He realized where his priorities were, and he came to see me." Some Ventrue even prefer to think that all this power is an inherent part of their superior nature rather than some mental trick or "mystic curse."

This section presents a few optional systems, again for use at the Storyteller's discretion.

FORTITUDE

Members of the clan often handwave the physical prowess they possess, but they relish its uses. More than a few anarch uprisings have ended the moment some punk Lick went berserk, only to realize that his Ventrue foe hadn't suffered even a scratch. The uses of the clan's unnatural resilience are obvious, and they need little discussion except to point out one tactic. In such base displays as combat, many Ventrue pretend to suffer more damage and pain than they actually do. Doing so keeps their enemies off guard and keeps the true limits of the Discipline a secret. As another Ventrue saying goes, "Never let them take your true measure."

DOMINATE

The Ventrue ability to Dominate others is a mixed blessing that's useful when all else fails, but easy for lazy and boorish Ventrue to come to rely on. Without a doubt, it is one of the most useful talents a Kindred can possess. Many sires encourage their progeny to attain mastery in this art, with a stern warning against its casual use and abuse. This vital skill comes in handy time and again when dealing with mortals and even other Kindred. As a tool for preserving the

Masquerade, it is penultimate, second only to not breaching the Masquerade in the first place. Ventrue become particularly adept at weaving their mental suggestion into normal speech patterns. A talented Ventrue can integrate commands so subtly over the course of a long, normal conversation, that the subject has no idea what is happening. The Ventrue might ask the same question several times before phrasing the inquiry with a mesmeric command attached to it. The target thinks he has simply slipped up or been fooled into revealing something he didn't mean to, but he has no idea that coercion of any kind took place.

Presence

The mystical force of personality most Ventrue acquire is a more subtle power than Dominate, even in its rawest form. Mortals who fall under its sway seldom think anything supernatural is going on at all, nor do they have any evidence to suggest that anything particularly untoward has happened. The one problem with Presence abilities is that they too often become overwhelming. Sometimes a Ventrue does not wish to scare a mortal into abject terror or cause someone to develop a love-like attachment to her. In these cases, the Ventrue have learned to use more subtle applications of their power.

System: At the Storyteller's discretion, the player may spend a Willpower point after making a too-successful Presence roll (one that would yield an effect that exceeds the player's desired effect) and negate the extra successes, leaving her exactly enough to generate her intended result. The player may do so only once per scene. Presence is simply doing what it had been developed to do by Caine himself.

Curse the Laurel (Fortitude Level Seven)

This fearsome power allows the Kindred to overcome one of the traditional banes of the undead: the feared stake. With this mastery of Fortitude, the Ventrue may subsume a stake that pierces her heart, reshaping that dead organ slowly and insulating it from the offending wood. Once a given stake has been turned away with this power, it remains within the Kindred's body, and it may even be visible beneath layers of clothing.

System: The player spends a permanent Willpower point and rolls Stamina + Survival (difficulty 9). The number of successes indicates the length of time that elapses before the Kindred's body rejects the stake, allowing her to rise from immobilization.

Each use of this power affects only one stake. If the Kindred suffers the same fate again, she may make a new attempt if the player chooses to spend the Willpower again. If the roll to use the power is a botch, the body does not expel the stake, and no further attempt may be made against that particular stake.

One success	One year
Two successes	Six months
Three successes	One month
Four successes	One week
Five successes	One night

After the stake has been turned away from the heart, it remains in the Kindred's body, overgrown by dead flesh and probably protruding at an unsettling angle. The Kindred may cut the stake out at any time she wishes thereafter, suffering two health levels of aggravated damage in the process.

MET System: To use this power, the Kindred must spend one permanent Willpower Trait and succeed in a Static Physical Challenge (nine Trait difficulty). If successful, he spends one to five temporary Physical Traits with the following results:

One Trait	One year
Two Traits	Six months
Three Traits	One month
Four Traits	One week
Five Traits	One night

The power works in the same fashion as the Storyteller version in all other particulars.

NEW MERIT

The following Trait, like all Merits and Flaws, is optional for use in a Storyteller's chronicle. For more details on Merits and Flaws, see **Vampire: The Masquerade**, p.295-296.

PARAGON (6-PT. SOCIAL MERIT)

The Embrace has awakened within you an aspect of personality that others find particularly compelling. You may select one Background from the following group: Allies, Black Hand Membership, Clan Prestige, Contacts, Fame, Herd, Influence, Mentor, Resources, Retainers, Sabbat Status or Status. Your maximum Trait score in that Background may exceed your normal generation limit by one. For example, a 10th-generation Kindred may take this Merit and enjoy the benefits of a Contacts Background of 6. You may take this Merit for only one Background, which may drop (and thereafter possibly rise again) at the Storyteller's discretion. Players should choose this Merit only for a Background that makes sense — a Camarilla archon is unlikely to have a Black Hand Membership Background of 7, for example.

MET System: This Merit allows the player to choose one Background Trait (*Allies, Black Hand Membership, Clan Prestige, Contacts, Fame, Herd,* Influence — any one area — *Mentor, Resources, Retainers*) for his character to excel in. The player can purchase one Background Trait beyond the maximum normally allowed by Generation. For example, a player who plays a ninth-generation Ventrue may select *Resources*, allowing him to purchase six *Resources* Background Traits for his character. As stated previously, the Background should make sense.

DENIAL OF APHRODITE'S FAVOR (DOMINATE ●●●, FORTITUDE ●●●)

Developed centuries ago, this power protects the Ventrue from the skills at which they and the Toreador excel. While the powers of Presence may be more subtle than those of Dominate, they are no less effective. Denial of Aphrodite's Favor allows the Ventrue to protect himself from emotional manipulation with the same efficacy that his generation affords him against Dominate.

System: Once learned, this power negates the effects of Presence Levels One through Three used by any Kindred of higher generation than the Kindred. Thus, a ninth-generation Ventrue would be unaffected by a 12th-generation Kindred attempting to use Dread Gaze upon her.

It costs 20 experience points to learn this power.

MET System: This power allows the Kindred to ignore the use of *Awe, Dread Gaze* or *Entrancement* by any vampire of higher generation than the Kindred.

Denial of Aphrodite's Favor costs 10 Experience Traits.

LIFESONG (DOMINATE ●, PRESENCE ●)

This power allows the Ventrue to assess any single statement made by the subject and look for the essence of that subject's being beneath the words she speaks. The Ventrue needs to speak no words himself; he simply interprets the statement offered to him.

System: The player makes an Intelligence + Empathy roll (difficulty equal to the subject's Manipulation + Expression). With even a single success, the Ventrue determines the subject's Demeanor from the statement, finding profound meaning in the most common of utterances. This power works only upon living creatures — Kindred lack the spark of life that colors the words they speak.

It costs four experience points to learn this power.

MET System: This power requires a Mental Challenge (retest with *Empathy*) to discern the target's Demeanor. As stated previously, the power does not work on Kindred.

Lifesong costs two Experience Traits.

CHAPTER THREE: OF AUGUST BLOOD

He takes great pride in doing things like… ordering a $40 million Gulfstream V jet by e-mail, or buying a twenty-four-thousand-square-foot mansion and leaving it nearly empty of furniture. His motto, his philosophy, his raison d'être, can be summed up in three little words: Because I can.
— Mike Sager, "Yeaahhh, Baaaaabyy"

To many Kindred, the Ventrue clan has the distinction of being The Man, the power that is, the omnipresence of paranoid or overbearing princes and the stodgy voice of pragmatism that prevents the other childer of Caine from enjoying the few moments of undeath not punctuated by loneliness and hunger.

But consider unlife from the perspective of the Ventrue themselves. Many Blue Bloods spend their unlives held to traditions and a noble obligation that they never asked for. Childer suffer their elders' demands of service, fealty and duty, warned that chivalry and legacy binds them. Those same elders plot and scheme against each other and anyone else who crosses their paths, stabbing others in the back for resources, power, contacts — anything that could conceivably give them an edge over the *next* rival. Being Embraced by a Ventrue is not unlike being drawn into an abusive family; having to subsist on blood and never see the sun only adds insult to the injury.

The truth of all clans extends to the Ventrue: Any automatic assumption one has for them based on their lineage sells them short. Over the years, the clan has certainly harbored its share of egomaniacal rogues and arrogant *aristos*. It has also numbered racketeers, murderers, saints and champions. The ranks of financiers and politicos hide individual artists, thieves and soldiers. Many would-be usurpers realize too late that the Ventrue is not the man who stands before him but the woman who stands, smiling, behind him, providing him with the power he needs to fulfill his desires.

The following, then, is a small cross-section of the cosmopolitan ranks of Clan Ventrue. Take them at face value, if you wish — but only at your own risk.

GAMBLER

Quote: *You know what? I don't think you've got it. You didn't draw that seven did you? All you're holding is a busted straight. Go ahead. Fold. There's a good boy.*

Prelude: To hear people tell it, the gambling industry takes in more money than print, radio, television and movies combined. That's a lot of money. You wanted your share. Hell, you wanted more than your share.

Before your Embrace you'd never gambled in your life. Gambling was for suckers. The house had everything stacked in its favor. Gambling was no way to get rich, and rich is just what you wanted to be in your previous life. So you took the traditional route: business school, MBA, full-service stockbroker. *Yawn.* You hated every minute of it. People talk about the excitement of the market, the ups and downs, but to you it was just numbers on a screen. You like to see cash in hand and deal with people face to face. You're a born salesman, but the fact is, the real money — the drop-dead, I'm-a-fucking-millionaire money — is all part of a larger picture. You can't get it selling cars or houses or even airplanes. (You know; you tried all three.)

Then came your Embrace and initiation into Clan Ventrue and your training. Wow. *Wow.* More than you could have ever imagined. You could control people's thoughts! You could change their memories! You could even make them like you! Money… hell, money would just come to you. Or so you thought. Except the other Ventrue in the city had all the lucrative domains locked up. You had no avenues open and nowhere to go. Nowhere except the casino, as it turned out.

Thus went your introduction into the world of underground gambling, and you've been delving deeper and deeper ever since. Back-room card games, casino games, alley games — you know how to buy the odds on all of them. Now you run your own business that takes and covers bets on everything, including (and especially) the local racetrack and sports teams. With a visit to the jockey, the star player or the coach, you

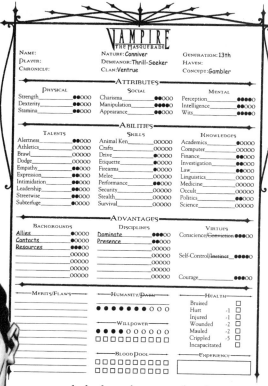

can not only find out the game plan, but you can make them change it. The fix is in, and you put it there.

Concept: You're a gambler but not a risk-taker. You never bet unless you know the outcome. Although you present yourself to the world as an unpredictable thrill-seeker, you're actually as cold and calculating as they come. It's all about setting the odds in your favor, whether it's a card game or high Kindred politics.

Roleplaying Hints: You look to succeed in the most unlikely ways — there's always an angle that no one else has figured yet. Never show concern, never let them see how hard you have to work to make things go your way. As far as the rest of the world can tell, everything comes naturally to you, and you act like you expect just that.

Equipment: Deck of cards, a wad of bills that could choke a horse, slick clothes and an attitude to match

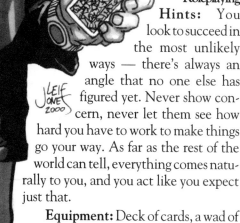

VAMPIRE
THE MASQUERADE

NAME:
PLAYER:
CHRONICLE:

NATURE: Conniver
DEMEANOR: Thrill-Seeker
CLAN: Ventrue

GENERATION: 13th
HAVEN:
CONCEPT: Gambler

ATTRIBUTES

Physical		Social		Mental	
Strength	●●○○○	Charisma	●●○○○	Perception	●●●●○
Dexterity	●●○○○	Manipulation	●●●●○	Intelligence	●●○○○
Stamina	●●○○○	Appearance	●●○○○	Wits	●●●●○

ABILITIES

Talents		Skills		Knowledges	
Alertness	●●○○○	Animal Ken	○○○○○	Academics	●○○○○
Athletics	○○○○○	Crafts	○○○○○	Computer	○○○○○
Brawl	○○○○○	Drive	●○○○○	Finance	●●○○○
Dodge	○○○○○	Etiquette	●●○○○	Investigation	●●○○○
Empathy	●●○○○	Firearms	●○○○○	Law	●●○○○
Expression	●●○○○	Melee	○○○○○	Linguistics	○○○○○
Intimidation	●●○○○	Performance	●●○○○	Medicine	○○○○○
Leadership	●●○○○	Security	○○○○○	Occult	○○○○○
Streetwise	●●○○○	Stealth	○○○○○	Politics	●●○○○
Subterfuge	●○○○○	Survival	○○○○○	Science	○○○○○

ADVANTAGES

Backgrounds		Disciplines		Virtues	
Allies	●○○○○	Dominate	●●●○○	Conscience/~~Conviction~~	●●○○○
Contacts	●○○○○	Presence	●●○○○		
Resources	●●○○○		○○○○○		
	○○○○○		○○○○○	Self-Control/~~Instinct~~	●●●●○
	○○○○○		○○○○○		
	○○○○○		○○○○○	Courage	●●●○○

Merits/Flaws	Humanity/~~Path~~	Health	
	●●●●●●●○○○	Bruised	□
		Hurt -1	□
		Injured -1	□
	Willpower	Wounded -2	□
	●●●●●○○○○○	Mauled -2	□
	□□□□□□□□□□	Crippled -5	□
		Incapacitated	□
	Blood Pool	Experience	
	□□□□□□□□□□		
	□□□□□□□□□□		

LEIF JONES 2000

PREACHER

Quote: *God has shown me the sin in your hearts! Hear His words as I speak them to you and rejoice, for I shall show you the road to Heaven!*

Prelude: As the third son of a very religious, conservative, middle-class family, you grew up in churches. Of course, you went the opposite way: leftist, atheist and argumentative.

Then it was time for life in the real world. You started working for a weird one — a mysterious, eccentric businessman you never saw in person for the first year. His was interesting work, analyzing business plans and corporate takeovers, liaising with lawyers and representatives from other companies. Strangest of all, the businessman had numerous ties to various church groups, and he donated money to every denomination in the city.

When the night came that your employer finally revealed his Ventrue nature, you were naturally more frightened than intrigued. By the following sunset, you were immortal, and your soul was (theoretically) damned forever.

For the first time in your life… er, unlife, you're doing something that would make your father proud: You're a preacher. In fact, thanks to your Kindred abilities, you're one of the best, most

highly attended preachers in the city. Thousands flock to hear you tell them the word of God… and who to vote for and what to think. As your flock grows, your inner circle of adherents grows as well. Men and women are willing to lay down their lives for you and follow you against Satan's armies. Even politicians are coming to you, asking you to help get out the vote for their cause. And you thought Sunday school was pointless and boring.

Concept: Your influence within the local religious community has raised more than a few eyebrows. As a high-profile, public figure, you're attracting more attention than most of your elders consider wise. Once your Kindred powers become great enough, you can disappear safely behind the scenes. But for now, they require your personal attention and touch.

Roleplaying Hints: You started your religious career as a firebrand and rousing speaker, and you can still preach a killer sermon when you need to. Now, though, you've toned it down a bit, becoming the respectable zealot. You speak softly, with a voice calm and treacle, deceptive words. Think Jerry Falwell and Mr. Rogers rolled into one devilish persona.

Equipment: Cross, Bible, cell phone and electronic organizer with the number of every Republican leader in the city

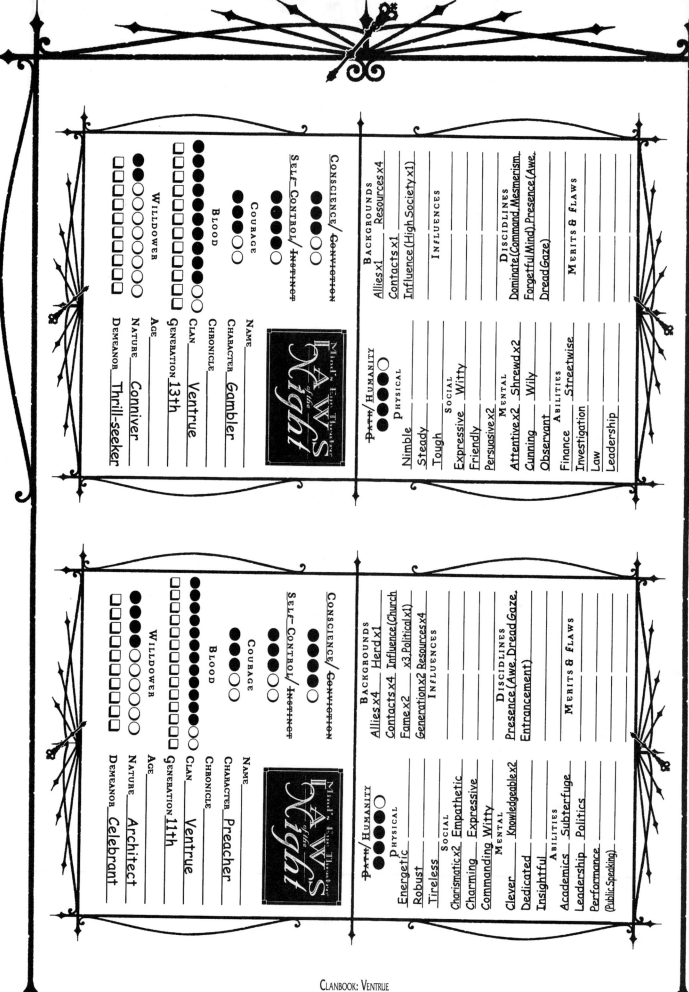

Generalissimo

Quote: *All right, gentlemen, this is the plan. You follow this plan to the letter, and we won't have any problems. You deviate from this plan, and your biggest problem isn't those Camarilla pussies, it's the guy standing in front of you right now. Do I make myself clear?*

Prelude: You wanted to make the military your life, and indeed that's just what you did. You enlisted at age 17, fought in Vietnam, then transferred to Europe where you served for most of the rest of the Cold War. Then, it was on to Washington, the Pentagon, the rank of lieutenant and… that was it. After 22 years of service, they forced you into a pension at age 40. Now what? Disgruntled and unable to find work in civilian life that could keep you happy, you'd just about come to the end of your rope. You'd even started looking at mercenary companies in the back of those God-awful magazines.

Then things changed. A beautiful woman showed up at your door one night and, you, to your surprise, just let her in. The two of you talked until just an hour before dawn. Just talked. And you revealed everything there was to know about yourself. Not only couldn't you help it, you didn't want to. You were glad to finally get it all off your chest.

These nights, three years later, you know the truth. She sought you out because of your background, because you knew how to lead but had no one to command. She was looking for a commander, a leader in a time of crisis and her search brought her to you. She could make you into everything she needed. She told you all this, flat out. She was going to train you to lead again in a new kind of war. A secret war fought in the night and over centuries.

Now, it's like you've started all over again. Your Embrace made you a newbie, a trainee. And you certainly didn't know a damn thing about being a vampire. Now you do, though. You're part of a clan that's dedicated to taking back the ground it lost long ago. You've got a noble heritage and fine traditions, just like you had in the army.

Concept: You loved the army, every God-damned minute of it. You

loved the authority, the discipline and the ability to give an order and expect it to be carried out. Now the enemy is Camarilla "Kindred" and the slumbering blood-gods, instead of the Viet Cong or Saddam Hussein. You've moved up quickly in just three years, and you already hold the honorific of True Sabbat. You're a ductus, and maybe you'll be a priscus one night. You've got your sights set on the very top, and if it takes 500 years to get there, so be it. Until the elders rise, you've got all the time in the world.

Roleplaying Hints: You are a leader. You expect those below you to follow your orders without question or delay. You are also a follower. When a leader gives you a task, your whole being focuses on getting it done. You are, in essence, the perfect soldier. The only thing is, leading is a whole lot better than following….

Equipment: Colt M1911A1, black hummer, flak vest (just in case)

VAMPIRE THE MASQUERADE

NAME:
PLAYER:
CHRONICLE:

NATURE: Autocrat
DEMEANOR: Fanatic
CLAN: Ventrue

GENERATION: 10th
HAVEN:
CONCEPT: Generalissimo

ATTRIBUTES

Physical		Social		Mental	
Strength	●●●○○	Charisma	●●●●○	Perception	●●○○○
Dexterity	●●●○○	Manipulation	●●○○○	Intelligence	●●○○○
Stamina	●●●●○	Appearance	●●●○○	Wits	●●●○○

ABILITIES

Talents		Skills		Knowledges	
Alertness	●○○○○	Animal Ken	○○○○○	Academics	●●○○○
Athletics	●○○○○	Crafts	●○○○○	Computer	●○○○○
Brawl	●●○○○	Drive	●○○○○	Finance	○○○○○
Dodge	●●●○○	Etiquette	○○○○○	Investigation	○○○○○
Empathy	○○○○○	Firearms	●●○○○	Law	○○○○○
Expression	●○○○○	Melee	●●●○○	Linguistics	○○○○○
Intimidation	●●●○○	Performance	○○○○○	Medicine	○○○○○
Leadership	●●●○○	Security	○○○○○	Occult	●○○○○
Streetwise	○○○○○	Stealth	●○○○○	Politics	●○○○○
Subterfuge	○○○○○	Survival	●●○○○	Science	●○○○○

ADVANTAGES

Backgrounds		Disciplines		Virtues	
Generation	●●○○○	Dominate	●○○○○	Conscience/Conviction	●●○○○
Mentor	●○○○○	Fortitude	●○○○○		
Sabbat Status	●●○○○	Presence	●●○○○		
	○○○○○		○○○○○	Self-Control/Instinct	●○○○○
	○○○○○		○○○○○		
	○○○○○		○○○○○	Courage	●●●○○

MERITS/FLAWS

HUMANITY/PATH
Power and the Inner Voice
●●●○○○○○○○

WILLPOWER
●●●●●○○○○○
□□□□□□□□□□

BLOOD POOL
□□□□□□□□□□
□□□□□□□□□□

HEALTH
Bruised □
Hurt −1 □
Injured −1 □
Wounded −2 □
Mauled −2 □
Crippled −5 □
Incapacitated □

EXPERIENCE

Silicon Success Story

Quote: *You see the microprocessors…? All right, let me try to explain it this way. Imagine this box is a magic machine — no, it's not really magic — full of millions of tiny investment bankers doing your taxes for you…. Ok fine, it's magic.*

Prelude: The magazines all say that nowhere in the history of the world has more money been made faster than in Silicon Valley during the late 1990s. Well, it may or may not be true so far as the world is concerned, but it was sure as hell true for you. At 27 years old, your net worth was just shy of $33 million. Not bad for a guy who never finished college. You thought that you were made for life. You had conquered the world and mastered your chosen field, so now it was time to enjoy it.

You'd cashed in your Yahoo! shares, paid the IRS its cut and still had more millions than you were likely to spend. Not that you didn't try — you bankrolled an entertainment portal company almost solely out-of-pocket. Then, one of the biggest venture-capital guys on Sand Hill Road asked if he could meet you for dinner one night. Sure, you said, why not?

Well, it turns out that you weren't the only guest. There was another guy, a young-looking suit from back east. Very corporate; very prim and proper. The suit started asking questions about what you thought the next big thing was going to be, what you knew about cryptography, vulnerabilities within the company you'd just helped start and a ton of other questions you normally would never have answered. Without really thinking about it, you told this guy everything he wanted to know.

The same thing happened the next night and the next and the night after that. One night, you never returned home at all.

Now you're Kindred, just like the man in the suit who sired you. You work for him, and you're working harder than ever, only instead of writing code you're handling computer problems for a group of 500+-year-old vampires who don't even know what a computer looks like. With these guys, $33 million is chump change, and you're at the bottom of the pile again.

Concept: The Ventrue have opened your eyes to possibilities beyond mere money. They have real power, the power to make people do things, to make people respect them, to buy the world if they want. Now that power can be yours as well, if only you have the balls to take it. You've been told that accumulating *dignitas* takes decades, even centuries. But

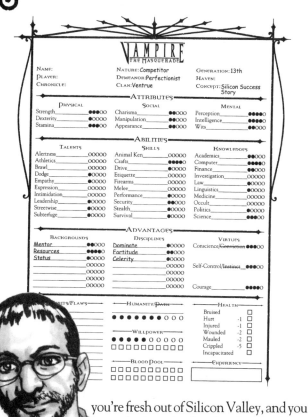

you're fresh out of Silicon Valley, and you don't wait decades for anything, especially some centuries-outdated business model. You've already learned more about the Ventrue through their computers than they want you to. Now all you need to do is figure out how to use that information to your advantage.

Roleplaying Hints: You're not the most socially adept creature, mostly because you don't care. You see the world and the people in it as problems to be solved and code to be written. You have little patience, especially for ignorance and incompetence.

Equipment: Kick-ass computer on a T3 line, PCS phone, beeper, Palm Pilot, electronic organizer and any other gizmo that'll save you 15 seconds in a night

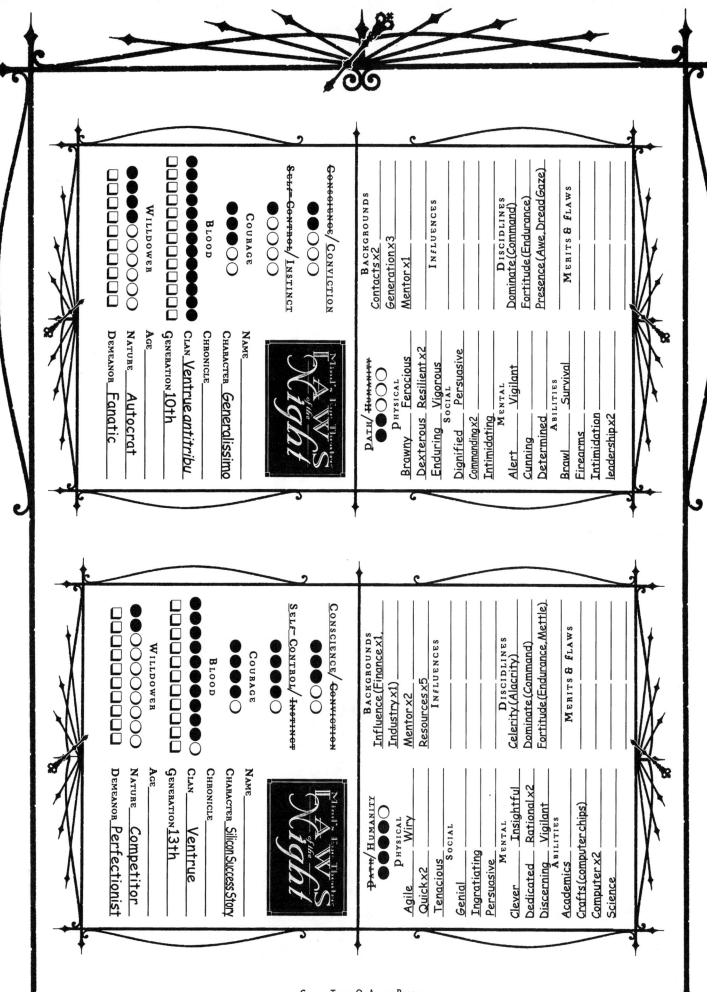

Mind's Eye Theatre — LAWS of the Night

NAME ___

CHARACTER __Generalissimo__

CHRONICLE ___

CLAN __Ventrue antitribu__

GENERATION __10th__

AGE ___

NATURE __Autocrat__

DEMEANOR __Fanatic__

PATH/HUMANITY

PHYSICAL: Brawny, Ferocious, Dexterous, Resilient x2, Enduring, Vigorous

SOCIAL: Dignified, Persuasive, Commanding x2, Intimidating

MENTAL: Alert, Vigilant, Cunning, Determined

ABILITIES: Brawl, Survival, Firearms, Intimidation, leadership x2

BACKGROUNDS: Contacts x2, Generation x3, Mentor x1

INFLUENCES

DISCIPLINES: Dominate (Command), Fortitude (Endurance), Presence (Awe, DreadGaze)

MERITS & FLAWS

CONSCIENCE/CONVICTION

SELF-CONTROL/INSTINCT

COURAGE

BLOOD

WILLPOWER

Mind's Eye Theatre — LAWS of the Night

NAME ___

CHARACTER __Silicon Success Story__

CHRONICLE ___

CLAN __Ventrue__

GENERATION __13th__

AGE ___

NATURE __Competitor__

DEMEANOR __Perfectionist__

PATH/HUMANITY

PHYSICAL: Agile, Wiry, Quick x2, Tenacious

SOCIAL: Genial, Ingratiating, Persuasive

MENTAL: Clever, Insightful, Dedicated, Rational x2, Discerning, Vigilant

ABILITIES: Academics, Crafts (computer chips), Computer x2, Science

BACKGROUNDS: Influence (Finance x1, Industry x1), Mentor x2, Resources x5

INFLUENCES

DISCIPLINES: Celerity (Alacrity), Dominate (Command), Fortitude (Endurance, Mettle)

MERITS & FLAWS

CONSCIENCE/CONVICTION

SELF-CONTROL/INSTINCT

COURAGE

BLOOD

WILLPOWER

Eyes of the Ephors

Quote: *May I get you anything else, sir? No? I'll leave this tray here in case you want some more. I'll be right outside the door if you need me.*

Prelude: Your unlife began three decades ago, but it has been slow going for you ever since. You grew up the last scion of a fading noble family. Your name had all the right syllables and titles but none of the money to back them up. By the time you'd graduated from school and were casting about for universities, father had gone from being a drunk to a member of some strange religious sect. The bank took the house, and you were left as alone as you'd always been.

Except for Uncle Karl. A long-time friend of your father's, the years had been kind to him. You received an invitation to come hunting at his rural estate as a graduation gift from an old family supporter. "Uncle Karl" is, in fact, a powerful Ventrue and a leader in the clan's complex hierarchy. His sprawling estate covers several thousand acres and hosts regular Ventrue gatherings.

Karl himself did not sire you. "Karl" is not even his true name, although you could not say what his real name might be. He hosts a number of Ventrue of all generations at his sanctum, sometimes a dozen at once, maybe more. He asked one of his younger guests to sire you. It seems that Karl does not trust anyone but Kindred to serve him, but he does not think it wise to bestow his powerful blood indiscriminately upon neonates destined for nothing but service.

Despite your initial resentment, you served your hosts well, and some of them even came to trust you in time. When you managed, through sheer happenstance, to overhear a private conversation between two guests that interested your master greatly, you passed on the information and earned the best reward possible: your freedom. Karl began training you for service in the outside world of Kindred politics.

Concept: You want to do the best you can to escape from under your master's thumb. That means acquiring *dignitas* on your own merits through the normal means. If you play your cards right, you can use your elder connections to further your personal career.

The only danger comes if your elders discover how you're using them. Will they reward your initiative or punish you for your insolence?

Roleplaying Hints: You are out on your own now, with substantial financial and political backing from Karl and his estate. This existence is not true freedom, however. In fact, it's utter dependency. Although none of the local Ventrue know it, your only real purpose in unlife is to report information to Karl (and the *ephors*, by extension). Although you are proud of your heritage, you have no use or feelings for the Ventrue with whom you share the city. Every bit of gossip and every iota of scandalous information that you relay proves your worthiness and helps you rise within the Ventrue ranks.

Equipment: Leased Bentley, extensive designer wardrobe, secure PCS phone, miniature cassette recorder, stake, personal organizer

DOMAIN-RAIDER

Quote: *Now, officially, the janitorial staff doesn't work for the police department. The janitors work for the city. Technically speaking, they're not part of your domain.*

Prelude: You have no intention of waiting, not one more moment than you have to. You came into Clan Ventrue like many neonates: a promising businesswoman snatched up by elders who needed someone who could understand and exploit the new market opportunities. You were never meant to be much more than a flunky, an eternal second-stringer to add to your sire's coffers. They cursed you with immortality and expected you to pay off the debt. Once you've done that (i.e., once you're not the expert on the next hot new market thing), it's either sink or swim on your own.

Except you're ready to swim *right now*. Swimming means building your own fortune, your own network of contacts and eventually your own brood of aides to make your calls and take your meetings. It's certainly a dream worth striving for, one your elders even encourage you to have. They just expect you to take a few decades to achieve it. Not gonna happen that way.

Why the big wait? The clan elders have everything all tied up and claimed as part of their respective domains. Hands off, no trespassing, this means you, fuck off. Fine. You just had to work a little harder here and there. Nobody ever made any rules against watching what would slip through those elders' talons and taking what they can't keep nailed down.

As you should have realized from start, the only reason young Kindred had any influence at all was because it's impossible—even for an elder Ventrue—to have his thumb in every pie in all but the smallest cities. In the end, though, most of the "scraps" are more trouble than they're worth. Shaking down the Chili's and the Blockbuster in the suburbs is small potatoes. If you're going to make it big, you'll have to do it by taking from those who've actually got something worth taking. The problem is, you can't go head-to-head with an elder yet. First of all, he'd probably smash you like a bug. Second, it's against the dignities or something, and the last

thing you want to do is to cause a public ruckus, because it's the quickest way to make sure that the elders notice you.

Concept: You've devoted your time to finding unique, technically legal methods for stealing from other Kindred. You do nothing to interfere with, steal or otherwise sway an elder's contacts. Of course, this tactic makes for dangerous enemies, but maybe a couple of new associates in high places as well. Next point on the agenda: Find a new target and pluck it for your growing collection.

Roleplaying Hints: You like to act quickly, decisively and ultimately with certainty. You don't rush in, but you don't hesitate when the time comes. Always act with respect toward your elders — even when your hand's in their pocket. The key to your success is acting like everything you do is perfectly legal and acceptable, even when it's not.

Equipment: Leather appointment book, rolodex of city employees and union bosses, late-model Audi for business meetings, ragged Ford pickup for meeting less sophisticated types

---

Character Sheet

VAMPIRE
THE MASQUERADE

Name: Nature: Rogue   Generation: 12th
Player: Demeanor: Pedagogue   Haven:
Chronicle: Clan: Ventrue   Concept: Domain Raider

ATTRIBUTES

Physical
Strength ●●○○○
Dexterity ●●●○○
Stamina ●●●○○

Social
Charisma ●●●○○
Manipulation ●●●●●
Appearance ●●●●○

Mental
Perception ●●●○○
Intelligence ●●●○○
Wits ●●●●○

ABILITIES

Talents
Alertness ●●●○○
Athletics ○○○○○
Brawl ○○○○○
Dodge ○○○○○
Empathy ●○○○○
Expression ○○○○○
Intimidation ○○○○○
Leadership ○○○○○
Streetwise ○○○○○
Subterfuge ●●○○○

Skills
Animal Ken ○○○○○
Crafts ○○○○○
Drive ●○○○○
Etiquette ●●●○○
Firearms ○○○○○
Melee ●○○○○
Performance ○○○○○
Security ●●○○○
Stealth ●●○○○
Survival ○○○○○

Knowledges
Academics ●○○○○
Computer ○○○○○
Finance ●●●○○
Investigation ●○○○○
Law ●●●○○
Linguistics ●○○○○
Medicine ○○○○○
Occult ○○○○○
Politics ●●○○○
Science ○○○○○

ADVANTAGES

Backgrounds
Allies ●●○○○
Contacts ●●○○○
Generation ●○○○○
Influence ●●○○○
Resources ●●○○○
_____ ○○○○○
_____ ○○○○○

Disciplines
Presence ●●●○○
_____ ○○○○○
_____ ○○○○○
_____ ○○○○○
_____ ○○○○○

Virtues
Conscience/~~Conviction~~ ●●○○○
Self-Control/~~Instinct~~ ●●●●●
Courage ●●●●○

Merits/Flaws

Humanity/Path ●●●●●●○○○○

Willpower ●●●●●○○○○○ / □□□□□□□□□□

Blood Pool □□□□□□□□□□ / □□□□□□□□□□

Health
Bruised □
Hurt -1 □
Injured -1 □
Wounded -2 □
Mauled -2 □
Crippled -5 □
Incapacitated □

Experience

LEIF JONES 2000

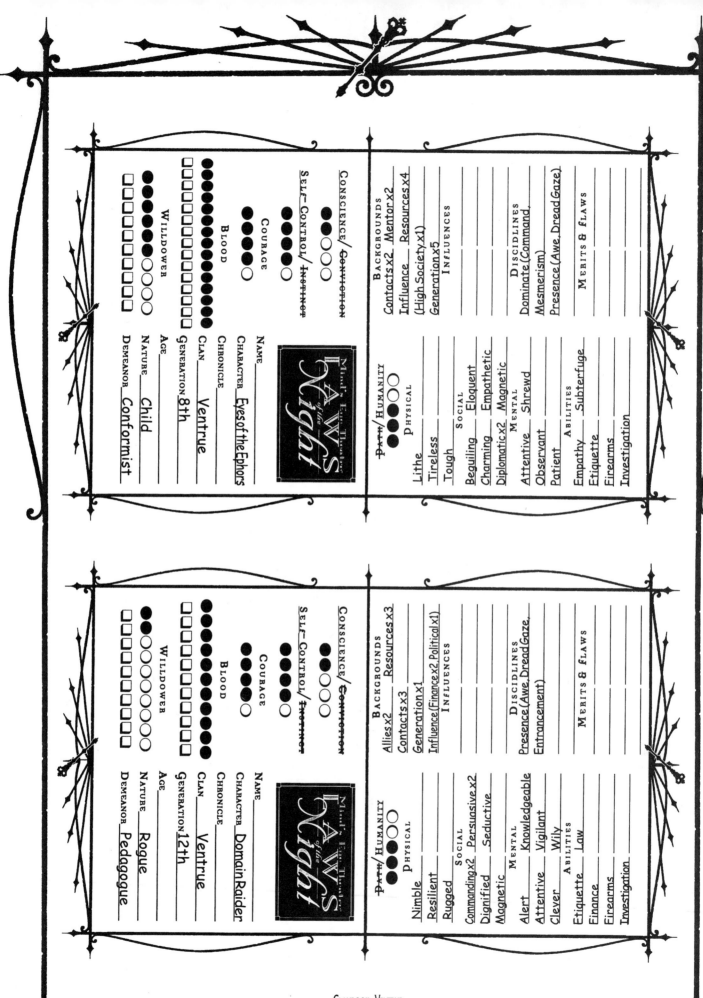

Mind's Eye Theatre — LAWS of the Night

NAME _____
CHARACTER __Eyes of the Ephors__
CHRONICLE _____
CLAN __Ventrue__
GENERATION __8th__
AGE _____
NATURE __Child__
DEMEANOR __Conformist__

CONSCIENCE/CONVICTION ●○○
SELF-CONTROL/INSTINCT ●○○
COURAGE ●●●●○
BLOOD ●●●●●●●●●●
WILLPOWER ●●●○○○

PATH/HUMANITY ●●●○○○

PHYSICAL
Lithe
Tireless
Tough

SOCIAL
Beguiling   Eloquent
Charming   Empathetic
Diplomatic x2   Magnetic

MENTAL
Attentive   Shrewd
Observant
Patient

ABILITIES
Empathy   Subterfuge
Etiquette
Firearms
Investigation

BACKGROUNDS
Contacts x2   Mentor x2
Influence   Resources x4
(High Society x1)
Generation x5

INFLUENCES

DISCIPLINES
Dominate (Command,
Mesmerism)
Presence (Awe, Dread Gaze)

MERITS & FLAWS

Mind's Eye Theatre — LAWS of the Night

NAME _____
CHARACTER __Domain Raider__
CHRONICLE _____
CLAN __Ventrue__
GENERATION __12th__
AGE _____
NATURE __Rogue__
DEMEANOR __Pedagogue__

CONSCIENCE/CONVICTION ●●○○
SELF-CONTROL/INSTINCT ●●○○
COURAGE ●●●○
BLOOD ●●●●●●●●●●
WILLPOWER ●●●●●○○○

PATH/HUMANITY ●●●○○

PHYSICAL
Nimble
Resilient
Rugged

SOCIAL
Commanding x2   Persuasive x2
Dignified   Seductive
Magnetic

MENTAL
Knowledgeable
Alert   Vigilant
Attentive   Wily
Clever

ABILITIES
Etiquette   Law
Finance
Firearms
Investigation

BACKGROUNDS
Allies x2   Resources x3
Contacts x3
Generation x1
Influence (Finance x2, Political x1)

INFLUENCES

DISCIPLINES
Presence (Awe, Dread Gaze,
Entrancement)

MERITS & FLAWS

REMOVER

Quote: *Time to die, motherfucker.*

Prelude: You knew the score since before you were old enough to screw — nobody ever fucks with the guy who has the power. Everybody in your neighborhood talked about being thugs. Everybody had their line of hardcore bullshit to tell any time somebody talked smack.

They were all liars, of course. If you stood up to them, they backed down like the pussy-ass niggaz they were. You made your reputation by doing just that: standing up to the loudmouthed bitches and giving them an unholy beat-down if they didn't recognize.

The sad thing was, you knew you weren't going to make it. You were smart enough to realize that somebody badder than you is always going to be out there, and thug life means that you would run across him sooner or later.

Turns out, it wasn't a him, but a her — some crazy white bitch from a gang

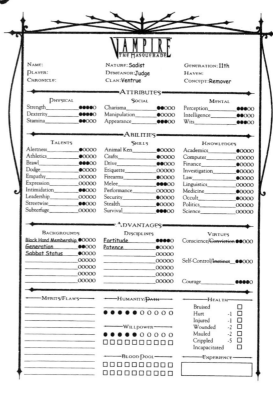

called the Sabbath. You hit her clear in the face six, maybe seven times, but she just stood there, laughing, calling you out. When you went for shot number eight, she grabbed your wrist, jerked that shit backward, *hard*, and pulled your arm out of socket. Then she laid down a beating a motherfucker's never had in his *life*.

Concept: Since your Embrace, you've joined your sire's gang, and you soon found yourself talking to one of the fucked-up "gangs-within-the-gang" or some shit. Motherfuckers called themselves the Black Hand. It sounded good enough to you — a chance to do what you were good at and earn props doing it. Still, that first kill was rough — but they get progressively easier, now that you know not to care. Or so they keep telling you.

Roleplaying Hints: You're fucking invulnerable, if not on your own, then with the Sabbat crew behind you. These Black Hand bitches keep telling you that the kill is more important than all your posturing, but that's because they're old and they've lost touch. Everyone on the street knows that it's what juice all the bitches know you can turn loose on them that matters. They've got to know you're hard, like they've got to know you earn the bank.

Equipment: Cell phone, Lincoln Navigator, Tommy Hilfiger and Hugo Boss wardrobe, two beepers, cheap pistol, Roman-style *gladius* (for when the business is Cainites)

HISTORIAN

Quote: *I think you'll find that precedent is against you, sir. The third childe of a prince has always had the rights my friend here asserts. It's tradition.*

Prelude: You never expected, nor wanted an exciting life. What you like best are stories: reading them, telling them, discovering new ones. The best stories, of course, are the true ones. That's why you went to graduate school and became a professor: so you could get paid for telling true stories.

You were always a bit of a maverick in your department (your one concession to an exciting life). Instead of wars, politics or sweeping social movements, though, your research focused on the strange and bizarre: ancient magical practices, cryptozoology, myths of fairies and monsters. None of it was true, of course. No such thing as magic existed, and monsters resided solely in fairy tales. The fact that people actually believed in these things, that they let these beliefs run their lives — now, *that's* a good story.

Except of course, as it turned out, it wasn't a story at all. It was the truth. You took an interest in vampire myths. The more you dug into the subject, the more interesting it became. On a trip to Katmandu, you dropped your research on legends of hairy hominids in the Indian subcontinent and turned exclusively to vampires.

Five months later, you had nearly enough for a great book, maybe even a popular book. Then one night, you received a call from the — as you now know — inevitable visitor. What you did not know at the time was that he was a Ventrue, sent by the city's concerned prince to check up on you and make sure you hadn't found anything you shouldn't. As it turns out, you'd managed to find quite a bit that you shouldn't. You knew about Caine, about clans, about the Inquisition, even about the Camarilla. Hey, you're good at what you do. It turns out you'd uncovered some stuff even *he* didn't know. It wasn't long before he Embraced you.

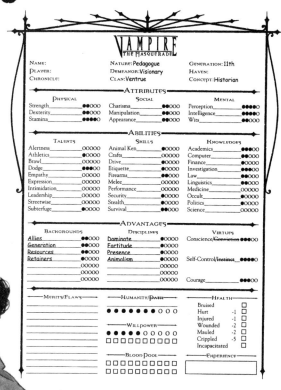

Concept: You spend your nights researching Ventrue history, searching for ancient artifacts and occasionally helping your fellow Kindred in disputes with other members of the clan or the race of Caine. But the Ventrue blood in you is beginning to sour. You're growing tired of helping others. It's time to start helping yourself. It's time to add some judicious excitement to your own, personal story.

Roleplaying Hints: You are quiet, watchful and ultimately as ambitious as any of your breed. You've fought for tenure before, and the game of Kindred politics isn't that different. Wait for the moment to reveal what you know, and use it to its fullest respect. You have the authority of knowledge, something you're not slow to lord over the less informed.

Equipment: Library of Ventrue and Kindred history, laptop with a concordance of clan traditions and precedent, diary of every offense every Kindred in the city has made that you know about, Japanese sedan

---

VAMPIRE THE MASQUERADE

NAME: NATURE: Pedagogue   GENERATION: 11th
PLAYER: DEMEANOR: Visionary   HAVEN:
CHRONICLE: CLAN: Ventrue   CONCEPT: Historian

ATTRIBUTES

Physical	Social	Mental
Strength ●●○○○	Charisma ●●○○○	Perception ●●●●○
Dexterity ●●○○○	Manipulation ●●○○○	Intelligence ●●●●●
Stamina ●●●○○	Appearance ●●○○○	Wits ●●○○○

ABILITIES

Talents	Skills	Knowledges
Alertness ○○○○○	Animal Ken ●○○○○	Academics ●●●○○
Athletics ●○○○○	Crafts ○○○○○	Computer ●●○○○
Brawl ○○○○○	Drive ●○○○○	Finance ●○○○○
Dodge ●●○○○	Etiquette ●○○○○	Investigation ●●●○○
Empathy ○○○○○	Firearms ●●○○○	Law ●●○○○
Expression ○○○○○	Melee ○○○○○	Linguistics ●●○○○
Intimidation ○○○○○	Performance ○○○○○	Medicine ○○○○○
Leadership ○○○○○	Security ○○○○○	Occult ●○○○○
Streetwise ○○○○○	Stealth ●○○○○	Politics ●●●○○
Subterfuge ●○○○○	Survival ●●○○○	Science ○○○○○

ADVANTAGES

Backgrounds	Disciplines	Virtues
Allies ●●○○○	Dominate ●○○○○	Conscience/~~Conviction~~ ●●○○○
Generation ●●○○○	Fortitude ●○○○○	
Resources ●●○○○	Presence ●○○○○	
Retainers ●○○○○	Animalism ●○○○○	Self-Control/~~Instinct~~ ●●●●●
○○○○○	○○○○○	
○○○○○	○○○○○	
○○○○○	○○○○○	Courage ●●●○○

MERITS/FLAWS	HUMANITY/~~PATH~~	HEALTH
	●●●●●●●○○○	Bruised ☐
		Hurt -1 ☐
	WILLPOWER	Injured -1 ☐
	●●●●●○○○○○	Wounded -2 ☐
	☐☐☐☐☐☐☐☐☐☐	Mauled -2 ☐
		Crippled -5 ☐
	BLOOD POOL	Incapacitated ☐
	☐☐☐☐☐☐☐☐☐☐	EXPERIENCE
	☐☐☐☐☐☐☐☐☐☐	

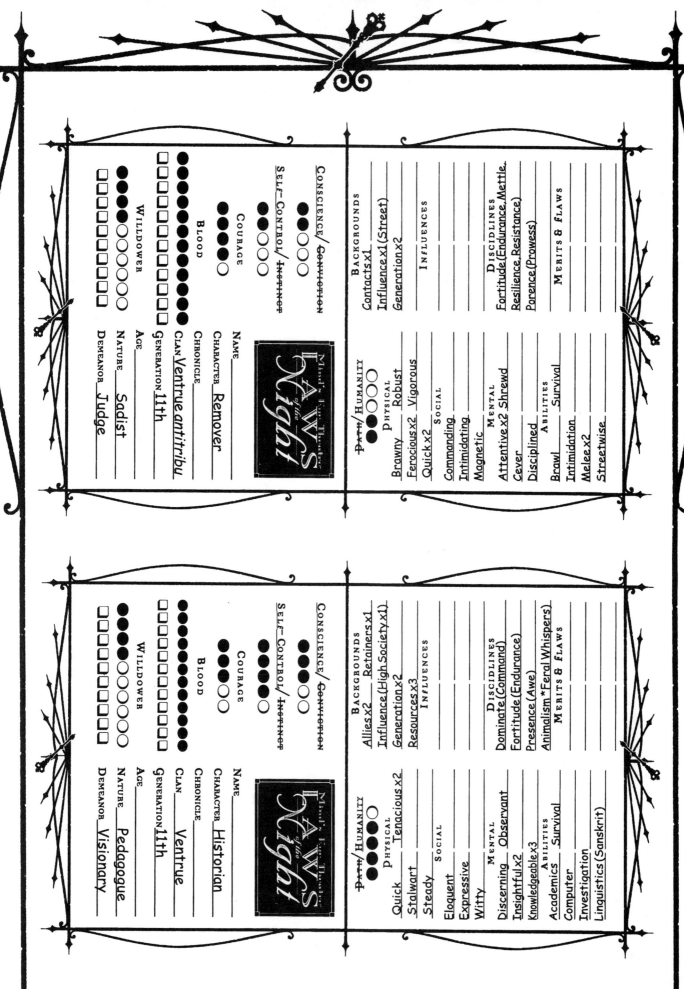

Mind's Eye Theatre — LAWS of the Night

Top Character Sheet

Name ___
Character **Remover**
Chronicle ___
Clan **Ventrue antitribu**
Generation **11th**
Age ___
Nature **Sadist**
Demeanor **Judge**

Conscience/Conviction
Self-Control/Instinct
Courage
Blood
Willpower

Backgrounds
Contacts x1
Influence x1 (Street)
Generation x2

Influences

Disciplines
Fortitude (Endurance, Mettle, Resilience, Resistance)
Potence (Prowess)

Merits & Flaws

Path/Humanity

Physical
Robust
Vigorous
Brawny
Ferocious x2
Quick x2

Social
Commanding
Intimidating
Magnetic

Mental
Attentive x2
Shrewd
Clever
Disciplined

Abilities
Brawl Survival
Intimidation
Melee x2
Streetwise

Mind's Eye Theatre — LAWS of the Night

Bottom Character Sheet

Name ___
Character **Historian**
Chronicle ___
Clan **Ventrue**
Generation **11th**
Age ___
Nature **Pedagogue**
Demeanor **Visionary**

Conscience/Conviction
Self-Control/Instinct
Courage
Blood
Willpower

Backgrounds
Allies x2 Retainers x1
Influence (High Society) x1
Generation x2
Resources x3

Influences

Disciplines
Dominate (Command)
Fortitude (Endurance)
Presence (Awe)
Animalism *Feral Whispers

Merits & Flaws

Path/Humanity

Physical
Quick Tenacious x2
Stalwart
Steady

Social
Eloquent
Expressive
Witty

Mental
Discerning Observant
Insightful x2
Knowledgeable x3

Abilities
Survival
Academics
Computer
Investigation
Linguistics (Sanskrit)

Vitaephile

Quote: *Oh, a fine vintage, that one. A saucy young French from Bordeaux. Rosemonde was her name, I believe.*

Prelude: In life, you were an account executive for a radio station. You had a natural gift for gab, for reading people and convincing them that radio ads would serve their needs. For you the job was always just a way to put food on the table. Not just food, but wine, too. Actually, wine *especially*.

You loved wine. You loved the taste, the effect, the history, the culture, the snobbery. Selling air-time made you a wealthy woman, but it was all so you could improve your cellar.

Then you met your future sire, who had been watching you and playing the part of a sommelier at Harold's Studio downtown. It was a "deal-breaker" at first. What was the point of being immortal if you couldn't enjoy a good Bordeaux? You couldn't see one at all. Then you tasted blood, not for the first time, but for the first time when you didn't have the Beast inside you howling for sustenance. It was delicious, divine, inspiring — sensual. Wine paled to nothing in comparison. You were hooked.

For you, vitae has become an obsession. You've made contact with other Ventrue throughout the world who share your tastes. Moreover, you've made a point of learning the tastes of every other Kindred in the vicinity, and many throughout the world. This knowledge, coupled with your passion for finding the best

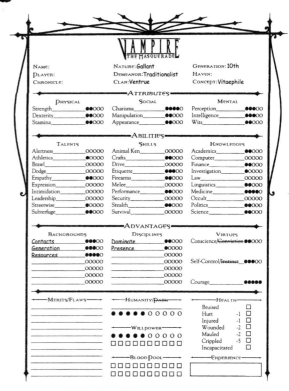

blood available, has led you into a unique niche: purveyor of fine vitae.

Concept: You watch mortals, seduce them to your haven, feed them certain foods or chemicals, subject them to certain stimuli — you're even doing research on a long-term breeding project to bring out certain nuances in their vitae. Like a vintner, you monitor every step, producing blood that tastes not only delicious, but complex. Most of the time, the herds from which you draw your blood don't even know what's going on. Of course occasionally, for an especially rare vintage, you take a mortal and keep it under controlled circumstances, nurturing it along until it's just right.

Roleplaying Hints: Other Kindred, not only Ventrue, pay premium prices for your intoxicating blends. Wealthy beyond your needs, you seldom take money in exchange for your wondrous vintages any longer. Instead, you trade blood for favors. More than a few Kindred in the city have become…*enthusiastic*…about your vitae, unable to resist its charms and unable to find it anywhere but from you. Thus far, your specialty has earned you much praise and recognition, but you know that the true market remains untapped. Fine Kindred vitae is far more tantalizing and far more dangerous….

Equipment: Shunts, needles, syringes, air-tight flasks for storing your samples, English luxury sedan with a refrigeration unit built into the trunk, wine cellar at your haven

DIABLERIST

Quote: *It's the Blood, baby… the power's all in the Blood, and don't let any craven elder tell you otherwise.*

Prelude: Nothing about your Embrace ever signified that you'd be destined for anything other than the most common and unpleasant unlife. It was a prosaic affair: Your sire met you at a nightclub, convinced you to return to his lair, fed on you and then Embraced you in a fit of self-loathing and remorse. How utterly uninspired. So mundane, in fact, that you didn't even feel much sympathy for him when he met his final reward.

In fact, your sire was more lackadaisical than anything else. Sure, he instructed you in the ways and traditions of the Kindred. He explained the noble legacy of the Ventrue, which was actually a bit ironic, because he was neither rich nor particularly guileful. He even warned you of the dire amaranth — much to his own dismay.

When you parted ways, you fell in with a crew of anarchs for a while. Not that they were particularly useful, but they did let you in on the truth about diablerie. The night you went with them on one of their elder raids was the night your eyes truly opened. Within a month, you visited the same fate upon your own sire. And then another Kindred. And then another…

Concept: You are a rogue and an anathema, availing yourself of the blood of elders in your own quest for power. Those who know you for what you are usually hate you, but you know they feel that way because they fear you. In your mind, you are bold and innovative, throwing off the hypocritical social contracts the elders impose

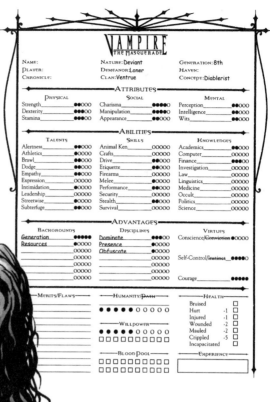

VAMPIRE		
THE MASQUERADE		

NAME: NATURE: Deviant GENERATION: 8th
PLAYER: DEMEANOR: Loner HAVEN:
CHRONICLE: CLAN: Ventrue CONCEPT: Diablerist

ATTRIBUTES

PHYSICAL		SOCIAL		MENTAL	
Strength	●●○○○	Charisma	●●●●○	Perception	●●○○○
Dexterity	●●○○○	Manipulation	●●●○○	Intelligence	●●○○○
Stamina	●●○○○	Appearance	●●○○○	Wits	●●○○○

ABILITIES

TALENTS		SKILLS		KNOWLEDGES	
Alertness	●●○○○	Animal Ken	○○○○○	Academics	●●○○○
Athletics	●○○○○	Crafts	○○○○○	Computer	○○○○○
Brawl	●●○○○	Drive	●●○○○	Finance	●●○○○
Dodge	●●○○○	Etiquette	●●○○○	Investigation	○○○○○
Empathy	●●○○○	Firearms	○○○○○	Law	○○○○○
Expression	○○○○○	Melee	●○○○○	Linguistics	○○○○○
Intimidation	○○○○○	Performance	●●○○○	Medicine	○○○○○
Leadership	○○○○○	Security	○○○○○	Occult	○○○○○
Streetwise	●○○○○	Stealth	●●○○○	Politics	○○○○○
Subterfuge	●●○○○	Survival	○○○○○	Science	○○○○○

ADVANTAGES

BACKGROUNDS		DISCIPLINES		VIRTUES	
Generation	●●●●●	Dominate	●●●○○	Conscience/~~Conviction~~	●○○○○
Resources	○○○○○	Presence	●●○○○		
	○○○○○	Obfuscate	●○○○○		
	○○○○○		○○○○○	Self-Control/~~Instinct~~	●●●●○
	○○○○○		○○○○○		
	○○○○○		○○○○○		
	○○○○○		○○○○○	Courage	●●●●●

MERITS/FLAWS

HUMANITY/PATH ●●●●○○○○○○

WILLPOWER ●●●●○○○○○○

BLOOD POOL

HEALTH
Bruised ☐
Hurt -1 ☐
Injured -1 ☐
Wounded -2 ☐
Mauled -2 ☐
Crippled -5 ☐
Incapacitated ☐

EXPERIENCE

upon their childer to protect themselves. To others, you are the Devil herself, waiting in the shadows with a smile to collect their souls and send them to Hell. In fact, you know that it's only a matter of time before someone "does something" about you or the Beast claims you utterly — but you'll be damned if you'll give up easily. Until then, it'll be one wild, bloody ride.

Roleplaying Hints: You drink the vitae of Kindred for the rush. In fact, you don't even limit yourself to lower-generation blood anymore. Sometimes, you drink from Kindred just because their blood is so much more delectable than the thin, soupy blood of mortals. You hunt other Kindred with stealth, catching them in the late hours as they return to their havens or before they depart for the night. You've given your coterie no reason not to trust you — well, besides the fact that they're terrified that you'll come after them one night — but you can see the suspicion and fear in their eyes. It used to make you feel remorseful. Now it just makes you dismissive of their cowardice.

Equipment: Note pad with scribbled reminders and clues about other Kindred's havens, stakes, ornate knife, Jaguar stolen from a diablerized elder

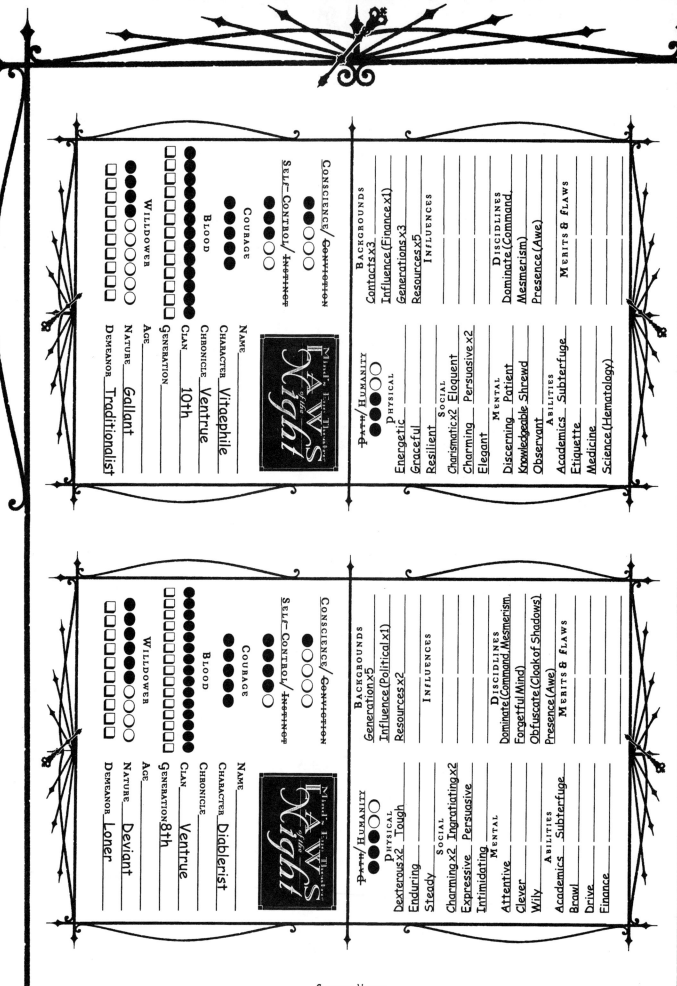

Sample Brood: Bilé's Gambit

Contrary to popular opinion, the Blue Bloods do not simply move into a city and "control" all of the mortal resources by "manipulating" everyone they see, insisting that everyone acknowledge their authority. Attaining prominence, power and *dignitas* requires more than some vague notion of supremacy. It requires precise action in the realms of finance, society and politics. Police departments don't just roll over for the toughest Kindred to barge past their precinct doors, his eyes ablaze with Dominate and his mien exuding Presence-fired charisma. Indeed, many Ventrue specialize, focusing on the resources that they can best turn to their profit. A venture-capitalist may work hard at creating a new financial base for himself in a new city; a politico might extend favors to election hopefuls or silence threats to incumbents in return for that official's debt. Many times, these individuals form coteries or consortiums (see Chapter Two), which not only allow them to present a more stable front to rivals, it sometimes allows them to usurp influence traditionally claimed by more established Kindred.

Being the sect champions of the Masquerade has taught the Ventrue valuable lessons about keeping a low profile and using deception to their advantage. Therefore, while closely tied in private, the members of this brood display little concern or care for each other when other eyes are watching. The brood operates relatively independently, each facing the city's problems and opportunities from a different angle. This strategy is typical of Ventrue in a new city, although few realize it because the clan makes such a show of their high finance and upper-class connections. While anti-clan sentiments focus on the "official" Ventrue presence, the brood's less obvious members have more freedom for their own pursuits. When and if the coterie's true nature is revealed, it is usually too late: The Ventrue have already accomplished their goals.

João Bilé, the Man Behind the Curtain

Background: Embraced nearly a century ago in Brazil, Bilé has only recently realized the chance to make a name for himself. He's paid his dues, fulfilled his obligations and capitalized on his opportunities. Now, as new territory opens up, he has a chance to establish a brood and domain, perhaps even a princedom for himself. Bilé has learned a great deal at the feet of his sire and elders, and he now seeks to put that knowledge to the test. He has devised an intricate yet flexible plan for this grand new venture.

Bilé has decided to conceal his own presence in the city, and he plans to work through his three childer as

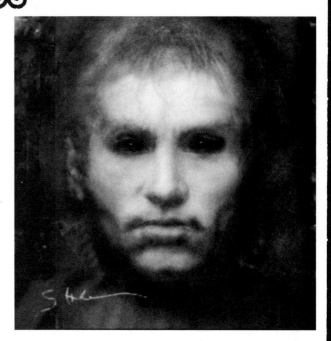

much as possible. To this end, he has taken up the role of servant and counselor to his eldest, Michael Brandeis. While Michael assumes the role (and inherits the enemies) of a prominent Ventrue, Bilé can work behind the scenes. He presents this switching of roles to Michael as a great opportunity for the young Ventrue, although the youth suspects that Bilé's motivations are not entirely altruistic.

As for the other two childer, Robin and Margarida, Bilé has equally duplicitous plans for them. Robin comes to the city an acknowledged Ventrue, ostensibly from another city and setting herself up in opposition to Michael. Bilé plans to promote her as the loyal opposition, a way to find out what influences other Camarilla members might devote themselves to nurturing. Margarida comes to the city as a Caitiff. Bilé has not even told his other two childer about his third progeny. He plans to have Margarida ingratiate herself with the ranks of the anarchs, Brujah and possibly even any Sabbat in the region, wherein she can provide him with news on the plans of each dissenting faction.

Image: In public, the tall, thin, Bilé stands stooped over, his thin lips drawn back in a fawning smile. He looks to be the doting mentor in every respect, accepting his own decline and lending his experience to better his ward's endeavors. Away from other Kindred, João stands erect, taller than his progeny, which allows him to glare down at them should they earn his derision. His salt-and-pepper hair and stern gaze give him an avuncular look that sets some Kindred at ease.

Roleplaying Hints: Before an audience, you defer to Michael in all things and seldom even meet the eyes of others. Take on an entirely meek and unassuming demeanor. When in private, your attitude changes entirely. You command your brood, your childer, with confident authority. Bark orders and become indignant if they're not obeyed without question. You care only a little for the unlives of your brood. They are tools first and family a distant second, which is an outlook you do little to hide from them.

Sire: Therése Maurier
Nature: Competitor
Demeanor: Conformist
Generation: 9th
Embrace: 1911
Apparent Age: late 40s
Physical: Strength 3, Dexterity 2, Stamina 4
Social: Charisma 3, Manipulation 5, Appearance: 2
Mental: Perception 4, Intelligence 3, Wits 4
Talents: Alertness 3, Brawl 2, Empathy 1, Expression 2, Intimidation 4, Leadership 4, Style 2, Subterfuge 3
Skills: Crafts 3, Drive 1, Etiquette 3, Performance 3, Stealth 2
Knowledges: Academics 2, Bureaucracy 2, Computer 1, Finance 3, Investigation 2, Law, 2 Politics 4
Backgrounds: Contacts 1, Resources 4, Retainers 2, Status 3
Disciplines: Auspex 1, Dominate 4, Fortitude 4, Presence 3
Virtues: Conscience 1, Self-Control 5, Courage 5
Morality: Humanity 5
Willpower: 6

MICHAEL BRANDEIS, THE PROTÉGÉ PROGENY

Background: Michael Brandeis has been Kindred for only 10 years, all that time under the secret tutelage of his sire João Bilé. No one outside of Clan Ventrue (and few inside) knows that Bilé is actually Michael's sire, which has been part of Bilé's plan since before Michael's Embrace. As a result, Michael has earned quite a reputation for one so young, acquiring numerous contacts and accolades in his brief unlife. Outwardly, he seems to be a prototypical Ventrue: calm, assured and decidedly self-confident.

Inside is a different matter entirely. In fact, Michael can scarcely make a move without his sire's permission or guidance. Bilé overwhelms him like an abusive parent. João assures the young Kindred constantly that he is worthless, and that Final Death would find him in a matter of hours without Bilé's protection and guidance. For many years, Michael believed just that. He obeyed his sire's orders to the letter, always playing the dutiful childe.

Now, with a new city lying open before him, Michael feels the first spark of rebellion. He sees the opportunity,

but he also sees the danger. He has begun to realize that Bilé has placed him in the forefront as a kind of lightning rod. These nights are dangerous, and Michael is beginning to suspect that he might not survive them if things continue on. For the time being, he plays his assigned role, letting the world think of Bilé as his aged counsel and of himself as the master. Should events present him with a chance to make that illusion real, he might just take advantage, if he can summon the courage to do so.

Image: Michael is a handsome man, with sandy hair and green eyes. He affects conservative clothes and manners, in order to play his role better. Michael stands just under six feet tall, with broad shoulders and an athletic physique. His eyes, however, let perceptive people know that beneath his calm veneer lies either doubt, fear or… something less definable.

Roleplaying Hints: You have a dry wit and a generally likeable personality when you choose to show it. You play your role as a leading Ventrue to the hilt, almost to the extent of a parody of your elders, the veriest stereotype of others' prejudices. From your royal airs and high-class sensibilities, one would never suspect that you become as submissive as a chastened child in private with Bilé. If anything, the hidden spark of rebellion in you makes you even more deferential in Bilé's presence since you fear that your sire will find you out.

Sire: João Bilé
Nature: Masochist
Demeanor: Architect
Generation: 10th
Embrace: 1989
Apparent Age: early 30s

Physical: Strength 2, Dexterity 2, Stamina 2
Social: Charisma 4, Manipulation 2, Appearance 4
Mental: Perception 3, Intelligence 2, Wits 3
Talents: Athletics 1, Expression 3, Grace 2, Leadership 3, Streetwise 1, Subterfuge 3
Skills: Drive 2, Etiquette 2, Firearms 3, Performance 2, Stealth 1, Survival 1
Knowledges: Academics 2, Computer 1, Finance 3, Law 2, Linguistics (French, German, Portuguese, Spanish) 3, Occult 1
Backgrounds: Allies 1, Contacts 4, Herd 1, Mentor 2, Resources 4
Disciplines: Presence 4, Dominate 2
Virtues: Conscience 3, Self-Control 4, Courage 3
Morality: Humanity 7
Willpower: 4

Robin Withers, the Rival

Background: Robin Withers served as legal counsel to politicians and businessmen, as a high-powered attorney who put her career before all else. When she "died" in a car accident at age 40, the legal community mourned her passing. Her rebirth into vampiric undeath did not receive nearly as much attention. Robin is Bilé's true favorite childe, the one he hopes to have sitting at his right side when all his ambitions become reality. As such, he spoils her (at least by his standards), allowing her more freedom than he allows his other two childer.

Robin herself appreciates the trust and confidence her sire vests in her, and she strives to please him. She comes to the city with a carefully contrived back-story. Even a detailed investigation into her past shows no connection with Bilé or Michael. She has existed apart from her sire for close to nine years, making a name for herself on her own. She has come to this newly opened city as a foil to her "elder," Michael. Although she supports him publicly, as a good Ventrue should, she grumbles privately to other Kindred about his incompetence. She seeks allies among the Toreador, Tremere and Nosferatu, binding the clans together in their general distrust of the megalomaniac Ventrue.

Her ambitions do not extend beyond those of her sire. She sees Bilé's scheme as brilliant, and she plans to play her part in it as best she can. She'll follow his lead and earn the comfortable benefits thereafter. As long as she believes that her sire offers the best chance for achieving wealth, she will follow him wherever he directs her. Should he ever betray her trust, she would have no qualms about turning against him. As for her "brother" Michael, she holds him in slight regard. He is but a pawn who's useful but ultimately disposable.

Image: A soft-looking woman in her 40s, Robin did not have much time for the gym or beauty salons when she was alive. From a certain perspective, she looks very much like a middle-class mother of three. She uses this disarming appearance along with a pleasant, matter-of-fact attitude to win over potential allies and make enemies underestimate her. In truth, she has a killer instinct, and — as her court record shows — she knows how to win.

Roleplaying Hints: You come across as a confidante, trusting (falsely) in others with the hopes of luring them into trusting you. You allow others to see your ambition, but not so much that it puts them off. Read other Kindred and determine just how much change they desire, then offer them just enough to earn their confidence. Greed is good, you've found. Other Kindred always want something, and you're able to promise it to them. Sometimes, you even deliver.

Sire: João Bilé
Nature: Competitor
Demeanor: Conniver
Generation: 10th
Embrace: 1976
Apparent Age: mid 40s
Physical: Strength 2, Dexterity 2, Stamina 2
Social: Charisma 2, Manipulation 4, Appearance 2
Mental: Perception 4, Intelligence 3, Wits 4
Talents: Alertness 2, Dodge 2, Intimidation 2, Leadership 3, Subterfuge 4
Skills: Drive 2, Security 2, Stealth 1

Knowledges: Academics 3, Bureaucracy 2, Finance 3, Investigation 2, Law 4, Linguistics (Portuguese) 1, Politics 3

Backgrounds: Contacts 3, Mentor 1, Resources 4, Status 1

Disciplines: Auspex 1, Dominate 3, Obfuscate 2, Presence 2

Virtues: Conscience 3, Self-Control 5, Courage 4

Morality: Humanity 6

Willpower: 5

MARGARIDA CORDEIRO, THE OUTCAST

Background: Margarida Cordeiro is an uncommon Ventrue, cut from a different cloth than her brood siblings. Although she currently dresses and acts the part of a disenfranchised Gen-X punk, that's all it is: an act. In fact, Margarida is an actress. When Bilé conceived his plan, he knew he'd need to Embrace men and women capable of staying "in character," acting their part for months or even years at a time. Therefore, he found Margarida's talents most appealing, and he Embraced her into his brood secretly, something only his own sire knows about.

Having taken on the role of an anarch Toreador, Margarida acts the part with consummate skill. She has no contact with her fellow childer, and she reports to Bilé only via dead-letter drops, e-mail and other anonymous means. Although Bilé has quite explicit plans, Margarida has most of her time to herself to pursue her charge in her own way. An accomplished mimic and judge of character, she can blend easily into many social circles. She has already managed to earn herself acceptance among the local anarchs.

Bilé has given Margarida permission to do whatever she has to do to maintain her cover. She plots actively with her cohorts, breaking the traditions of Kindred and men with relative abandon. She has killed police officers, perpetrated arson and even committed diablerie (unknown to her sire). Margarida knows that she is a valuable asset to Bilé and that he'll use his influence to help her out if she finds her way into any serious trouble with the authorities, which may well happen, given her new reckless bent. This assurance makes her all the more willing to "go wild" with her new friends, a trait they have come to respect in her. Of course, she passes on all the information she gathers to Bilé who then distributes it to Robin or Michael as he sees fit.

Image: Margarida is a strikingly beautiful, dark-haired woman. She currently shaves her long hair each night and festoons herself with piercings and other appropriate accouterments.

Roleplaying Hints: In your role as an anarch, you are a loud, wild bully. Brash is an unlifestyle, not an attitude.

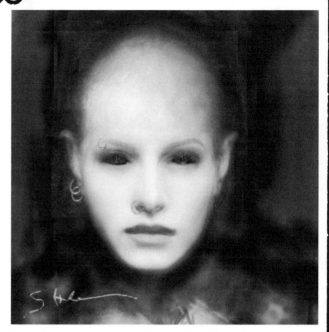

In reality, you are actually a calm, thoughtful woman. You view Bilé as an employer more than a father figure, and you harbor no feelings for your two broodmates.

Sire: João Bilé

Nature: Thrill-Seeker

Demeanor: Fanatic

Generation: 9th

Embrace: 1993

Physical: Strength 2, Dexterity 4, Stamina 3

Social: Charisma 4, Manipulation 3, Appearance 4

Mental: Perception 2, Intelligence 2, Wits 3

Talents: Alertness 1, Athletics 2, Brawl 1, Dodge 2, Empathy 3, Intimidation 1, Intuition 2, Subterfuge 3

Skills: Animal Ken 1, Crafts 1, Drive 1, Firearms 1, Melee 2, Performance 2, Stealth 1

Knowledges: Academics 1, Investigation 4, Linguistics (English, Spanish) 2, Politics 1

Backgrounds: Allies 2, Contacts 1, Mentor 1, Resources 1, Retainers 1

Disciplines: Celerity 1, Presence 2, Fortitude 3

Virtues: Conscience 3, Self-Control 4, Courage 4

Morality: Humanity 7

Willpower: 4

THE REVERED CASTE

Leaders behind the scenes, plotters too cagey to leave traces of their passing, wielders of vast wealth and bearers of tremendous influence — the Ventrue are all of these things and more. Like their ideological opposites, the Brujah, Clan Ventrue is a clan of contradictions. To hear them tell the tale, they rule other Kindred, while all but the most deluded know that rulership is practically outdated in the modern nights. Indeed, the successful Ventrue has either made her fortune in the past and survives on her bounty of *dignitas*, or she adopts the tactics the modern world demands. All but gone are the nights of Cainite lords issuing terrible decrees from craggy castles. These Final Nights demand subtlety and grace. The Ventrue warlord has given way to the Blue Blood advisor; nobles have stepped aside for power-brokers. Such are the demands of the Masquerade, which the Ventrue must uphold to truly prosper. The following, then, are a few of the most noteworthy Ventrue, outstanding in either their excellence at contemporary tactics or so adept at the old ways that the secret world around them still acknowledges their greatness.

FABRIZIO ULFILA

Clan Ventrue has rarely tied itself too closely to the Church, finding it infested with Tremere, Toreador, Giovanni and Lasombra. Even those few who have made places for themselves within the mighty Catholic Empire have remained at the lower echelons, playing at jyhad from within holy walls at the local level. Fabrizio Ulfila, however, is the exception to this trend. He is quite a potent exception at that.

Some Kindred whisper that Ulfila holds each of the cardinals in debt, that he has the keys to a vast library of documents held as heretical by the Church, and that even the Pope himself stands accountable to this venerable Cainite. While these rumors are almost certainly exaggerated, Fabrizio has remained an active and powerful figure in the Catholic Church for centuries. As any Kindred associated with a mortal institution for centuries must, Ulfila remains hidden. When he seeks to act, he does so through telephone calls invoking favors, ghoul attendants or quiet influence leveled against capable Church officials. Over the centuries, Ulfila has been the impetus behind papal bulls, official declarations of dogma and even more dire events. Some hold him accountable for the Fourth Crusade, and still others for the Inquisition itself.

Whether these claims are true or not, Ulfila doubtless has the clout to make such things happen should he so wish. The Cainite's connections seemingly have no limits. He is known to consort with a coven of Catholic mages, and he has alluded to boons owed him by Ambrogino Giovanni and a host of former justicars.

Detractors claim that Ulfila's power has waned in the modern nights, and that the Church is no longer as relevant as it was during the nights of his meteoric ascent. Fabrizio simply smiles at these doubts. As the Final Nights approach, he has seen more and more of the desperate become devout, either hoping to hedge their bets or experiencing true epiphanies. While the world itself may indeed have become more secular than during the Long Night of the Dark Ages, it has also become far more populous, and the ranks of the faithful have swelled despite the fall of the ratio. It is upon the backs of those followers that the House of God is built — as well as the foundation of Ulfila's influence.

ANUSHIN-RAWAN

As one of the greatest champions of the merits of Elysium, the Kindred Anushin-Rawan has garnered great status and support among Camarilla Kindred. In particular, many Toreador honor her in addition to her Ventrue clanmates. During the late 1950s, Anushin-Rawan combined the resources of several Ventrue partners in the interest of purchasing Yiaros, an island near Greece.

Establishing the island as her own personal domain and haven, Anushin-Rawan also declared the entire island an Elysium. Although she looks unfavorably upon Kindred using her haven as an asylum, she has recently opened the island to all Cainites of the Camarilla. In truth, Anushin-Rawan prefers the company of invited guests, with whom she spends nights in song and revelry. Although officially unpopulated, Yiaros has become home to a small community of *psaras* fishermen. From the ranks of these people, Anushin-Rawan populates the ranks of her manor's servants, pleasure-slaves and professional vessels.

Almost three centuries before she purchased the island, Anushin-Rawan visited Yiaros and disseminated her blood through pirates taking shelter on the island. Thereafter, she provided the ghoul pirates with concubines, who promptly began populating the region. Unknown to the majority of the other Ventrue (let alone other Kindred), when Anushin-Rawan bought the island, she had fed its secret inhabitants vitae so long that the descendants of the original pirates and concubines had become a revenant family. While Kindred scholars debate the probability of this claim being true, Anushin-Rawan knows its truth for certain, as Yiaros is home to a few lingering fae and their magical presence gradually twisted the islanders from mere ghouls to hereditary revenants.

To those who know her, Anushin-Rawan seems to have purely selfless motives in mind. True, she grows wealthy from international interests, but no one has ever breached the traditions of Elysium in her island domain, and she has never asked a guest for anything in return. (Although she has asked numerous odious coteries of Kindred to leave, at least one of which turned out later to be Sabbat.) Others, though, question her generosity, even if they have no idea about her revenants. What gain does it offer her besides status and fame?

True to her diplomatic origins — her release was a gala affair attended by almost one hundred Kindred luminaries of the time — Anushin-Rawan simply dismisses naysayers as pessimists. She has gone to great lengths to create a pleasant haven for Kindred who wish to escape the ugliness of the Jyhad. Why would anyone wish to denigrate that?

JAN PIETERZOON, CHILDE OF THE CAMARILLA

Background: To Jan Pieterzoon, Gehenna and the *Book of Nod* are superstitious drivel belonging in the Dark Ages. Jan understands that Kindred are paranoid and petty —his grandsire was killed over a vendetta. Talk of Gehenna and ravenous Antediluvians only feeds this paranoia and results in factionalism, fear and paralysis. The Final Nights are here because foolish elders project their fears and read too much into coincidences and random chance. Jan is not blind, however. He knows that something is happening, but it is no more apocalyptic than simple change in Kindred social conventions. It happened before in the legends of the Kindred, as it did in Constantinople and during the Anarch Revolt. Instead of hiding from "Gehenna," Jan believes that the Camarilla should embrace change, evolve and adapt to the new millennium. If it does not, Jan fears that the Camarilla will crumble and face a self-fulfilling Gehenna.

Jan has acquired no small amount of media influence to further his goal of eradicating Kindred superstition. The Ventrue is on a book-burning crusade. He wants the Inner Circle to punish all references to the *Book of Nod* since such references only feed the apocalyptic fear gripping Kindred society and make it harder for the Camarilla to remain dominant. He has gathered Cainite scholars and scientists to find "scientific" explanations for vampires — hoping that a secular explanation will quell fears of Gehenna.

Despite being immersed in Byzantine Kindred treachery since the very night of his Embrace, Jan Pieterzoon remains committed to the *noblesse oblige* that characterizes the most august of Ventrue. He truly believes that Ventrue *dignitas* includes guiding other wayward Kindred. He subscribes to the crumbling ethic of leadership over greed, counsel over dominance. Nevertheless, Pieterzoon isn't naïve. He understands that most Kindred are too short-sighted to know what's best for them. To this end, he's willing to indulge in the race of Caine's petty deceptions and grand jyhads as long as they accomplish the necessary end — the preservation of the Kindred and their secret ways.

Image: With a face framed by spiky blond hair and deep blue eyes, Jan Pieterzoon is an archetype of Scandinavian stock. He often colors his hair when traveling, as many Kindred find his look a little less than traditional and a bit shocking. Jan is a complete clotheshorse, wardrobing himself in tailored suits of the finest subtle fabrics and accessories of high quality.

Roleplaying Hints: Your stake in the game is a great one, and you know full well that you are probably in over your head. Still, calm must prevail. If you let others know that you doubt the extent of your capabilities, they will

bring you down like sharks drawn by the scent of blood. Your sire, Hardestadt, left you a tremendous legacy to satisfy, and you don't fear failure for its own sake as you do his disappointment should you be unable to succeed at the tasks for which he chose you.

Clan: Ventrue

Sire: Hardestadt the Younger

Nature: Idealist

Demeanor: Director

Generation: 7th

Embrace: 1723

Apparent Age: late 20s

Physical: Strength 3, Dexterity 3, Stamina 6

Social: Charisma 4, Manipulation 5, Appearance 3

Mental: Perception 5, Intelligence 4, Wits 3

Talents: Alertness 4, Athletics 2, Brawl 2, Dodge 2, Empathy 4, Expression 3, Grace 4, Intimidation 4, Leadership 4, Streetwise 1, Style 4, Subterfuge 6

Skills: Drive 2, Etiquette 4, Firearms 1, Melee 4, Performance 4, Stealth 2, Survival 3

Knowledges: Academics 4, Computer 2, Finance 5, Investigation 3, Law 4, Linguistics 4, Politics 4, Science 2

Disciplines: Auspex 1, Dominate 4, Fortitude 5, Obfuscate 2, Obtenebration 1, Potence 3, Presence 4

Backgrounds: Contacts 5, Herd 2, Influence 3, Mentor 5, Resources 5, Retainers 2, Status 4

Virtues: Conscience 3, Self-Control 4, Courage 3

Morality: Humanity 6

Willpower: 7

Ventrue

NAME: **NATURE:**   **GENERATION:**
PLAYER: **DEMEANOR:**   **SIRE:**
CHRONICLE: **CONCEPT:**   **HAVEN:**

ATTRIBUTES

PHYSICAL
Strength_____ ●OOOO
Dexterity_____ ●OOOO
Stamina_____ ●OOOO

SOCIAL
Charisma_____ ●OOOO
Manipulation_____ ●OOOO
Appearance_____ ●OOOO

MENTAL
Perception_____ ●OOOO
Intelligence_____ ●OOOO
Wits_____ ●OOOO

ABILITIES

TALENTS
Alertness_____ OOOOO
Athletics_____ OOOOO
Brawl_____ OOOOO
Dodge_____ OOOOO
Empathy_____ OOOOO
Expression_____ OOOOO
Intimidation_____ OOOOO
Leadership_____ OOOOO
Streetwise_____ OOOOO
Subterfuge_____ OOOOO

SKILLS
Animal Ken_____ OOOOO
Crafts_____ OOOOO
Drive_____ OOOOO
Etiquette_____ OOOOO
Firearms_____ OOOOO
Melee_____ OOOOO
Performance_____ OOOOO
Security_____ OOOOO
Stealth_____ OOOOO
Survival_____ OOOOO

KNOWLEDGES
Academics_____ OOOOO
Computer_____ OOOOO
Finance_____ OOOOO
Investigation_____ OOOOO
Law_____ OOOOO
Linguistics_____ OOOOO
Medicine_____ OOOOO
Occult_____ OOOOO
Politics_____ OOOOO
Science_____ OOOOO

ADVANTAGES

BACKGROUNDS
_____ OOOOO
_____ OOOOO
_____ OOOOO
_____ OOOOO
_____ OOOOO
_____ OOOOO
_____ OOOOO

DISCIPLINES
_____ OOOOO
_____ OOOOO
_____ OOOOO
_____ OOOOO
_____ OOOOO
_____ OOOOO
_____ OOOOO

VIRTUES
Conscience/Conviction ●OOOO

Self-Control/Instinct__ ●OOOO

Courage_____ ●OOOO

MERITS/FLAWS
_____
_____
_____
_____
_____
_____
_____
_____

HUMANITY/PATH
O O O O O O O O O O

WILLPOWER
O O O O O O O O O O
☐ ☐ ☐ ☐ ☐ ☐ ☐ ☐ ☐ ☐

BLOOD POOL
☐ ☐ ☐ ☐ ☐ ☐ ☐ ☐ ☐ ☐
☐ ☐ ☐ ☐ ☐ ☐ ☐ ☐ ☐ ☐

HEALTH
Bruised		☐
Hurt	-1	☐
Injured	-1	☐
Wounded	-2	☐
Mauled	-2	☐
Crippled	-5	☐
Incapacitated		☐

WEAKNESS
Feeding Restriction

Ventrue

Other Traits

_____ OOOOO	_____ OOOOO	_____ OOOOO
_____ OOOOO	_____ OOOOO	_____ OOOOO
_____ OOOOO	_____ OOOOO	_____ OOOOO
_____ OOOOO	_____ OOOOO	_____ OOOOO
_____ OOOOO	_____ OOOOO	_____ OOOOO
_____ OOOOO	_____ OOOOO	_____ OOOOO
_____ OOOOO	_____ OOOOO	_____ OOOOO

Rituals

Name	Level
_____	_____
_____	_____
_____	_____
_____	_____
_____	_____
_____	_____
_____	_____
_____	_____
_____	_____
_____	_____
_____	_____
_____	_____
_____	_____
_____	_____
_____	_____
_____	_____
_____	_____

Experience

TOTAL: _____

TOTAL SPENT: _____

spent on:

_____

_____

_____

_____

Derangements

_____

_____

_____

_____

_____

_____

_____

_____

_____

Blood Bonds/ Vinculi

Bound to	Rating	Bound to	Rating
_____	_____	_____	_____
_____	_____	_____	_____
_____	_____	_____	_____
_____	_____	_____	_____

Combat

Weapon	Damage	Range	Rate	Clip	Conceal

Armor

_____

_____

_____

_____

Ventrue™

Expanded Background

Allies
_____
_____
_____
_____

Contacts
_____
_____
_____
_____

Fame
_____
_____
_____
_____

Herd
_____
_____
_____
_____

Influence
_____
_____
_____
_____

Mentor
_____
_____
_____
_____

Resources
_____
_____
_____
_____

Retainers
_____
_____
_____
_____

Status
_____
_____
_____
_____

Other
_____
_____
_____
_____

Possessions

Gear (Carried)
_____
_____
_____
_____

Feeding Grounds
_____
_____
_____

Equipment (Owned)
_____
_____
_____
_____

Vehicles
_____
_____
_____

Havens

Location
_____
_____
_____

Description
_____
_____
_____

Ventrue™

History
Prelude

_____
_____
_____
_____
_____
_____
_____
_____
_____
_____
_____
_____
_____
_____
_____
_____
_____

Appearance

Age_____   _____
Apparent Age_____   _____
Date of Birth_____   _____
RIP_____   _____
Hair_____   _____
Eyes_____   _____
Race_____   _____
Nationality_____   _____
Height_____   _____
Weight_____   _____
Sex_____   _____

Visuals

Coterie Chart   Character Sketch